THAT GENTLE TOUCH

THAT GENTLE TOUCH

BEVERLY C. WARREN

DOUBLEDAY & COMPANY, INC.

GARDEN CITY, NEW YORK

1984

Library of Congress Cataloging in Publication Data
Warren, Beverly C.
That gentle touch.
I. Title.
PS3573.A769T45   1984   813'.54
ISBN 0-385-19133-2
Library of Congress Catalog Card Number 83–14032
Copyright © 1984 by Beverly C. Warren
All Rights Reserved
Printed in the United States of America

First Edition

THAT GENTLE TOUCH

CHAPTER 1

Somewhere in her dream the telephone was ringing, and she kept calling for someone to answer it so she could sleep. It had been an unusually long day and she was exhausted. But the piercing, persistent ring screeched unabated. A limp arm groped for the cold plastic receiver and she brought it to her ear, then moaned a garbled hello.

"Doc! I've got trouble out here. You've got to come right away or I don't think Cathy will make it through the night. She needs help and now!" The voice was anxious, breathless and desperate.

"Who is this?" Her voice was thick and raspy with sleep.

"This is Jake . . . the McBride place. I have to get back to her so hurry, Doc . . . hurry." Abruptly the connection was severed.

Nicole Winters let the receiver slip from her hand into the golden hair fanned out over the pillow. With uncommon effort she raised one eyelid to peer lazily at the clock on her nightstand. One o'clock in the morning! Sighing deeply, eyes closed, she swung her legs over the edge of the bed, sat up and replaced the receiver. She shook her tousled head as if it would create an instantaneous awareness, then stumbled into the bathroom. It was her week to be on night call, and she could only conclude that the fates had decided to make all emergency calls happen at night for the entire week.

Grimacing as she looked in the mirror through squinted eyes that resented the intrusion of the bright fluorescent light, she shoved her long blond hair behind her ears, then turned the cold water tap on. She cupped her hands to catch the water, then splashed her face several times before her eyes would open to a sharp focus.

Back in the bedroom, she slipped on a pair of heavy blue corduroy jeans, a cotton blouse and a thick turtleneck sweater. After tugging on her fleece-lined boots, she pulled her long hair back into a ponytail. She didn't have time to braid and skewer it in a bun at the nape of her neck as she usually did. She went to her medical bag and surveyed its contents. Satisfied that she had what was necessary—standard items she might need were always kept in the back of her station wagon—she snapped it shut and grabbed her thick nylon parka.

It was a black, moonless night. Even the stars were hiding, as though they had inside information regarding the atmosphere. She sniffed the dank, soggy air and could almost feel the incipient snow in her nostrils. She had only been in Vermont a few months, but being born and raised in upper New York State, she knew the scent of snow. After zipping the parka, she drew the hood over her head, then proceeded to her car.

Nicole tossed the black leather bag, a gift from her brothers upon her graduation, onto the passenger seat as she slid behind the wheel of the six-year-old station wagon. She had been lucky to find the car. There weren't too many vehicles in her price range that ran. Its greatest flaw was its tendency to be whimsical when it came to starting.

Before turning the key in the ignition, she raised her eyes to the heavens and said aloud, "Dear Lord, please let it start." When the engine roared to life, she smiled, patted the dashboard and gave a silent thank you.

She had never been to the McBride place before but had studied all Dr. John Carey's routes, clients and their special needs. She was a thorough, efficient person, traits that had served her well throughout her schooling. Occasionally her curiosity had placed her in a predicament or at odds with a fellow human being, especially when she was very young. Her older brothers were always telling her to mind her own business and not to ask so many questions. But she was stubborn and headstrong, characteristics she tried to temper as she grew older, with minor success.

With watchful eyes she scanned the roadside for a familiar sign. Dr. Carey had pointed out the McBride place to her once when he was taking her on one of his routine calls. Dr. Carey, she mused, a wily, sometimes cantankerous sixty-one-year-old teddy bear with a predilection for doughnuts. She felt lucky indeed when he chose her to be his assistant out of all the other applicants for the position. Of course her magna cum laude degree from Cornell University had helped, along with her obviously zealous attitude during the interview. She sometimes wondered if Dr. Carey hadn't been laughing a bit at her ardor and enthusiasm. But she got the job, and that was all that counted.

She liked Essex Junction, even though it wasn't the megalopolis she had dreamed about and the salary wasn't phenomenal. But she loved the open, friendly people, and Dr. Carey had been kind enough to secure reasonable rooms for her with a widow: a bedroom, a living room, a kitchen and a bathroom—all with her own private entrance through a side porch.

If her memory of the maps served her right, the McBride place would only be another mile down the road. She glanced at the clock on the dashboard, the only item on the car that seemed to run with perfection, and was pleased to note she had made good time. When her eyes returned to the road, the huge structure loomed before her.

She parked the car and went in to be greeted by an effusive, nervous and perplexed man.

"Where's Dr. Carey?" he asked with anxious impatience.

"I'm Dr. Winters, his assistant." Her voice rang with authority. She was getting used to the initial hostility her presence aroused. She had confidence in her ability, and, when she was given time, it soon became apparent to those around her.

"I don't know." He scratched his head in doubt. "I'd rather Dr. Carey was here. I don't think a woman can handle it."

"Mr. McBride, I assure you I know exactly what I'm doing. Surely you have enough faith in Dr. Carey to know he wouldn't take on someone who couldn't handle the job." Nicole had come up against this kind of resentment before and had learned to handle it with graceful aplomb.

He pursed his lips and quietly looked at her, his ruddy face screwed up in distrust. "I dunno . . ."

"It's not doing your Cathy any good for us to stand here debating my qualifications. Where is she?"

He heaved a heavy sigh of resignation. "This way. By the way, I'm not Mr. McBride. I'm Jake Douglas. Call me Jake. Everyone else does."

With bag in hand, Nicole followed the stocky young man while pushing the hood of her parka back with one hand, then unzipping the nylon jacket.

"There she is, Doc. I don't know what to do for her," he said, shaking his head ruefully, his sandy hair flopping about like a dust mop.

"How long has she been like this?" asked Nicole, removing her parka and looking for someplace to hang it.

"I'll take that," said Jake, his hand closing over the weighty jacket. "As for Cathy, I don't rightly know. After supper I started to watch the news on television. I must have fallen asleep, really asleep. By the time

I got around to looking in on her, she was like this. I did what I could but nothing seemed to help. That's when I called you."

"Well, we'll have to get her on her feet," said Nicole, her brow wrinkling with concern. "Do you have any molasses, Jake?"

"Yeah. I think so."

"Get it, will you? And bring me a pail of hot water."

"Whatever you say, Doc." He trudged off with long, heavy strides, carrying her jacket with him.

Elation trickled through Nicole. He had called her Doc several times, signifying his acceptance of her as a professional. She exhaled with satisfaction, for that was the first step in establishing a doctor-client relationship. Her fingers caught the hem of her sweater and she yanked it off, eager to get to work. She viewed her patient with a practiced eye and got a strong educated feeling as to the nature of the trouble. She rolled the sleeves of her cotton blouse as high as she could get them. A bubbling energy and an unquenchable vitality were integral ingredients in her expression and the way she moved. Her love of her specialized work was clear and unmistakable.

"Here's your water, Doc. What do you want me to do with the molasses?" asked Jake, setting down the pail of water and waving the can of molasses in the air.

"Get a good scoop of grain in front of her, then sprinkle the molasses over it. It that doesn't get her up, I've got a sling in the car. I'd like to try the easy way first," said Nicole as she watched Jake carry out her instructions.

She held her breath as he sprinkled the aromatic molasses over the grain, slowly releasing its pungency as the huge holstein cow got to her feet to devour the delectable treat before her.

"That did it, Doc." Jake threw her a smile and a nod, then joined her at the rear of the black and white cow. Automatically Jake grabbed the animal's tail and held it to one side as Nicole soaped and scrubbed her entire arm in the pail of tepid water.

She reached down into the cow's womb until her arm could go no farther. "The calf is breeched. No wonder your Cathy is all worn out." The weak, shallow contractions were a boon for Nicole, and between each one she managed to move the calf around inch by inch until her fingers slid over the young animal's head. With delicate precision she coaxed the head to lie forward in the proper channel. The only remaining problem was the feet. They were pointed down into the womb, making it difficult for the cow to expel the calf, as if it were still presenting its back to the birth canal.

When Jake asked if he could help, Nicole shook her head, breathing in great gulps of air as if the extra oxygen would pump up the strength of her muscles. With a huge intake of breath, her hand stretched down to touch the bony hoof. It kept slipping from her grip as she struggled to bring it forward. In a desperate effort she grappled with the elusive hoof until she thought her arm would fall off from the exertion. She caught a look of doubt in Jake's eyes, so she set her teeth on edge, determined not to let the cow defeat her—for if she failed now it would be all over town in no time and her reputation as a veterinarian would be tarnished before her career really had had time to get off the ground.

Sheer stubbornness gave her the strength and tenacity to get a good grip on the small, slippery hoof and draw it forward to rest under the calf's head. As if it realized Nicole's dedicated perseverance, the other hoof obeyed the demands of her hand without a fight.

As she slowly withdrew her arm, she settled the calf's head on the two front legs now poised toward the exit of birth. As her hand slipped down to grasp and hold the two hooves, she said, "Jake, there's a nylon rope in my bag. Would you please get it? She's too weak to expel the calf on her own now."

Jake nodded and was soon back with the nylon rope and handing it to Nicole. She looped it above the calf's hooves and pulled tight to make sure it was secure.

She pulled her arm free from the beleaguered cow with a loud sucking noise. "Hold tight, Jake," she said, handing the rope to him, then soaped her arm and dried it on a gray, well-worn towel Jake had brought into the main barn for her. "Okay, now. When I say pull, you pull with everything you've got and hold it, stopping when I say stop," she ordered as she placed her hand on the side of the cow's stomach in order to feel whatever slight contractions might emanate.

"I'm ready, Doc," said Jake, holding the rope firmly after having twisted it around one of the barn's supporting beams for leverage.

Nicole waited until she felt the cow's hide tighten. "Pull!"

"The feet are out, Doc!" Jake informed her.

"Stop and hold it. Don't let them slip back in," she warned. It was several seconds before she yelled "Pull!" again.

When the calf's head cleared the opening, Nicole smiled in triumph.

The rest of the animal slithered out without consequence into the dry straw. Nicole went down on her knees beside the newborn calf and cleared the mucus from the animal's mouth and nose while Jake went to get a burlap bag. He wrapped the bag around the calf and carried it to the mother's head, where the black and white cow proceeded to lick her newborn offspring with maternal devotion.

"Well, Doc, that was a good night's work—or should I say morning?" called Jake over the stanchion, his ruddy face cracking into a smile as he watched the calf slip and slide to its feet. "And a fine heifer to boot."

"I'm always happy when things turn out for the best," said Nicole, feeling quite satisfied with herself. "I'll wash up and be on my way."

"There's hot water and soap in the milk room, Doc."

Nicole nodded and headed for the milk room, grabbing her bag and sweater as she walked through the barn, her step light, her mood almost giddy as her nostrils inhaled the sweet odors of hay and silage.

Thoroughly scrubbed, she was about to slip her heavy sweater back on when Jake's frantic cries bounced into the milk room and stopped her. She hung the sweater on the hook over her parka, clutched her bag and dashed back into the main part of the barn. Her soft amber eyes widened in alarm when they caught sight of the cow's rigidly arched back. She rushed to Jake's side behind the cow, opened her bag and threw a six-inch curved needle and some heavy nylon thread into a jar of alcohol.

"Looks like she's going to have another one, Doc," observed Jake, his weathered face pinched with worry.

"I'm afraid not, Jake. There was only one calf in there. Of that I'm certain. I saw this once before in veterinary school. Your Cathy is about to throw her uterus out," she said, swirling the needle and cord in the alcohol with her forefinger. Quickly she took them out and threaded the needle deftly. "Hold her tail."

"Will it hurt her, Doc?"

"No. She's much too numb in the area now." With sure, steady hands Nicole swiftly sewed the entrance to the birth canal in strong, careful cross-stitching. Securing the ends of the cord firmly, she cut the heavy thread. "There . . . that should do it. Leave the stitches in for a few days. You can call me when you think she has completely settled down, and I'll take them out or you can do it yourself."

"Will she be able to have another calf?" He looked troubled.

"Oh, sure. The cow I saw who had expelled her uterus went on to have several more calves. We did have to watch her and routinely sew her up after calving." Nicole smiled. She'd never forget the time the professor had let her and a fellow student struggle with the cumbersome uterus that was like a mountain of slippery, weighty Jell-O before demonstrating the proper procedure for getting the massive object back into the cow. "Well, I guess everything is under control now." She stroked the animal's back tenderly and released a sigh of a job well done, then bent over, replaced the needle and snapped her bag shut.

Jake walked her back to the milk room, where she washed up, then donned her sweater and parka. Saying good night, Nicole opened the milk room door.

"Oh no!" she exclaimed, frustration etched in her voice as she watched the snow swirl thick with angry vengeance. With her half-bald tires, it would take her forever to get home, if she made it at all. She had bought cheap retreads at the beginning of winter, hoping they would last. She hadn't expected a snowfall when spring was just around the corner. Her only consoling thought was that tomorrow was her day off and she could sleep for twenty-four hours if she wanted to.

"Looks real bad out, Doc," commented Jake as he poked his head out the door.

"You can say that again," she said despondently, her eyes trying to pierce the density of the rapidly falling snowflakes.

"If you like, we have a couch you could use. This will be over by morning—or I should say daylight," offered Jake.

"I couldn't impose on you like that." It was a tempting proposal. Morning was only a few hours away, and falling snow didn't hold quite the terror in broad daylight that it did at night. It would probably be the sensible thing to do, she thought.

"No trouble at all, Doc, and I'd feel a lot better about it. I'd feel terrible if something happened to you. Wait here while I get some milk into the calf, then I'll take you to the house."

"But won't your wife . . ." He disappeared into the barn before her words of protest could reach his ears.

As she waited for Jake, a mood of contentment cloaked her. This was her first serious big-animal case, and she had handled it with adroit professionalism. She was pleased with and proud of her performance. She was doing what she had always dreamed of doing and was good at it. It was a marvelous sensation.

She peeked at the snow again. Though she didn't approve of thrusting herself on strangers, she rationalized that this time it was a sensible decision. The thought of driving on those winding, slick, hilly roads in foul weather at night sent a shudder through her.

Coming back into the milk room, Jake motioned for her to follow him. She tossed her medical bag into the car, then trudged behind him as he covered the short distance from the barn to his two-story wood-frame house. Following his lead when they reached the covered porch, she removed her snowy boots along with her white-dusted parka. He quietly directed her into the living room, indicating the two woolen afghans at the foot of the couch. Whispering a thank you and a good night, Nicole spread the afghans over the couch, then curled under them as Jake tiptoed up the stairs. She didn't have to wait long for sleep. It descended on her like an impenetrable fog.

The aroma emanating from the kitchen spread its tentacles through the house. Nicole's deep sleep became shallow as the delicious smells assailed her nostrils. Her eyes fluttered open, and at first she was surprised by her unfamiliar surroundings. She sat up, placing her sock-covered feet firmly on the carpeted floor and focusing her hazy attention on the room until the memory of the previous evening came back to her. This was Jake's home.

She shook her head to clear the cobwebs of sleep from her brain, then carefully folded the hand-knit afghans and placed them at the foot of the couch, where she had found them. Her nose and the rumble in her stomach propelled her to follow the scent into the kitchen.

"Well, good morning, Dr. Winters. Jake told me how he had to call you last night and what a fine job you did on Cathy. Then that sudden squall. I'm Jake's wife, Milly," said the neat, dark-haired woman, wiping the flour from her hands on a printed cloth apron, then extending one to Nicole in greeting.

"How do you do, Milly. I really appreciate the use of your couch last night," said Nicole, grasping the woman's hand.

"Oh . . . only too glad to be of help."

"This kitchen smells heavenly," commented Nicole, taking in the aromas.

"I'm making some bread and pies. With two young boys and Jake to feed, nothing seems to last very long. I'll fix you some breakfast. You must be starved. It's ten in the morning."

"I didn't know it was so late. I appreciate the offer of breakfast, but I really must be on my way. Again, I'm most grateful for the use of the couch."

"Please, do stay. I don't get much company out here and it would give me a good excuse to sit down and chat for a while. Please."

The look of entreaty on the woman's face was so genuine, Nicole relented. "All right. But don't fuss. Coffee will be fine."

"The bathroom is the second door on the right down the hall if you want to freshen up while I get a fresh pot of coffee brewing," said Milly brightly as pleasure filled her face.

Returning from the bathroom, her face shiny clean, Nicole took the seat Milly indicated. A plate filled with scrambled eggs nestled against two slices of ham was placed before her. Alongside the plate of buttered toast was a small crock of strawberry jam.

"You're new to these parts, aren't you, Dr. Winters?" asked Milly, pouring them each a cup of coffee. "How do you like Essex Junction?"

"Very much, even though I've only been away from New York for two months." Nicole greedily attacked the breakfast. She was hungrier than she had thought.

"Coming from New York, you must miss the excitement and glamour of the big city."

Nicole gave a little half-laugh. "Whenever I mention I'm from New York, people assume I mean New York City and expect to hear all about Broadway and Chinatown. It comes as a disappointment when they learn I've never been in the city. New York is a very large state, and I come from Lowville in the upper part—a town very much like Essex Junction: small, quiet and bitterly cold in the winter. So you see I feel very much at home here," Nicole concluded, then proceeded to polish off the blood-warming breakfast.

Milly smiled. "I never would have taken you for a small-town girl, what with being a veterinarian and all. It just goes to show people are not always what they appear to be." She sipped her coffee thoughtfully as she watched Nicole devour the food she had prepared. "Can I fix you some more ham and eggs?"

"Goodness, no. I've eaten more than I should already," said Nicole, placing her splayed hands on her flat stomach. "That strawberry jam was the best I've ever tasted."

"Thank you. It's homemade. I have a good-size strawberry bed out in back," said Milly.

"How old are your boys?" asked Nicole as Milly poured more coffee for them.

"Five and seven. The oldest is starting to be of some help to his father in the barn. By the way, Jake said you worked hard last night and did a real professional job."

A pink glow settled high on Nicole's cheeks. She never did know how to respond to a compliment. "You and Jake have a nice place here and a fine herd of holstein cows."

"They're all registered holsteins—purebreds with pedigrees as long as your arm. We're buying them on the installment plan. Jake hopes to work the twenty-five head up to fifty."

"Why is it called the McBride place when it belongs to you and Jake?" asked Nicole.

"Oh, we don't own the farm. It belongs to Jason McBride."

"Who is Jason McBride?"

"Jason McBride is somewhat of an enigma. I don't think anyone knows who he really is, even though his family has owned the place for generations and generations. He owns almost a thousand acres of prime land around here. He lives in the big white house down the road a bit. You probably haven't noticed it, for it is set quite a way back from the road and is hidden by maple trees and high juniper bushes," replied Milly.

"Then Jake is Mr. McBride's herdsman?"

"No. We sort of rent the place."

"Sort of?"

"We don't pay cash money rent. We pay in goods—milk, veal, beef, pork, chickens and eggs. We raise a few pigs and Angus steers for meat. It's been a real good arrangement for us."

"You and Jake must love farming," stated Nicole.

"Oh, we do. We had a small farm and worked our tails off, only to find we were sinking deeper and deeper into debt. Finally the farm and its contents were put on the auction block. Frankly, I don't know what we would have done if it hadn't been for Mr. McBride. He offered us this place, had the barn modernized with a pipeline for the milking machines to deliver the milk directly into the big stainless steel milk cooler in the milk room, all the modern equipment to run the place— and he put up the money for the initial herd," explained Milly.

"You mean this McBride foots all the bills?" asked Nicole, wondering why she hadn't heard of this strange philanthropist before. In a small town one gets to hear most everything about the town and the people in it in a very short time.

"Not really. He gets a fair value in goods for rent, but all the animals are ours. We keep the profit from them. We pay Mr. McBride the sum of two hundred dollars a month, interest-free, until the debt for the cows is paid off, which will be in another year and a half. The land, buildings and equipment remain his in title. It all has something to do with taxes." Milly shrugged. "We're happy with the arrangement, so that's all that counts. It's helped to give us a real good start."

"He sounds like an eccentric old millionaire," said Nicole, her eyes twinkling with amusement.

"Millionaire, yes. Eccentric, maybe. But old . . ." She shook her head. "He's somewhere in his mid- or late thirties. I'm not very good at guessing ages."

"With that kind of money, I suppose he's a jet-setter of sorts," commented Nicole, envisioning a playboy trying to tuck in all the thrilling experiences life has to offer before being overwhelmed with old age.

"No. At least I don't think so. From what I've heard, he's somewhat of a recluse, some kind of electronic genius. Designs microchips for computers. Something like that," replied Milly.

"Then he must work for the computer complex on the edge of town," remarked Nicole.

"He does some work for them, but I've heard he is more of a freelancer. Gossip has it he does secret work for the government. Elsie, the postmistress, says he gets all kinds of mail from California and Washington, D.C.," said Milly in a conspiratorial tone.

"Sounds intriguing. You and Jake must know him pretty well."

"Not really. Jake knows him better than I do but Jake isn't one for talking about people. The times I've come in contact with McBride, he gave me the impression of being a pretty cold fish. It's like there's a stone wall around him and if you tried to get through all you'd do is smash your head on it. Don't get me wrong. He's polite and friendlylike, but there is something very impersonal about him. I can't put my finger on it."

"More than likely his business is so demanding that his mind is constantly preoccupied. Perhaps with his creative powers he has to maintain a certain detachment from the world around him to be able to concentrate to the fullest," offered Nicole as she started to rise from the table. "I'm so glad to have met you, Milly, and I can't thank you enough for everything, especially the excellent breakfast."

"Oh, it was my pleasure. It was nice to have someone to chat with for a change, Dr. Winters."

"Do call me Nicole. Dr. Winters sounds a little too formal for all the hospitality you've shown me."

"That's a pretty name . . . Nicole." Milly smiled.

"I suppose it's time to face the snow," said Nicole with a sigh.

"There's not much to contend with, and it looks like all the roads have been cleared. It was one of those last bursts of winter. Looks worse than it actually is. It won't be long and spring will be here." Milly began to clear the table, stacking the dishes in the sink while Nicole went to peek out the window.

"You're right, Milly. There's not much on the ground at all."

"I hope you won't get in trouble with Dr. Carey for staying and chatting with me. Once I get to talking I seem to forget the time."

"Today is my day off so I can spend it as I wish," said Nicole, heading for the door to the covered porch. "Thanks again, and I've enjoyed meeting you, Milly."

"Drop in anytime you're out this way." She wiped a stray tendril of hair from her face with the back of her hand. "Oh . . . are you going to the barn?"

"Yes. As long as I'm here I thought I'd take a look at the cow and see how she is doing. Besides, my car is parked at the milk room."

"Will you do me a favor?"

"Sure."

"Have Jake send my youngest home. He followed his father down to the barn this morning before I could grab him, and I know he gets under Jake's feet even though Jake is very patient about it. Tell Timmy I need him to help me feed the chickens. It's one of his favorite chores and will bring him scurrying," requested Milly.

"Will do," said Nicole with a smile as she went through the door. She tugged the high boots onto her feet, then slipped on her parka. Shoving her hands into the pockets, she headed for the large red barn now clearly visible in the morning sun.

Milly was right, thought Nicole. One could almost smell the promise of spring in the air even though it was still crisp with a decisive chill.

After entering the barn, Nicole called down to Jake, who was at the other end. "How's the patient this morning?"

"Fine. Just fine," replied Jake, coming to meet her. "I hope Milly gave you something to eat."

"She prepared a feast for me," said Nicole, stopping at the cow she had doctored last night. "Well . . . she looks fit. Is she off her feed any?" She ran her hand over the short-haired hide gently, petting the animal as one would a dog or cat.

"Nope. And the calf is doing well, too. Bright as a new silver dollar."

"Don't hesitate to call me if anything happens." She turned to leave, then remembered Milly's request. "By the way, your wife wanted me to tell you to send your youngest boy home."

"Bobby!" Jake shouted.

"Yeah?" A small voice responded from the depths of the barn.

"Where's your brother?"

"He went down to the stream to sail his boat," was the reply.

"Well, go fetch him. His mother wants him."

"But I'm feeding the calves," moaned the young voice.

Jake shook his head, then said to Nicole, "There just aren't enough hours in the day."

"If you'll tell me where the stream is, I'll go tell him," offered Nicole.

"Oh, I don't want to put you out, Doc. You have enough work of your own to do."

"It's my day off and a walk would do me good after that breakfast Milly cooked for me. Besides, I'd enjoy it."

"Well . . . I dunno . . . I'd appreciate it, though." He followed her outside and, with his arm extended, pointed. "See that line of trees at the end of the field?" Nicole nodded. "Well, go down to the trees and you'll find a path that will take you directly to the stream. He'll be at the bottom of the path, more than likely. He's been told never to go any further than that and he minds pretty well."

With a brisk stride, Nicole walked across the winter-killed field, taking deep breaths of the clean air. After last night the day had turned out to be quite beautiful. She thought of Jake and Milly and what nice people they were. In fact, everyone in Essex Junction had been warm and friendly toward her, making her feel like an integral part of the community. Even the young women she had met when she joined the Young Women's League had treated her like a long-lost friend.

Her mind wandered to the man Milly had spoken of—Jason Mc-Bride—a wealthy computer genius whose world was outside the pale, who seemed to divorce himself from the day-to-day trappings of society. Maybe Milly was exaggerating. As she tried to visualize such a man, her mind was diverted by a new notion: computerized veterinary medicine. The possibility intrigued her.

Coming to a halt at the barrier of trees, Nicole began to look for the path. Finding it easily, she started down, becoming alarmed at the sound of muffled crying originating somewhere inside the leafless trees and myriad conifers, which barred any clear view of the area.

Quickly rushing down the path, it didn't take her long to find the source of the sobs. A small boy in a bright orange jacket sat at the base of a blue spruce tree, weeping spasmodically.

"You must be Timmy," said Nicole gently.

The tearstained face looked up at her, and the sobs increased in intensity.

Nicole squatted to be on his level and smiled. "Now what is all this weeping about?" she asked softly.

Between sniffles and sobs he managed to choke out, "I lost my boat."

"Oh, dear. That is tragic."

"I can't go downstream to look for it or my dad will be mad. I'm supposed to stay by the path," he blurted out in sobbing gulps.

"Tell you what," she began in soothing tones. "I'll go look for your boat if you'll go home and help your mother feed the chickens."

The eyes widened. The tears stopped. "You will?"

"On my honor. I'll bring it to the house the minute I find it," promised Nicole.

"You will?" The eyes remained wide, and he wiped the tearstained rosy cheeks with the back of his mittened hand.

Nicole nodded, stood and offered him her hand, which he took to pull himself up. "Now you run along home, because your mother is waiting for you to help her."

A smile brightened the child's face and he started to race along the path toward the open fields. As Nicole watched him, he suddenly turned and shouted, "You won't forget the boat?"

"No . . . I won't forget," she called as he once again scampered off in the direction of home.

With a sigh and a shake of her head, Nicole continued down the path toward the stream, wondering how she had let herself be dragged into what was probably a futile search. The toy boat would be long gone by now. But she had given her word and she would do her best to try to find it.

The trees and shrubs began to thin out to reveal a fast-flowing stream in front of her, its crystal-clear, shallow waters gurgling over small rocks. She proceeded along the bank, made slippery by the dusting of snow from the previous night, which was beginning to melt in the rising temperatures. She scanned the water and both shores with sharp eyes for some sign of the toy boat.

The bank of the stream sloped higher and higher as she moved along, leaving her a three-foot-wide path beside the streaming water. The miniature river was getting wider and wider and deeper and deeper. Nicole began to doubt if she'd ever find the child's lost boat. With dismay she glanced at the steep rise of the land with its gnarled trees and shrubs to what seemed to be a clear meadow at the crest.

The path grew narrower, and Nicole feared she would have to give up the search. When it seemed she could go no farther, her eyes spied a speck of bright red wedged between some branches of a tree that had succumbed to the whims of nature and partially fallen into a section of the stream. Her hand reached into the chilling water and clasped a plastic object that, when she drew it out, proved to be the young boy's red and white toy boat.

With a smile of triumph, Nicole stared at the incline and decided it might be quicker to climb the slope to the meadow. She had come some distance and thought it best to get her bearings. For all she knew she might have circled around, bringing her nearer to the barn than before.

Stuffing the toy boat into the ample pocket of her parka, she began the ascent, using the shrubs and low branches to assist her light body upward and prevent any slipping back on the slimy ground. Her final leap to the top did not bring the result she had expected. Instead she was dazed and astounded by the spectacle before her.

CHAPTER 2

The huge black stallion rose violently and pawed fruitlessly at the empty air before him, his nostrils flaring as a startled whinny issued from his throat. Steam curled in the chilled air from the majestic animal's excited breath. The ebony sheen of his well-brushed coat matched the wildly strewn mane of its rider.

Nicole took in the awesome sight with a mixture of wonder and admiration. The horse was a beautiful specimen, and she knew she had frightened the poor beast out of his senses. But her attention was soon held by the rider astride the magnificent steed. He was clad in a heavy black turtleneck sweater and tight black denim pants that were half covered with glossy black boots. It was Satan himself on horseback, she thought with a twinge of amusement as she blatantly returned his naked stare.

His sharp-boned, craggy features were made gaunt by deeply etched furrows slashing from his high cheekbones down to his strong, square chin. The sharp contour of his high-bridged nose was well defined as it rested above wide lips, the upper one a thin line over a full lower lip. Both were set in a grim, foreboding expression. The thick, unruly raven hair was tempered by wings of gray at his temples. Under dark, heavy eyebrows, black stars emitted a peculiar reflected light that seemed to be indigenous only to those deep-set eyes.

The stallion's eyes were still wild with unsettled frenzy, his lips drawn back by a tight pull on the reins as his hooves pawed at the ground with righteous indignation. He pranced sideways as his master directed him closer to Nicole, who was still somewhat in awe of the satanic appearance of the large stranger whose dark eyes were cold and haughty as they searchingly glared down at her oval face. He placed his large hands on the leather-wrapped horn of the saddle and quietly appraised the golden-haired young woman before him. Nicole raised her chin and returned the stare with matched defiance.

"What the devil are you doing here? And who the devil are you?" The deep voice was as ominous as its owner.

"I was looking for a boat!" snapped Nicole, irritated by the man's abrasive attitude. The irritation was replaced by a feeling of foolishness when she realized the import of her words and the ironic smile that almost threaded its way over the stranger's lips. Quickly she added, "A toy boat."

"Aren't you a little old for playing with boats in a stream?" His voice was soft but held a satirical note.

"I wasn't playing with it, and I think it's rather silly of you even to suggest I was."

"I could hardly think otherwise, learning you were wandering about the stream looking for a toy boat, now could I?"

With her hands in her pockets, she drew herself erect. "The young Douglas boy lost it, and I promised him I'd look for it, if you must know," she said with an impatient sigh. There was something about the man that touched a raw nerve in her. She couldn't put her finger on it, but the sensation was strong and disturbing.

"And did you find it?"

"Yes." The word was sharp and quick as she spoke, then withdrew the toy boat from her pocket and held it up as evidence of her statement.

"Other than looking for lost toys, what are you doing here? I haven't seen you in this area before."

"I'm Dr. Carey's new assistant," she stated matter-of-factly.

"You're a veterinarian?" His dark eyebrows lifted in mild surprise.

"Yes. I've been tending to one of Jake Douglas's cows, if it is any of your business."

"A . . . little thing like you grappling with cows? Come, come, Miss . . . ?"

"Dr. Winters," she corrected him firmly. "A veterinarian doesn't need brawn but brains. Now if you'll excuse me, I have better things to do than subject myself to your rude questioning."

Nicole felt a need for immediate flight. She didn't like the unsettling scrutiny of his inky eyes or his arrogant manner. Forgetting the skittish horse, she made a quick darting movement, which once again spooked the animal into rearing restively and lurching in Nicole's direction.

She hopped backward to avoid any chance encounter with the lethal hooves, only to lose her balance on the rim of the slippery incline. She tumbled down the rough embankment unceremoniously, her limp body coming to rest in the cold, clear water of the stream. She never felt the wet, chilly water soaking through her clothes, for her head had struck a low-lying branch as she toppled down the stubbled and jagged slope.

Nicole shut her eyes tight, as if it would relieve the relentless pounding in her head. A man . . . a horse . . . a boat. What happened to the boat? It had been in her hand when she lost her balance and fell. She remembered the feeling of helplessness as she started to slide down the bank, but nothing after that. Her mind recognized that she was in a warm bed, but she had no inkling of how she got there. Perhaps Jake had found her and brought her to his home. Her one day off ruined because of that insufferable man and his horse.

Her eyelids trembled as she tried to open them. She could only manage a slight squint. Her half-open eyes peered with blurred vision at the large, shadowy form at the foot of the bed. Like outspread wings, hands grasped each of the tall poster rails at the foot of the bedstead. The dark apparition gave the appearance of a huge bird of prey about to swoop over her. Her eyes closed tight, as if to banish an unwanted dream, then opened with a little more vigor and clarity of vision. Concentrating on the dark giant figure, she saw the image gradually take shape as its sharpness increased.

"It's you," she gasped, recognizing the face that had an offbeat handsomeness to it as the coal-black eyes gazed down at her with concern. She began to lift her head from the downy pillow, but the effort caused her head to throb painfully. She winced, closed her eyes and let her head rest on the pillow. "What happened?"

"You hit your head on a branch when you fell, and it rendered you unconscious," he said quietly.

Her eyes flew open when she felt the bed sag. The tall stranger had sat down beside her. "Where am I? And who are you?"

"I'm Jason McBride, and this is my home. Under the circumstances I thought this was the best place for you."

"Under what circumstances?" She felt groggy, and sporadic aches assailed her body.

"You rolled down the embankment and into the water. By the time I got you out, you were thoroughly soaked. I thought it expedient to get you out of those wet things and into a warm and dry bed."

"You . . . you . . ." Her hands darted under the covers, feeling the long flannel nightgown covering her otherwise naked body. She looked up at him obliquely.

"My housekeeper, Mrs. Beaton, undressed you and prepared you for bed," he said, answering the question in her eyes.

Her tense body relaxed. "I'm sorry to have been a nuisance to you. As a rule, I'm not that clumsy."

"It was my fault. I should have had more control over the horse. How do you feel?"

"My head hurts, and I think I have a few bruises," she replied honestly. "I'm sure I'll mend, though."

"I'm sure you will, too. The doctor said you have a mild concussion and some minor bruises but no broken bones. He was more concerned about you catching pneumonia. By the time we reached the house, you were quite blue with the cold," explained Jason, touching her forehead with the back of his hand.

"The doctor's been here? How long have I been out?" Her forehead felt scorched where his hand had grazed it. The man was making her uncomfortable in a way she never had been before. Having three brothers, she had always been completely at ease with any man. Now she felt a tightness in her that wouldn't go away.

"About five hours."

"Five hours," she repeated loudly, then wished she hadn't, for it only served to echo through her already aching head. In a softer tone she said, "I have to get home. I certainly can't stay here. I've imposed long enough."

As she began to raise herself on her elbows, Jason's hands came down on her shoulders, gently forcing her back onto the bed.

"The doctor said you should stay in bed for at least twenty-four hours. Give your head a chance to heal and make sure nothing else develops. Seeing I was the cause of your misfortune, I intend to make sure that his orders are carried out to the letter."

"I can rest as easily at home and would feel much better about it. I don't want to intrude here. Besides, I have to be at work tomorrow morning."

"I've called Dr. Carey and explained what happened. He'll be over later this evening to see how you are. And you are in no way intruding.

In fact, Mrs. Beaton is delighted that you are here. It gives her a chance to practice her nursing skills. And, young lady, I'm used to having my own way."

"So am I." Regardless of the throbbing in her head, Nicole struggled to sit up and looked into those eyes with a mutinous glare. "I would like my clothes. They should be dry by now."

He rose and took a deep breath, his face set like rugged granite. "It's out of your hands. Your clothes will be returned when you are fully rested."

"I'm fully rested now." She swung her legs over the edge of the large four-poster bed and stood, but her legs quickly buckled beneath her. She would have crumpled to the floor if Jason hadn't caught her. Her breath caught in her throat. She felt as though pulsing electrons were dispersing wildly throughout her when her body came in contact with his, and the heat that emanated from that contact caused a rush of dizziness. Get a hold of yourself, she thought as she braced her hands on the hard sinews of his forearms. This is utter foolishness. It's not the man; you're only weaker than you thought. "Maybe I will rest for a few hours. But after that I'm definitely going home."

"We'll see about that," he said, assisting her back into the bed. "I'll go downstairs and see if Mrs. Beaton can fix you a light supper."

Undaunted, Nicole began to rise from the bed again. "I'll go downstairs. I don't want to be putting you people out."

He sat down on the bed again, effectively barring her from rising. "Haven't you heard one word I said?" he asked with exasperation, his eyes sparkling like black pearls. "You are to stay in bed. If you don't give me your word that you will, I won't leave this room and we'll both starve to death."

"All right," she said grudgingly. "But I'm leaving in a few hours."

A slight ironic smile feathered across his wide lips, and he sat gazing at her for several moments before leaving the bed and walking to the door. When his hand touched the knob he turned, eyed her critically, then quietly went out of the room, closing the door softly behind him.

Nicole studied the room from the great four-poster bed and found it to be utterly charming. Through two large windows the fading sun still managed to flood the spacious room with a misty light. There was a small cherry-wood writing table, a mirrored dressing table and an oversized chest on chest. A chaise longue flanked the decorative fireplace, the latter dominating the room with its pilastered frame and ornate mantel. Pale green, white and gold were the colors used on the walls and echoed in the drapes and carpet. It was a tasteful, attractive and restful room, most definitely feminine, and she wondered who the occupant was. Whoever it was won her admiration for the choice of decor. But her head ached too much for her to ponder the question in any depth.

The two doors on either side of the fireplace piqued her curiosity. Probably closets, she said to herself. All in all, the room had a calming effect on her, and she nestled in the bed with a sweet serenity.

As she began to doze, there was a light rap on the door before it opened, bringing Nicole fully alert. A short, stocky woman in her late fifties bustled in carrying a tray.

"I'm glad to see our patient is awake. You gave us quite a scare, you know, so cold you were and still." She placed the tray on the small table next to the chaise longue, then assisted Nicole in sitting up, fluffing the pillows behind her. "I've brought you some homemade chicken soup and a biscuit or two. Nothing too heavy."

"You must be Mrs. Beaton," said Nicole, her head throbbing unmercifully as the older woman brought the tray to her, snapped down the short legs and put it on the bed.

"That I am. My, you look so pale." Her wide brow crinkled, and her expression was stamped with distress. "The doctor said it was a wonder you didn't break any bones. A right nasty spill you had. Can you manage the soup by yourself?"

"Yes. I only have a headache," replied Nicole with a smile, noting how warm and friendly Mrs. Beaton was. She was about to ask whose room she was in when her eyes strayed to the door where the formidable outline of Jason McBride was framed as he lounged against the doorjamb.

"I think our guest was lucky not to have broken her neck," he said, his voice deep and strong.

"I've put an extra teacup on the tray for you, Mr. McBride," said Mrs. Beaton, turning to him momentarily, then shifting her gaze back to Nicole. "Eat every bit of the soup while it's hot. It'll do you more good than all the patent medicines in the world. And there's plenty more if you want it."

"Thank you, Mrs. Beaton." Nicole began to spoon the hot liquid into her mouth cautiously, testing the degree of warmth as she watched Mrs. Beaton leave the room and the McBride man stride across the room to the writing desk, where he easily lifted the chair in one hand and brought it to the side of the bed.

"You don't mind if I join you for a cup of tea, do you?" asked Jason, his eyes skimming over her face appreciatively.

"Not at all. I'd be grateful for the company. I'm not used to staying in bed like this. I'm sure after I have the soup I'll be up and about and on my way. I really can't thank you enough for all the attention you've shown me." She tackled the soup in earnest, along with a buttered biscuit, as Jason poured himself and her a cup of tea from the pot on the tray.

He waited until she had finished the soup, then asked, "Would you like me to get you some more?"

"It was delicious, but I've had enough for now, thank you."

"Is the head any better?"

"A little." She ran her hand over her long blond hair, which some-one had let loose from the ponytail, and felt the ugly swell on her skull. She frowned, her head aching with a dull pain from the mere touch of her hand. "There's quite a bump there."

Putting his teacup on the nightstand, he rose and bent over her, his fingers lightly tracing over the silken hair. "I guess there is. Lucky for you you didn't crack your skull open." He resumed his seat.

"Everything could have been a lot worse, I suppose," she said, then sipped at the tea. "I feel like a pampered princess sitting here being waited on hand and foot. You really shouldn't have bothered."

He waved his hand in the air as if to signal a dismissal of the topic. "How long have you been in Essex Junction, Miss Winters?"

"Two months. And it's Dr. Winters."

"I'm sorry, Dr. Winters."

Nicole extended her cup, which Jason promptly filled with more tea.

"Where do those doors at the fireplace lead?" she asked.

"One is a walk-in closet and the other is the bathroom," he replied, his eyes never leaving her face.

"Oh." She paused. "This is a very lovely room. Whose is it?"

"Yours for the time being. It was my grandmother's and her mother's before her. The house dates back to the early nineteenth century," he said flatly.

"Then you've been here all your life?"

"No. I was born and raised in Boston. I came back about six years ago, when my parents died. I had the house completely modernized when I moved in, yet it retains the flavor of the period."

"If the rest of the house is as charming as this room, then it must be quite a house."

"When you are well enough, I shall be happy to show it to you," Jason stated, the corners of his lips turning up slightly.

"Do you live here alone?"

"With the exception of Mrs. Beaton, yes." His dark eyes became somber. "You're a very inquisitive young lady. You are my guest, not my interrogator."

"I'm duly chastised," she said with a tilt of her head and a broad smile. She cautioned herself not to tilt her head so strongly again. It seemed to augment the ache.

"And you? Where are you from originally?" he asked.

"Lowville in upstate New York. It's about fifty miles north of Utica —a small town, somewhat like Essex Junction."

"And what made you become a veterinarian?"

Nicole smiled whimsically. Now he was putting the shoe on the other foot. "My father has a small dairy farm. Animals all over the place. Being the only girl, I didn't have to do many of the farm chores, so I had the leisure to make all the animals my private pets. It seemed the natural choice of a career when the time came for me to choose."

"You have brothers?"

"Three. All older."

"Why didn't you set up a practice in Lowville?"

"The area had all the vets it needed. Young ones at that. I sent out forty resumés to practices looking for assistants and only received four replies. Most of them didn't take too kindly to having a woman for an assistant, especially when it came to big-animal work. The first interview I had was a disaster. The chemistry wasn't there, if you know what I mean. Though I didn't say so, I thought the man abrasive and too money-oriented for my tastes. I'm sure he found me overly confident and too assuming. The minute I met Dr. Carey I knew I liked him. He was kind and treated me like another professional right away. My instincts have proved to be correct, and we get along famously."

"You sound like a very headstrong woman," observed Jason, his dark eyebrows raising in mock amusement.

"I don't like my qualifications being pushed aside because I'm a woman. I'm good at what I do and am not afraid to say so," said Nicole with conviction.

"If you're finished, I'll take these things downstairs and you can lie down again," said Jason, rising from his seat and lifting the tray from the bed.

"Yes, I'm finished. Please thank Mrs. Beaton for me and tell her the soup was excellent."

He nodded, balanced the tray with one hand while he opened the door and closed it after him.

Now was the time, she thought. She slipped from the bed, lifted the hem of the long nightgown and treaded her way to what she hoped was the bathroom door. She grasped the knob firmly and leaned heavily against the door, for there was a whining dizziness making her head spin. Fortunately it was the bathroom. She gripped the rim of the porcelain sink to steady herself. She splashed her face with cold water until it tingled, then dried it with the towel that hung alongside the sink. She knew she had to sit down for a minute or two before searching for her clothes. Better yet, she thought she had better lie down, for a flash of heat swirled through her and she felt faint.

Halfway toward the bed she sneezed. It felt as though the top of her head had fallen off, rolled across the floor, bounced against the wall, then vaulted back atop her skull. She closed her eyes and held her head with both hands to make sure it was still there. With a suddenness that startled her, strong arms were raising her body off the ground and moving her toward the comfort of the bed.

"I should think with a medical background you would have more sense than to get out of bed," scolded Jason as he placed her on the bed, brought the covers over her, then sat down. "Will I have to stand guard over you?"

"I'm not an invalid, you know." Her eyes flashed with indignation.

"I wouldn't speak too soon if I were you." His hand covered her forehead, and his dark eyes clouded with uncertainty. "I think I'd better have the doctor come back. You're feverish."

"It's the hot tea and the hot soup. It's time I got out . . . out . . ." Before she could finish her sentence she was caught up in the throes of another sneeze. Jason shook his head soberly and went into the bathroom, quickly returning with a box of tissues. She gratefully took one and said, "Thank you" with a nasal twang.

"At this moment you're not the paragon of health you think you are," he commented.

"She could do with a good rest. She's been overworking herself," said the small, wiry man coming through the open door, his white hair dancing about his head like a cloud. "Good evening, Mr. McBride. I hope your patient hasn't been too difficult. She can be quite stubborn when the mood suits her."

"I think I can deal with her. I'm not known for a vacillating personality," said Jason, shaking the older man's hand.

"Well, how are you feeling, Nicole?" asked Dr. Carey.

"Fine. I've had excellent care and will be back on the job first thing in the morning," replied Nicole, her voice ringing with determination.

"I won't hear of it. You take the rest of the week off," insisted Dr. Carey.

"I couldn't leave you stranded like that," cried Nicole, then promptly sneezed.

Dr. Carey reached down and took her wrist in his hand, studied her pulse, then placed her hand back on the bed and pursed his lips. "Hmmm. You have a fever, young lady. If you don't want to end up in the hospital, I'd advise you to stay where you are for a few days. I'm sure Mr. McBride won't mind, do you, McBride?"

"It's exactly what I've been trying to convince her to do," said Jason, staring at Nicole, his dark eyes unreadable.

"Then it's settled," said Dr. Carey with a nod of his head.

"It's far from settled," contradicted Nicole. "I'll do what I think is best, and the best thing for me is to get back to work."

"You'll stay here as long as needs be, and I don't want to hear any further arguments from you, Nicole," said Dr. Carey firmly. "You're not any good to me or yourself when you are only half functioning. I can make it for a number of days without you. Besides, that'll give me a good excuse to take a few days off myself when you're back to normal. I could do with a minivacation myself." There was a merry twinkle in his watery blue eyes.

"I'll hold you to that," said Nicole before she was burdened with an attack of sneezing. She groped for the tissues as her eyes filled with fluid.

"I think it's about time you took a good rest anyway. You've been pushing yourself much too hard ever since you came to work for me." Dr. Carey took her hand in his and patted it fondly. "I stopped in at

Jake's barn before coming on to the house. That was a fine job you did on the cow. I'm not sure I would have spotted that the animal was about to cast her uterus as quickly as you did."

"Of course you would have. You're just being kind," responded Nicole, swelling with pride.

"You know very well I call the shots as I see them. Well . . . I'd better be on my way. I wanted to see how you were and let you know I don't want to see you in the hospital at work until you're completely recovered." He peered at her over the top of his steel-rimmed glasses. "Promise?"

She nodded her head wearily and with resignation. "Promise." She was beginning to feel strange and fuzzy. She saw Jason follow Dr. Carey out the door with hazy eyes and then heard the muffled tread of their feet on the carpeted staircase. She absently plucked at the gathering of lace about the high collar of the nightgown, then at the ruffles of lace bursting from the full-length sleeves. As her head became suffused with a new kind of ache, the whole day took on a dreamlike quality, a shimmering mirage that had no basis in fact. She didn't notice Jason as he slipped back into the room. The light was dimming, and she reached for the box of tissues to relieve the clogging in her nose, only to knock it off the nightstand onto the floor. Through reddened, teary eyes she glanced at the tall, misty figure alongside the bed, proffering the box of tissues.

"When did you come back in?" she asked, taking several of the tissues.

"A short while ago," he replied as he turned on the lamp resting on the nightstand.

"Why didn't you say something?"

"I thought you might be asleep and didn't want to disturb you."

"I'm very sorry about all this. I haven't had a cold or been sick since I was a little girl. I feel terrible about you being stuck with me for the night."

"You seem to have a one-track mind, Dr. Winters. Your contrition was well noted some time ago." He positioned himself in the chair that still remained near the bed.

She blew her nose and sat quietly as Jason helped rearrange the pillows. Then she asked, "Does this nightgown belong to Mrs. Beaton?"

"No. It belonged to my grandmother. She was about your size, only taller. Periodically Mrs. Beaton goes through everything in here and freshens it up. I keep meaning to dispose of it all but haven't gotten around to it yet. Now I'm glad I didn't. It's finally served some useful purpose."

"I'm surprised you didn't clear everything out when you moved in," said Nicole in a raspy voice. The stuffiness in her head was spreading to her chest.

"There were a lot of papers to go through, and then there was my work. It seemed at the time that clothes and personal effects could wait." He stared at her curiously. "You seem uncomfortable. Maybe some diversion would help. I have a small portable television downstairs. Would you like me to bring it up to you?"

"I don't think so. Perhaps something to read, though," she countered.

"I'm afraid there are only histories and classics in the library. Nothing recent."

"One of the classics would be fine. You choose it."

He went to the door, but as his fingers touched the knob he turned and asked, "Do you play chess?"

"Not very well. I only have a rudimentary knowledge of it."

"Then I shall teach you the finer points." The door remained open as he left. It was some time before he came back balancing two mugs atop a wooden box supported by a sturdy board.

"Hot cocoa," he announced, putting his burden on the nightstand. He handed her a cup as he sat down and spread the chessboard on the bed, carefully arranging the pieces on their proper squares.

They played for several hours, Jason speaking only to inform her of how she should have played the pawn, the knight, the bishop or the rook. Though she did everything in her power to make well-considered plays, Jason handily won the two games. Seeing that she was no longer concentrating, he put the finely carved chess pieces back into their niches in the wooden box and folded the board.

"I think you've had all the lessons you can tolerate this evening. With a clear, concentrating mind, I believe you could make a formidable adversary," he said.

"I will. I can't let you win all the time." She gave him a weak attempt at a smile.

"I'll look forward to it. Get some sleep," he said softly, then left.

Nicole reached over to the lamp and switched it off, then fluffed the pillows. She gave her nose a good-night blow, then cuddled down under the covers. Sleep came quickly but soon turned fitful and disturbed. A dark rider on a dark horse raced through her mind, the ebony eyes of man and beast plundering her dreams and rest.

The sun streamed into the pale green room at an angle that penetrated Nicole's eyelids. She rolled in the bed to avoid it, but each roll only served to bring more consciousness to her awakening brain. Her lids were heavy as she opened them, and her throat was scratchy and tight. The ache in her head was gone, leaving a clogged, constricted sensation in its wake. Reluctantly she drew her feet from the bed, dumped them on the floor and sat on the edge for a moment. She drew in a deep breath, expelling it by coughing. Picking up the hem of the long nightgown, she stumbled into the bathroom and peered through half-closed eyes into the mirror. Her eyes were watery and red, with dark circles under them. She sneezed, coughed and rinsed her face with tepid water. She wanted to go back to work—or at least go home where she could suffer in silence and no one could see her pitiable condition. Damn . . . damn . . . damn, she said to herself.

Leaving the bathroom, she went to the window to see if the world still existed. Drawing back the lacy curtains, she gazed out over the expansive lawn, its newly green carpet exuding a tranquillity indicative of the calm before the onslaught of spring with its riotous display of colors and sweet aromas.

Her vision picked up a dark, hulking form coming toward the house. His long legs strode across the spacious lawn rapidly. His black hair glistened with tones of blue as the sun's rays scattered across the thick, wavy mass. His head was bent in thought, so she could not see the craggy face that was fast becoming entrenched in her mind. To her, he didn't seem to be the enigma everyone thought he was. But, then, did she really know the man? She studied him unseen at the window. In tight, faded jeans and pale blue sweater, the power of his wide shoulders and his bearlike chest was emphasized by lithe hips. There was a magnetism about the man that held her captive for a moment. Was it the way he walked—the confident stride, the measured determination of his gait? She was transfixed by the sight of him.

Suddenly he looked up toward the window, and Nicole dropped the curtain and stepped aside like a spy caught in the act.

Now why did I do that, she asked herself. Why didn't I wave and throw him a smile? Her mind raced down divergent avenues to explain her uncharacteristic reaction, only to become lost in a maze of inexplicable emotions. She gave a shrug, a sneeze and a cough as her hand flailed, reaching for the bedpost as she shuffled across the room. Her legs were increasingly unsteady and rubbery.

As she clutched the smoothly turned post, the bedroom door opened with a force that seemed to make the room tremble. Jason filled the open door frame, his face menacing.

"What are you doing out of bed?" The hard lines of his wide mouth were grim as the edges sank down to his rigid jaw.

She met his gaze with a hauteur of bravery as she drew herself erect with the aid of the bedpost, noting that his eyes were raking over her as though the nightgown didn't exist. She didn't realize the sun was behind her, revealing the outline of her well-rounded figure through the soft, delicate material.

"I had to go to the bathroom," she announced defiantly before she was seized with a fit of coughing.

In two strides Jason was across the room, scooping her into his arms. He placed her in the bed with a gentleness that belied his brusque manner. He drew the covers up to her chin, then placed his hand on her forehead.

"At least your fever is gone. How do you feel?" he asked.

"Fine."

"Liar."

Her nose tickled and she waved a frantic hand toward the box of tissues. Jason pulled out several and handed them to her just in time to contain the sneeze that finally erupted.

"I'm sorry I'm such a nuisance. It's only a cold, and if you'd take me home I could nurse it just as easily there." Her voice sounded funny to her: guttural, the words clipped, with a nasal twang.

"Nonsense, Dr. Winters. There's still a strong nip in the air. Exposure to it and the exertion of the trip might lead to more dire consequences, and I wouldn't want that on my conscience, too. I'll see if we have any cold tablets around. Are you hungry?"

"Yes." She was starved. As he started to leave the room, on impulse she called, "Mr. McBride."

"Yes?"

"Thank you." For a minute she thought he was going to flash a large, toothy smile. But he didn't, and she wondered what effect a broad grin would have upon his foreboding countenance. Jason McBride was not handsome in the classical sense. His bones were too sharp, the bridge of his nose too high. Not at all the sort of man she would feel attracted to. But there was something about his eyes that could transfix her, as if impaling her on mesmerizing spikes of iron. She sneezed and coughed at once, a feat she hadn't known was possible.

Within twenty minutes Jason reentered the bedroom and placed a small bottle on the nightstand. "Some antihistamine tablets. They may help. I've also brought you three books to choose from," he said, shuffling the leatherbound books in his hands. *"Jane Eyre,* the complete works of Sherlock Holmes and Hardy's *Tess of the D'Urbervilles.* Sorry there's nothing current."

"I've always wanted to read Sherlock Holmes but could never find the time." She smiled up at him as he put the books on the bed.

"Mrs. Beaton will be up with your breakfast shortly. I'll be gone for the day, but she'll take good care of you." He stood close to the bed and stared down at her, a strange incandescence flickering in his dark eyes. He cleared his throat and stepped back. "Get plenty of rest, and I'll see you later." He turned on his heel and quickly stalked out of the room.

Milly Douglas was right. There was an invisible curtain around the man. But what she had taken for arrogance earlier was instead a quiet reticence that appeared to be impenetrable even though he was friendly on the surface. She had the feeling gates of steel would snap shut, insulating him from any real personal contact, if one tried to invade the recesses of his personality. She knew his kindness and concern for her stemmed from a sense of guilt and duty. Yet for a split second when he had looked at her, she thought she had seen a softening, a suggestion of affinity. She shrugged and thumbed through the books, her hand grasping the one with the gilt imprint, Sherlock Holmes. She had put the others on the nightstand and opened the heavy tome when Mrs. Beaton came in with her breakfast.

"You poor child!" exclaimed Mrs. Beaton, setting the bed tray over Nicole's lap. "Mr. McBride told me what an awful cold you have developed. No wonder. You were chilled to the bone when he brought you back from the stream. It's a miracle you're not in the hospital with pneumonia."

"Thanks to your good nursing," said Nicole, her mouth watering at the sight of a small bowl of orange and grapefruit sections, all peeled and skinned, along with a soft-boiled egg, toast and coffee. "I have a feeling before all this is over I'm going to be thoroughly spoiled."

"It's a pleasure to have someone in the house to spoil."

"You have Mr. McBride. And isn't there a Mrs. McBride?" asked Nicole, her heart tightening as she waited for the answer. It was an involuntary reaction that puzzled her. Why should she care if there was a Mrs. McBride? It was hunger that caused the tenseness in her, she decided, and she cracked the egg open.

"There is no Mrs. McBride, to my knowledge. And Mr. McBride isn't that visible around the house. He spends a good deal of time in that laboratory of his."

"He has a laboratory here?"

"Yes." Mrs. Beaton went to the chaise and sat, lifting her legs to rest on the soft cushions.

"This looks like a big house for you to keep up all by yourself," remarked Nicole, finishing her egg and swallowing a cold tablet with some coffee before she began to spoon the tangy citrus pieces into her mouth.

"I really don't have all that much to do. A little dusting, some cooking and the laundry. There's an automatic washer and drier, so laundry is no big chore. The heavy cleaning and such are hired out."

Mrs. Beaton went on to tell Nicole of her small private apartment at the back of the house, her late husband, her son in the service and her daughter in California. No matter how hard Nicole tried to bring the subject around to Jason McBride, Mrs. Beaton remained steadfast in circumventing the topic. Nicole finally gave up and let the older woman go on about the town and its people.

The cold tablet had the desired effect, and Nicole's symptoms eased for the hour or more that Mrs. Beaton kept her company. When Mrs. Beaton left, Nicole started on the tales of Sherlock Holmes with relish.

Her lunch was duly brought at twelve noon, with the housekeeper rushing off, explaining her penchant for the daily soap operas and announcing proudly that she was the owner of a large color television set.

When the sneezing and coughing resumed, Nicole took a couple more of the cold tablets and opened the book again. In an hour or so her eyelids refused to stay open, and she dozed off.

The light tapping at the door became louder and more insistent. Nicole roused herself from the refreshing nap only to find that her head was once again congested.

"Come in," she called nasally. She ran her fingers through her tangled blond hair and, fluffing the pillows behind her, sat up. The door opened and her amber eyes widened at the sight of the unknown visitor. For some reason she had expected Jason McBride, even though he had said he would be gone for the day.

"I was in the neighborhood so I thought I'd drop in and see how my patient was coming along," said the young, handsome man coming to the side of the bed.

"You are?" Nicole managed to ask before a fit of sneezing gripped her.

"Dr. Stephan Baker at your service, Dr. Winters," he introduced himself, then picked up her wrist and studied his wristwatch. "Have you been seeing any spots? Blurred vision? Vertigo? Nausea?"

"No."

The well-manicured hand was laid over her forehead, then it dropped to the man's side. "I would say, with the exception of a bad cold, you have fully recovered from your fall." He smiled down at her, his white, even teeth sparkling under a full mustache.

"You seem quite young to be a doctor," observed Nicole. There wasn't a speck of gray in the full head of curly brown hair or a trace of lines around the clear blue eyes. She suddenly felt disheveled and self-conscious about her appearance. Funny, she didn't feel that way when Jason McBride was in the room.

"I'm thirty-one, if you must know. I could say the same of you, Doctor," he said and grinned.

"Touché," said Nicole, tossing the smile back at him.

"I've heard nothing but good things about Essex Junction's new woman vet. Frankly, I expected someone much older and sturdier. You look much too fragile to be wrestling with cows and horses."

"I manage," said Nicole, then blew her nose.

"Are you taking something for that cold?" he asked.

"Over there." She waved toward the nightstand.

Stephan Baker picked up the bottle of over-the-counter cold tablets. "These are as good as any." He replaced the tablets, then reached into his medical bag and removed a stethoscope. "Open the gown, please."

Nicole flushed as her fingers struggled with the tiny buttons down the front of the gown. She knew it was silly but she was embarrassed. If only he were a gray old man like country doctors should be, she thought. She unbuttoned enough for him to slide the stethoscope to her chest and winced when the cold metal touched her skin.

"Sorry." He listened to the instrument, then, removing it, said, "Your heartbeat is sound, and I'd say most of the congestion is in your head, for the lungs are quite clear now. You'll survive, I'm sure."

"That's good to know." Her fingers raced to rebutton the gown. "Am I fit to go home now?"

"What's the rush? Is McBride suggesting you leave?" His blue eyes enlarged under raised chestnut eyebrows.

"Oh, no," said Nicole quickly. "On the contrary, he insists I stay here in bed until I'm completely cured."

"Then don't look a gift horse in the mouth. Stay and rest until all the symptoms are gone."

"I don't like imposing on strangers."

"I know for a fact Mrs. Beaton is delighted to have you here. As for McBride . . . well . . . I don't think he pays much attention to anything outside his world of microchips," said Stephan Baker with a cynical smile.

"Do you know him well?"

"Hardly. It's my guess he's pretty much a loner. To my knowledge he seldom mixes with the people in town."

"Well, loner or not, he's been quite decent to me."

"I can see." Stephan looked around the room with admiration. "This is an exquisite room, much in keeping with the rest of the house, at least what I've seen of it. The furniture is of the highest craftsmanship, probably genuine antiques. It's a truly gracious place." He placed his stethoscope back in the bag and snapped it shut.

"Dr. Baker, will you please send the bill to my home? I wouldn't want it coming here by mistake," said Nicole. "Do you want the address?"

"You're living at the Widow Thompson's place, aren't you?"

"Yes." She gazed at him with amused wonder. "Word travels fast around here."

"Mrs. Thompson is a patient of mine and could do nothing but talk about her new tenant," he said.

"Nothing bad, I hope."

"Nothing but praise, I assure you. She was extremely happy to have a nice, quiet tenant who didn't have the television or the radio blaring at all hours of the day and night. I only wish she had described you. I wouldn't have waited so long to make your acquaintance and I would have made it under different circumstances. Well, at least we've met, and that's a step in the right direction. It is with regret that I must leave you now and get back to the office. As you well know, when duty calls . . ." His voice trailed off as he walked to the open bedroom door. He stood in the doorway and faced Nicole. "We have a lot in common, you know—both doctors and relative newcomers to Essex Junction. There must be a divine purpose there somewhere. Good-bye for now, Dr. Nicole Winters."

Nicole smiled as she watched the handsome young man leave. Maybe there was something in what he said. Even though they had divergent types of patients, he certainly understood what it was like to serve in the medical profession and the demands it made upon one's time and energy. He was the kind of man she had always thought she might fall in love with someday: clean-cut, handsome and very personable. Yes, Dr. Stephan Baker had impressed her.

It was precisely eight o'clock in the evening when Jason McBride came through the open door, board and box of chessmen tucked under his arm.

"Are you up to another lesson?" he asked.

"Yes," she replied enthusiastically. She had grown tired of reading. Her red, watery eyes were ready for it.

"You don't look too good. Perhaps I should let you rest." His expression was grim and dour.

"Oh, no. Please. I would enjoy it."

He brought the chair to the side of the bed, set up the board and, like before, only spoke to instruct her in the art of playing chess.

Occasionally Nicole found herself stealing small glances at his rugged face set stonily in contemplation as he studied the board. She had the bizarre urge to reach out and let her fingers trace over the gray strands of hair wisping at his temples, to touch the hard line of his square jaw. A tremor raced through her at the thought of it.

"Are you all right?" he asked, suddenly looking up at her.

She cleared her throat. His sudden acknowledgment of her presence had caught her off guard. She couldn't help but think the man didn't miss a thing and was quite sensitive to those around him. "Of course I'm all right."

"I saw you tremble. Are you cold? Do you have the chills?" His eyebrows clashed together over the high bridge of his nose in a dark frown.

"I'm perfectly fine." As if to make a liar out of her, her nose tickled and she proceeded to sneeze.

"I think we'd better call it an evening. I'll put the board on the desk, and we can pick up where we left off tomorrow night," he said, carefully lifting the chessboard. Then, with a brief good night, he was gone.

During the dead of the night, she was aroused by a tickling sensation in her throat. She coughed a few times, and it seemed to ease the scratchiness. As she rolled onto her other side, her half-open eyes caught a shaft of light glimmering under the closed bathroom door. She knew the bathroom was connected to another room, for she had tried to open the door on the other side, but it was locked. Seeing now that the bathroom was in use, it came to her that it must connect her bedroom to that of Jason McBride, for to her knowledge he was the only other person living in the main part of the house. Mrs. Beaton had her own apartment.

Hypnotized, she stared at the thin ribbon of light. When it vanished, she sighed and was about to close her eyes when she heard the faint metallic turn of the knob. Though it was dark, she instinctively knew the door was opening . . . opening into her room. Her heart pounded against her rib cage; her skin tingled up and down the length of her body with a novel excitement. Jason McBride was entering her room in the middle of the night.

CHAPTER 3

Holding her breath and feigning sleep, Nicole furtively watched the tall, shadowy form glide across the deep-piled carpet to loom at the foot of her bed. She tensed, wondering how long he was going to stand there and study her. What had prompted him to come into her room in the middle of the night? She was sure if she lay quietly, he would go away. But her affliction betrayed her, and several short sneezes were crowned with two deep coughs.

"Are you awake, Dr. Winters?" Jason whispered in a low, deep voice as he came to stand at the side of the bed.

"This darn cold doesn't seem to want to go away."

"I thought I heard you choking in here and thought I'd better check," he explained, turning on the bedside lamp.

"My throat was scratchy, and I was trying to cough it clear." She looked up at him, taking in the white shirt open to the waist, revealing a thick mat of curly black hair spreading across his deep chest. It, too, had sprigs of gray spattered through it.

"Did you take your pills?"

"I forgot. I'll take some now." She pushed herself upright in the bed.

"Never mind. I have something that might do you more good."

Jason went back through the connecting bathroom while Nicole, her curiosity unchecked, craned her neck trying to get a glimpse of his bedroom. But the angle was wrong. She couldn't see a thing.

He returned with a large brandy snifter in his hand. Sitting on the edge of the bed next to her, he said, "Here, try this."

"What is it?" she asked, not really caring. At this point she was willing to try anything that would get her back on her feet. She was eager to get back to work and home.

"Brandy," he replied, extending the glass toward her.

As she reached out to curl her hand around the bubble-domed glass, their fingers touched lightly. Nicole felt a peculiar spark ignite her fingertips and rush along her arm to disperse like a million charged ions throughout her body. It was a totally new sensation, and she didn't know what to make of it. She glanced at Jason briefly to see what kind of expression was registering on his face. It was impassive, and she quickly lowered her eyes to stare into the brandy as she tried to put a label on her reaction to his touch.

"Don't stare at it. Drink it," Jason ordered quietly.

She obeyed and crinkled her face at its pungent, acrid taste as it burned its way down her throat and splashed into her stomach with a fiery heat. She handed the half-empty glass back to him.

"All of it," he insisted, gently pushing the snifter back to her.

"Must I?" She grimaced.

"Yes."

Nicole took a deep breath, let it out slowly, then downed the brandy in one gulp. She shook her head and gave a little shudder. "I don't know how anyone can drink that stuff," she said raspily, holding one hand over her burning throat and thrusting the empty glass in Jason's direction.

"It's an acquired taste. I guarantee you'll feel much better in the morning." A vague smile hovered around his lips as he looked at her and used one lean finger to brush a stray tendril of hair from her cheek. He rose from the bed. "You'd better get under the covers and keep warm."

Nicole's head was beginning to spin, and the pillows felt good as she snuggled down into the bed while Jason drew the covers up to her chin. She looked up at him looming over her and gave him a silly grin. To her astonishment, he traced his fingers over her cheek and whispered a low good night. The light on the nightstand was quickly shut off, followed by the barely audible closing of the bathroom door.

The morning light once again spread its warmth over Nicole's face, and she stretched in the bed like a lazy, well-fed cat, a wide, contented smile gracing her lips. Reflexively her hand went to her cheek in remembrance. Had Jason really caressed her cheek, or had she dreamed it? Emitting a long, low sigh, she told herself it didn't matter. Jason McBride was not the man for her, and her thoughts quickly veered toward young Dr. Baker.

The day passed rapidly. Her congestion had eased considerably, leaving in its wake only the ragged remnants of the cold, a vague achiness and a sporadic cough that she could easily cope with. Fortunately, the sneezing had stopped.

She was feeling quite fit when Jason came in the evening to resume their chess game. She was in a lighthearted mood that Jason's sullen frame of mind couldn't alter. He wasn't his usual instructive self, playing the game with rare singlemindedness. He won handily, with the air of someone who had more important tasks at hand.

"Your cure for the common cold should be patented," she said gaily. "I'll be leaving tomorrow." She watched him pack the chessmen into the wooden box.

"I thought as much." His voice was icy, his expression dour.

"I should think you'd be delighted to rid yourself of an extremely poor chess player." Her attempt at levity fell on deaf ears. She became serious. "I can't tell you how much I've appreciated your generosity and kindness."

"Forget it." He snapped the wooden box shut, slipped the board under his arm and went out the door with a brusque good night.

Nicole stared at the empty doorway. Jason McBride was as insulated from the world around him as a bear in hibernation. Well, that's his problem, she thought, not mine. Yet her dreams had been filled with a man on a black stallion, her fingers throbbed where they had touched his, her cheek burned from his fleeting touch. She sighed. The whole thing was stupid! Her idleness had turned her brain to mush. Tomorrow she would go home even if she had to crawl. She punched the pillow with a mixture of determination and anger, never stopping to analyze why she was so angry.

"Mr. McBride tells me you are leaving us today," said Mrs. Beaton as she placed the breakfast tray on the bed, her face sagging dejectedly.

"Yes, Mrs. Beaton. Three days is enough to impose on anyone. You really didn't have to bring my breakfast up. I could have come down for it," said Nicole, smiling at the older woman who had practically waited on her hand and foot for almost seventy-two hours.

"I've enjoyed every moment of it. Your clothes are all cleaned and ready for you. I'll bring them up as soon as you've finished your breakfast." Mrs. Beaton took her usual position on the chaise and chatted away while Nicole consumed the breakfast.

When Mrs. Beaton left with the breakfast tray, Nicole could no longer contain herself. She headed for the bathroom, where she turned the shower to steamy warmth. The beads of water pelted her skin with a renewing force. Finding some shampoo, she cleansed her hair with a vigorous massage. The entire ritual was almost like a religious experience, Nicole thought. After a thorough rubdown, she wrapped one towel around her hair and the other around her body and was gratified to find that Mrs. Beaton had left her clothing on the bed along with a blow-dryer.

Fully dressed, her golden hair braided in one neat plait down her back, Nicole looked around the bedroom and had to admit that she had become fond of it. With the books Jason had lent her tucked under her arm, she closed the door behind her, then headed down the hall to the wide staircase as Mrs. Beaton entered the small foyer.

"You certainly look a lot different from when Mr. McBride brought you in," remarked the older woman.

"I feel a lot different. Is Mr. McBride in? I'd like to return these books and say good-bye," said Nicole, her heart racing in a most peculiar manner.

"He left early this morning. He put your car in the driveway, and I'll take care of the books." Cradling the books in the crook of her arm, Mrs. Beaton saw Nicole to her car, telling the young veterinarian not to be a stranger and to come and visit with her when she had the time.

Driving back to her home, Nicole made a mental note to call the local florist and have a bouquet of flowers sent to Mrs. Beaton. It was the least she could do. As far as McBride himself was concerned, she thought it best to let it go with the thank you she had already expressed. She tried to push McBride from her mind and concentrate on the handsome Dr. Baker, but the image of McBride's craggy face kept superimposing itself on that of the young doctor.

When she got home, Mrs. Thompson, her landlady, had back-to-back questions about the McBride place and the man—especially the man. Concerning the latter, Nicole felt there wasn't much she could tell her. Even three days in his company hadn't resolved the enigma of his true personality for her. But she did describe what she could of the house in lavish detail, which pleased Mrs. Thompson. When Nicole mentioned that Dr. Baker had attended her, Mrs. Thompson became a babbling encyclopedia and Nicole learned that the young doctor was considered the most eligible bachelor in town. Almost every young woman was eyeing him hopefully. Anxious mothers were forever inviting him to dinner, and his practice was flourishing. The information did not quell Nicole's wish to know him better; neither did she feel she was in a contest to snag him. She thought him a personable man with whom she had something in common.

Both men vanished from her mind when Dr. Carey took a few days off as he had promised. It seemed that the minute Dr. Carey was gone, animal disorders became epidemic. Between outlying farms and the hospital, she was kept on a dead run. She wondered how Dr. Carey had kept up the grueling pace when he was the sole practitioner. Her most heartwrenching case was the removal of some two hundred quills from a large dog of mixed parentage who had tangled with a porcupine. But no matter how arduous the work became, she loved every minute of it. It was a challenge that stimulated her every pore and excited her beyond imagination. Even when Dr. Carey returned from his brief hiatus, the days flew by, each one different from the last.

She was checking the day's schedule as Dr. Carey thumbed through the mail when the telephone rang.

"Is Peaches there?" asked the woman's high-pitched voice.

"Yes, Mrs. Strong." Nicole tossed a raised eyebrow at Dr. Carey, who smiled at her with a mischievous glint in his eye.

"Could I speak to her?" There was an urgent plea in the nervous voice.

"Mrs. Strong, she is—"

"Please. I have to talk to her."

Nicole could almost hear the tears in the woman's voice. She looked again at Dr. Carey with an expression of helpless impatience, which he returned with a nod.

"Just a minute, Mrs. Strong, I'll get her." Nicole went into the back room and, feeling totally idiotic, held the receiver to the clipped poodle's floppy ear. The animal yawned with disdain at the sound of its mistress's voice.

Nicole could hear the singsong voice mewling words of encouragement and endearment into the poodle's ear. Her eyes remained fixed on Dr. Carey, who was displaying great fortitude in keeping his laughter under control. When she finally caught the repeated phrase "Put the doctor back on, sweets," she lifted the phone back to her own ear.

"I'm here, Mrs. Strong."

"When will Peaches be having her surgery?"

"In an hour or so," replied Nicole.

"How long will it take?" There was a muffled sob.

"About twenty minutes to a half hour."

"I'd better come over so she won't be alone when she comes out of the anesthetic."

"That won't be necessary, Mrs. Strong. Besides, we wouldn't want to get her all excited so soon after surgery, now would we?"

"I suppose not." The sound of a deep, low sigh bounced along the telephone wires.

"You can pick her up first thing tomorrow morning. We open at nine, as you know," said Nicole, trying to inject some sympathy into her tone.

"I'll be there at nine sharp. You're sure she'll be all right and you'll take good care of her, won't you?"

"Of course we will. And she'll be fine, just fine."

When Nicole hung the phone up, Dr. Carey could no longer contain himself and burst into gales of laughter. As the merriment subsided, he removed his glasses and wiped a tear or two from his eyes.

"I was watching your face as you held the receiver to the dog's ear and would have given anything for a camera at that moment," he said with rippling glee.

"I'll confess, I did feel a little foolish."

"Well, you handled it very nicely. I no longer have the patience for all that silly business. I can understand an owner's concern for an animal, but when it's carried to absurdity I . . ." His voice trailed off, and with a shrug he threw his hands in the air.

It was about forty-five minutes after the surgery on the poodle and almost closing time for the hospital when a special messenger arrived with a large bouquet of mixed flowers. Nicole thanked the messenger and opened the card with the fuzzy notion that they were for her and possibly from Jason McBride. Her heart pumped with excitement until she read the card. She leaned against the counter beset with laughter, then handed the card to Dr. Carey, who was seated at his desk.

" 'To Peaches . . . Hope you feel a whole lot better and will soon be up and out, 'cause you're the kind of person who's so nice to have about. Mother Strong,' " he read aloud.

They both convulsed with laughter and didn't hear the door of the clinic open and footsteps treading on the tiled floor of the waiting room.

"Is this a private joke or can anyone join in?" asked a smiling Stephan Baker, coming to stand at the counter.

"Why, Dr. Baker. How are you?" Nicole's eyes still sparkled with mirth.

"Fine. And I see you have fully recovered. How are you, Dr. Carey?" Stephan asked, poking his head over the counter to meet the old vet's gaze.

"Since Nicole came to work for me, all my aches and pains have vanished into the wind. I won't be throwing much business your way, I'm afraid," said Dr. Carey. "Don't tell me you've brought an animal here for us to diagnose."

"No. I thought I'd deliver my bill to Dr. Winters and see if she'll have dinner with me tonight," Stephan explained as his eyes moved to Nicole's face.

"Good." Dr. Carey stood and stretched, then, rising from his seat, ambled into the back room.

"How about it?" asked Stephan.

"I'd like that," she replied, the laughter still rumbling deep within her.

"I'll pick you up at seven. Is that all right?"

"Fine." She watched him turn to leave. "Dr. Baker . . . you forgot to give me your bill."

"Oh, so I did." He reached down into his pocket and handed her the small white envelope. "See you at seven."

Nicole joined Dr. Carey in the back room, where he was bedding down the animals for the night. Seeing that he was almost finished, she went into the operating room and scrubbed it down for the next time it would be needed. Their good nights said and everything in order, Nicole headed home in a light, easy mood.

Thumbing through her wardrobe for a suitable dress, Nicole realized this would be the first formal date she had had since coming to Essex Junction. Her social engagements—those few she had had time for—had been funneled through the Young Women's League and consisted of group engagements. The men were nice, but there was no one in particular she had taken a fancy to. It was all plain, pleasant camaraderie.

She laid a dress of very sheer green wool on her bed, then unpinned the heavy, braided chignon at the nape of her neck. As she unbraided the plait, she walked into the bathroom, turned the shower on, then discarded her clothes on the floor.

With her freshly shampooed hair dry, her toilette complete, Nicole slipped into the green dress. Even though it was a few years old, it still looked good, she thought, her fingers deftly rebraiding her long blond hair. After securing the chignon, she inserted two small gold buttons in the pierced lobes of her ears. The high-heeled shoes felt peculiar after clomping about in sturdy flat shoes all week long. Her feet felt strained, and she hoped she would be able to walk properly. It wouldn't do to stumble about like a clumsy clod.

Stephan Baker was prompt, and Nicole was pleased when he held the car door open for her.

"You look quite lovely, Dr. Winters," he said, thrusting the key into the ignition once he had settled himself in the bucket seat.

"Thank you. You don't look so bad yourself, Dr. Baker," she replied, thinking how the dark brown suit, beige shirt and beige-and-brown striped tie accented his patrician good looks and coloring.

"Why don't we dispense with all this doctor nonsense? The name is Stephan, preferably Steve," he suggested as he put the car into gear and sped down the street.

"Sounds like a good idea, Steve. For tonight I would like to forget all about the medical profession."

"I don't think you really mean that. From what I've heard around town, you're a very dedicated vet," he said.

"I'll have to admit I do love my work." She smiled.

"The long hours? Being on call at all hours? The stringent social life?" he queried with a wry smile that was extremely becoming.

"You make it sound positively monastic. Is that the way you find it?" she countered.

"Some days it seems that way. But then we have totally different types of patients. Yours can't talk back to you."

"But their owners can and do."

The restaurant was not unusual. It typified the burgeoning popularity of steak houses with the standard all-you-can-eat salad bar. After their order was placed with the waitress, they helped themselves to the varied offerings at the salad bar, then resumed their seats, plates full of greenery.

"More wine?" asked Steve, raising the decanter of chilled white wine over Nicole's glass.

"Please. You said before you are a newcomer to Essex Junction. Where are you from originally?"

"From Worcester, Mass."

"However did you get here?"

"Heard about the old doctor here wanting to sell his practice and retire. The price was right, and I liked the idea of being a general practitioner in a small town. And the practice included not only a ready-made clientele but a house in which to live and fully equipped offices. As I said, the price was well within my reach, so I grabbed it," he explained.

"Wouldn't it be more lucrative practicing in a big city like Boston?" she asked.

"Definitely. But it would be a lot more expensive living in the city and getting set up on my own. Way beyond my means. I would have had to start as low man on the totem pole in an already established medical firm. That idea didn't appeal to me in the least. Besides, the benefits here are great."

"Oh?" Nicole looked up from her salad into the cool blue eyes across from her.

"They are very prompt at paying their bills. Yankee pride, I suppose. Anyway, the people themselves are most generous. I have on occasion received homemade bread, pies, casseroles, even a hand-knit pair of socks. Can you imagine those types of benefits in a big city?"

"Hardly." She smiled and pushed her empty plate aside as the waitress brought their steaks and baked potatoes. Conversation ebbed as they tackled the hot food but soon picked up as they aired their views on the community and the people in it.

"That hit the spot," exclaimed Nicole as she drained her wineglass.

"More?" asked Steve, reaching for the decanter, then stopping his hand in mid-air as Nicole shook her head. "Dessert? Coffee?"

"Just coffee, no dessert," said Nicole, leaning back against the leatherlike plastic of the booth, feeling physically and mentally content. The waitress cleared their table and promptly brought their coffee.

"By the way," began Steve as he stirred sugar into his cup. "I found out a few things about your benefactor, Jason McBride."

"Oh? What?" Her heartbeat intensified. It must be the wine, she thought, for Jason McBride was nothing more than a passing moment in her life.

"One of the vice-presidents of Bitron Computers was in for a routine checkup. We started talking, and McBride's name came up. It seems there is something very unsavory in McBride's past. No one seems to know exactly what it is, or they're not saying, but rumor has it he was discharged from one of the hi-tech firms in California, then disappeared into the woodwork for a number of years. I guess his startling genius for innovative creations got him back in the game. From what I've gathered, it all happened back when he was twenty-four or so. Thirteen, fourteen years ago."

"Whatever it was, it couldn't have been too bad. It doesn't seem to have affected his career in computers," defended Nicole, finding it hard to believe anything sinister about Jason McBride. "From all appearances he is a private man, but that doesn't necessarily mean he has a lurid past."

Steve shrugged. "I think he may have murdered someone years ago. Inadvertently, of course."

"What makes you say a dreadful thing like that?" she asked with perplexed anger.

"Well . . . when you were unconscious and I was examining you, McBride paced the floor like a condemned man. I got the impression that if anything happened to you, he'd be in big trouble. When I found out the circumstances of the accident and that you were a stranger to him, it started me thinking, especially because of what I had learned about him," said Steve, pausing to take a sip of his coffee.

"The man was only concerned for my welfare. I see nothing grisly about that." She was becoming indignant; Steve's accusations were unwarranted.

"You didn't see the look on his face." Steve looked at Nicole with a deep intensity in his blue eyes. "I have the feeling that somewhere in his past there might have been another accident, only it was a fatal one."

"How absurd! You certainly have a vivid imagination, Steve, for one who has been trained in the rigid discipline of the medical profession," declared Nicole, thinking that the entire notion was ludicrous. The topic was making her uncomfortable.

"It just seems to me that a man his age, with a house like that and no wife . . . well . . . something doesn't ring true." He finished his coffee.

"One could almost say the same of you," she blurted. "Perhaps the bachelor life is the one he enjoys most."

Steve smiled at her as if he knew she wanted to drop the subject. "Maybe you're right. Maybe I've read more into the man than is there. How about taking in a movie to round off the evening? There's a comedy playing at Cinema Four that is considered to be one of the best in a long time."

"Great. I could use a good laugh about now." It was true. The discussion regarding Jason McBride had disturbed her more than she cared to admit. The idea that there might be any truth to Steve's observations was repugnant to her, and she refused to acknowledge the possibility of a dark secret in McBride's past. She couldn't and wouldn't let such a thought dampen her spirits. After all, she hardly knew the man. A few games of chess? Three days in his home with only occasional encounters? That hardly created a relationship between them. She was being absolutely ridiculous.

The movie was indeed entertaining and deflected Nicole's mind from any thoughts of McBride. Steve Baker proved to be an amiable companion, and she invited him in for coffee when they arrived at her home without a second thought to any gossip such an act might provoke in a small town. He stayed for a little over an hour as they compared notes on medical studies at their respective universities.

Even though she had been looking into blue eyes all evening, when Steve left, black embers seared themselves into her brain. Why couldn't she stop thinking about Jason McBride? She was angry with herself for not being able to govern her own thoughts. With a shake of her head, she got ready for bed. Only when sleep claimed her did her mind release the image of Jason McBride.

Spring had definitely made its appearance as an abundance of daffodils, forsythia and other species of spring blooms dazzled all eyes with their colorful dancing in the wafting breeze.

"I have the papers from the state for testing herds, Nicole," said Dr. Carey, continuing to leaf through the mail as Nicole entered the office. "How would you like to cover that little chore for me?"

"Can't think of anything I'd rather do," she replied.

Dr. Carey pulled his glasses to the bridge of his nose and peered at her. "If you'd rather not . . ."

She smiled. "Really. I'd be delighted." Nicole liked going out to the farms, being in the fresh air, watching the countryside burst with spring, and she was fast becoming accepted by the farmers. Testing the bovine herds for brucellosis was a job that gave her more time to get to know the farmers and animals better. Every state required that dairy cows be tested to make sure they didn't have the bacteria, which seep into milk and can cause undulant fever in humans. The program had pretty well eliminated the disease.

"I only have fifteen herds this year. A lot of the smaller farms have gone out of business. Better make yourself a schedule so you can call the farmers the day before and let them know you're coming. They're a pretty cooperative bunch and will hold the cows in the barn for you." He handed her the papers. "Shortly after morning milking is the best time to test them. They don't like keeping the cows in the barn too long and don't take kindly to having the herd tested just before milking. It upsets the cows and affects milk production."

"I'll work it out tonight. Then if I have a problem, we can straighten it out tomorrow," said Nicole.

Most of the farmers milked at different times in the morning, so Nicole juggled distances and times, coming up with a schedule of three farms a day, giving her the afternoons to assist Dr. Carey in the hospital. She would complete the testing within the week. She purposely scheduled Jake's farm for last. Dr. Carey had given her that Friday afternoon off, and she thought she would visit with Mrs. Beaton and Milly for a little while.

She called Jake the day before and told him she would be there at ten in the morning to test his herd. Early Friday morning she showered and put on a fresh pair of jeans and a pale blue chambray shirt. Her blond hair braided, coiled and secured at the nape of her neck, she grabbed an old heavy jacket, for it was still chilly in the early hours of the morning. The weather didn't become balmy until the sun had climbed high in the sky. It was dark when she went to her battered station wagon, and it would be a few hours before daylight made its welcome appearance as she drove along the country roads to her first farm.

Her timing was off and she was twenty minutes late arriving at Jake's. Getting out of the car after parking it near the milk room, she tossed her jacket onto the seat, went to the rear of the car and pulled down the back door. She reached in for her canvaslike cover coat, which came down below her knees, and grabbed her high rubber boots in her other hand. After putting them on, she took a wire basket holding the vials for the blood samples and a clipboard with her papers on it from the depths of the old station wagon.

"I'm sorry I'm late, Jake," she said, entering the main section of the barn.

"Not by much. One year Doc Carey never did show up and I had the cows in for the better part of the day," replied Jake, scratching the mass of sandy hair on his head.

"That doesn't sound like Dr. Carey," said Nicole, her voice betraying her disbelief.

"Not his fault. On his way here his van broke down, and he had sprained his ankle while walking to a garage. A bad storm hit the night before and knocked all the wires down. He couldn't get a hold of me. One of those days when nothing goes right."

"Let's hope this isn't one of them." She smiled. "Shall we get started?"

Jake nodded. With brisk efficiency on both their parts, the samples were taken and the testing was completed in a little under an hour.

"Oh, by the way, Doc, Milly sent down a jar of strawberry preserves for you," said Jake, following Nicole into the milk room, where she proceeded to wash up. "She said you enjoyed it so much she wanted you to have a jar."

"That was nice of her. I thought I'd have a little visit with your wife, so I'll thank her in person," said Nicole, wiping her hands on the coarse paper towels in the dispenser.

"She'd love a visit from you." He handed her the jar, which Nicole slipped into one of the oversize pockets of her coat. Then he disappeared back into the barn.

The glass vials in the rack she was holding began to clatter when her eyes locked with the black embers of Jason McBride. He was leaning against her car, his brawny arms folded over his chest. She stood mesmerized by his presence until his sonorous voice brought her back to reality.

"I've been waiting for you, Dr. Winters," he said quietly, never changing his position as his eyes narrowed in appraisal of her form hidden beneath the voluminous coat.

"Why?" she asked, resuming her walk to the back of the car. She swung the door down and placed the blood samples and the clipboard on the floor of the station wagon. Taking the jar of preserves from her pocket, she balanced it on the edge of the flattened door while she removed the coat and boots, tossing them into the rear of the car. She grasped the jar and closed the car's rear door.

"Well?" she asked, coming to stand before Jason as he blocked the door to the driver's seat.

"I have need of your services." He looked down at her, his eyes traveling over her face as though it were a road map he was trying to memorize. "My horse seems to have a problem."

"I suggest you call Dr. Carey. His knowledge of horses is far more extensive than mine." There was a nervous fluttering inside her that refused to go away. His white shirt, unbuttoned at the neck and sleeves rolled to his elbows, revealed a mass of curly black hair sprouting from the V and the same thick, wiry hair clung to the heavy sinews of his forearms. The black jeans clung to his lithe hips, then swelled over the curves of his well-muscled legs. There was a virile magnetism about the man Nicole couldn't ignore.

"I don't think it is anything too serious, but I would like him looked at to be on the safe side. He seems to be favoring one leg, but I couldn't find anything wrong with his hoof or shoe. I'd appreciate it if you'd take a minute to look at him," he said in a hard, flat tone, his face expressionless as he continued to gaze at her.

She sighed deeply. "I'll have to move my car. It's blocking the milk room."

"The horse barn is behind my house." Jason hoisted his tall frame to a full standing position, looked at Nicole briefly, then went around to the other side of the car and got in at the same moment she did.

Nicole backed out of the graveled driveway onto the macadam road and headed for the large crescent driveway that led to the regal Mc-Bride home.

"Go past the main entrance. About a hundred yards farther down is a road that leads directly to the horse barn," Jason instructed, his long legs looking uncomfortably cramped in the pulled-up front seat.

Nicole spotted the turnoff and maneuvered the station wagon up a slight incline, bringing it to a halt before a neat white building trimmed in green. She followed Jason into the long structure, trying to keep up with his long, steady stride until he stopped abruptly before a closed stall.

"I'll bring him out. He's a bit skittish with strangers," he warned.

In silence she watched the tall man slip a bridle over the sleek ebony horse's head and marveled at the beauty of the animal when Jason led him out into the aisle of the barn. Her first meeting with the beast had been more of a confrontation.

"He's a beautiful animal," she commented.

"Yes, he is," agreed Jason, stroking the animal's neck.

Nicole put her bag down and slowly approached the horse, her hand unhurried as it went to pet the long face of the black creature. She stroked the silken hide with tempered, delicate caresses. His soft brown eyes no longer held the frenzy they had that day by the stream. They reflected a calm warmth.

"Could you walk him a bit so I can see how he favors the leg?" she asked.

Critically watching the animal as Jason led him around, she noted that the uneven gait was almost imperceptible.

"Did you see it?" asked Jason, bringing the animal to a halt before her.

"Yes. You have very keen eyes, Mr. McBride. Most owners wouldn't have caught it," she said, stroking the horse's cheek once again.

"Very little escapes me, Dr. Winters, I assure you."

Bending over with her back to the horse's head, she lifted the troublesome leg and carefully inspected the hoof. The animal was expertly shod. There were no blisters, boils or foreign objects in the hoof; neither was there any inflammation. She placed the hoof back on the cement, then ran her hand gently over the pastern and the fetlock up to the cannon, which was evidently tender, for the animal raised his leg slightly in protest. Her fingers probed the area with great delicacy, for horses were about the most dangerous of large animals to work on. Satisfied that nothing was broken or torn, Nicole rose and faced Jason with a smile.

"Anything serious?" he asked.

"No. It seems the tendon of the common digital extensor muscle has been bruised a little. I'll wrap it to prevent any further bumps aggravating it." She went to her bag and took a roll of cotton, some tape and scissors, then went back to the horse and kneeled. Taking a wide piece of cotton, she carefully wrapped several layers around the area between the hock and the fetlock of the lower back leg, then taped it. "There . . . that should do it. I wouldn't ride him for a few days, but do exercise him," she said, snipping the tape and rising.

Jason put the horse back in the stall and removed the lead halter. He watched Nicole return her materials to her medical bag, then said, "You must have a very gentle touch, Dr. Winters. Midnight doesn't usually behave that well when he's being examined." He shoved his hands deep into his pockets. "Do you ride, Dr. Winters?"

"Yes. First ponies, then my father bought a horse for me. Nothing grand like your Midnight. Just an old scrag, but I loved her."

"Come here." He motioned for her to advance to the next stall.

Nicole peered over the top of the door to behold an exquisite chestnut mare. "She's splendid. How many horses do you have?"

"Only the two."

The inquisitive chestnut came to thrust its head over the wooden door of the stall. Nicole responded by petting the muzzle of the docile animal. "She's quite friendly."

"She has a very mild and tractable disposition. When Midnight is fit for the fields again, would you care to go riding with me?"

"We'll see," she managed to say while her heart was screaming yes

. . . yes. "By the way, the horse barn looks so much bigger and longer from the outside than it is inside. Is it my imagination, or is it an optical illusion?" She didn't turn to look at him but kept her attention focused on the chestnut, who was relishing her gentle strokes.

"I see you have keen powers of observation also, Dr. Winters. Only half the building is a horse barn. The other half is my workshop. Mrs. Beaton likes to call it my laboratory."

Nicole faced him with a look of mild surprise. "Oh? A real laboratory? May I see it?"

A cloud of indecision stole across his face as if an inner struggle warred within him. "It wouldn't interest a layman."

"I'm hardly a layman. I've been in a number of laboratories, and they hold a fascination for me," she persisted.

"This one wouldn't," he said flatly and began to leave the horse barn.

Nicole grabbed her medical bag and pursued him. Her curiosity was now challenged. "I promise not to ask any foolish questions."

He half-turned and stared down at her, his dark eyes meeting hers as if they were trying to reach into her soul. He was like a big, wary animal, suspicious of the newcomer in his territory. His eyes slowly narrowed in contemplation; his mouth was set in a grim, hard line.

Nicole gave him her most ingenuous smile. "Please."

He took a deep breath, his wide shoulders heaving with the intake. "Very well. A brief glance around."

Reaching the other end of the barn, Jason withdrew a ring of keys from his pocket and, thumbing through them, selected the one that would open the door to the laboratory. He pushed it open and waited for Nicole to enter.

It was like stepping from one world into another. There were no wooden stalls, no smell of hay or manure. It was one vast, antiseptic room where white-paneled drop ceilings were studded with bright fluorescent lights. The walls were completely covered with pale green tiles, while the floor sparkled with linoleum a shade darker. Formica-topped benches, tables and compartmentalized cabinets stood throughout the expansive chamber. On most of the tables were large computers, small computers, gutted computers, wires, bits and pieces of unknown components. Everything was scattered about at random, and Nicole couldn't begin to absorb what her eyes beheld. She moved to a table that was in such disarray she could only conclude it was where Jason was currently working.

"Is this your latest project?" she asked, her fingertips tracing along the edge of the table.

"Partly. Does it overwhelm you?" he asked, his hands clasped behind his back as he moved next to her.

She looked up at him and smiled. "I'm afraid it does. You were right. This is not quite what I had expected in the way of a laboratory. No eerie bubbling brews and all that."

"Sorry to have disappointed you." He picked up a small item and studied it with intensity, then rummaged through some material like a man possessed.

Nicole could see he was lost in his world of computers, much as she could become lost in her work. She backed away from the table and started to leave.

"Where are you going?" he asked, his back toward her.

"I thought you might like to be alone to continue with your work."

"This might interest you, Dr. Winters. Come here, won't you?" As Nicole approached him, he held up a tiny square object for her inspection. "Hold out your hand."

She set her bag down and extended her hand to receive the microscopic object. "What is it?"

"It contains a minuscule new cryotron that will revolutionize the computer industry." He looked at it with the pride of a new father, then raised his eyes to Nicole's. "I can see you are totally mystified. Well, to be succinct, it's a device that makes use of the effects of low temperatures on conductive materials so that any change in a small magnetic field can control the change in large currents." He stared at her stonily for a moment. "It's rude of me to bore you with my little novelties."

"I don't find computers or their components boring, Mr. McBride, only beyond my mechanical comprehension. My courses in physics were rudimentary, but I understood what you were saying about the cryotron. I think computers would be of great use in veterinary medicine. But I doubt if there is any software in the science at present." She held the tiny object for him to retrieve. As he did, his fingers traced over the palm of her hand, causing a pink glow to flush her face and a lingering catch to form in her throat.

"That's an idea I might be tempted to work on for you," he responded, laying the object on the table.

"Is Mrs. Beaton home? I thought I might have a little visit with her while I'm here." Nicole was seized by a sudden impulse to get away from Jason McBride. His nearness, his touch were confusing her thoughts and emotions.

"Mrs. Beaton is expecting you."

"Expecting me?"

"Yes. I told her you would be staying to lunch."

"Oh, I couldn't."

"Why not? It is your afternoon off, isn't it?"

"Yes. But how did you know?"

"I called the office in regard to Midnight, and Dr. Carey told me you'd be at the farm around ten this morning. I felt I should at least give you lunch for intruding on your free time," he explained.

"I appreciate the offer but . . . really . . . I couldn't."

"You'll break Mrs. Beaton's heart if you don't. She's been cooking up a storm all morning." A smile flickered across his lips, softening his angular features. He walked to the door and held it open for her. "I insist."

"Well . . . I am hungry. It's been a long time since breakfast," she said, thinking, why fight it, especially when her stomach was growling so.

The path from the white barn led directly to the rear entrance of the house. Tantalizing aromas filled Nicole's nostrils the minute she and Jason entered the back foyer.

"Mrs. Beaton's in there," said Jason, nodding toward the kitchen door. "You have your chat, and I'll be down shortly."

"I'd like to wash up first."

"Second door down the hall on the left," he replied, then vanished through another door.

It was a small half-bath. She would have liked to have taken a thoroughly cleansing shower, but under the circumstances she would have to settle for a good wash of her hands, face and arms. At least her hair was still neatly secured at the back of her head.

Satisfied that it was all she could do for the moment, she went into the back hall and softly padded to the kitchen, where she was greeted with a hug and a kiss on the cheek from Mrs. Beaton.

"You could have knocked me over with a feather when Mr. McBride told me you were coming to lunch," said the beaming Mrs. Beaton. "I missed you when you got better and went home. And it was so sweet of you to send the flowers. They were lovely, just lovely. And they lasted for quite some time. Well, now, tell me how you've been doing. I heard you went out with that nice Dr. Baker. Dinner and a movie, no less."

"That's quite a network of information you have, Mrs. Beaton," said Nicole, her finely formed eyebrows arching with humorous surprise.

"Amy Heath, she works in the bank, was having dinner at the steak house when you and the doctor came in. And Mabel Grant's son works at the concession booth at Cinema Four. Dr. Baker's comings and goings are always noted around town with great interest, especially when he's with a young woman. I swear, every time the town begins to think he is going to settle down with one woman, he switches to another," declared Mrs. Beaton, then shook her head and pursed her lips.

"He probably likes to keep everyone guessing," suggested Nicole, amused by the older woman's eager interest in the young doctor. She wondered if Steve knew of the town's absorption in his personal life. "Anyway, Mrs. Beaton, it was only a date, not a lifelong commitment."

"Well now, don't you see? He had been seeing the Clarke girl for over three months now, and then he takes you out. Lucy Clarke thought her daughter had snagged the elusive and eligible young doctor for sure. Now he seems to be up to his old tricks again, switching lady friends," said Mrs. Beaton breathlessly, her eyes gleaming as if she had discovered the missing piece to a complex puzzle.

"You can assure everyone that I'm not in the market for a husband at the moment, and I certainly have no designs on Dr. Baker," consoled Nicole as she smiled, then gently patted Mrs. Beaton's arm in reassurance.

Mrs. Beaton returned Nicole's smile and, as if sensing Nicole's reluctance to pursue the topic, she changed the subject. "Is Mr. McBride's horse going to be all right? You won't have to put him to sleep or anything like that, will you?"

"Oh, no. The horse only has a mildly bruised tendon. He'll be fine in a day or so," replied Nicole.

"That's good to hear. He puts a lot of stock in that horse of his. He just loves those animals." Mrs. Beaton resumed her bustling about the kitchen, every move a calculated one.

"Is there anything I can do to help?" asked Nicole.

"You're a guest. Mr. McBride would be very put out if he thought you were working in the kitchen. Besides, I have everything under control."

"You're the boss."

"It's been a refreshing change to prepare a nice luncheon. Usually Mr. McBride comes into the kitchen at odd hours and fixes himself a sandwich or whatever he fancies at the moment. Not much of a challenge for me." As Mrs. Beaton passed one of the kitchen windows, she stopped, took a step backward and craned her neck to peer through the glass pane. "Oh, he's out there on the porch waiting for you. It's best you go out. Tell him lunch will be ready in a few minutes, will you?"

"Sure." Nicole looked around, perplexed. "How do I get out there?"

"Normally you would go through the dining room, but under the circumstances I think it would be easier if you used the kitchen entrance over there." She gave a directional nod of her head.

"Thank you. I'll see you later, Mrs. Beaton."

Jason stood as Nicole entered the large screened in area, the rubber soles of her sturdy shoes noiseless on the flagstoned floor. He pulled out a thickly padded wrought iron chair for her.

"This is a lovely place to eat," remarked Nicole as she took the proffered seat. Her eyes skimmed over the well-set table gleaming with fine bone china and delicate crystal, then moved to the array of various potted plants, some of which were beginning to bloom in bright colors. "It's so light and airy here, and the plants give it a nice touch."

"It faces south, getting a large share of the sun. When the weather starts to chill in the fall, the screens are replaced by insulated glass panels," said Jason, taking the seat opposite her, the glass-topped table the only barrier between them. "The plants are a hobby with me. Someday I hope to build a modest greenhouse where I can experiment with pollination. I suppose that seems a bit incongruous to you—a man who deals strictly with inert mechanical objects wanting to toy with living plants."

"Why should it?"

"You don't find it out of character?"

"A person's character has many divergent facets. Otherwise we'd all be clones of one another."

"And what are your out-of-character interests, Dr. Winters?"

"Animals have always been my main interest in life, and new aspects of medicine and treatment for them."

"Surely you must have a secret passion for something other than animals."

Nicole smiled faintly. "Well . . . I confess I have a positive mania for modern murder mysteries."

One dark eyebrow arched quizzically. With elbows resting on the filigreed iron arms of his chair, he steepled his fingers, brought them to his chin and contemplated the well-scrubbed, shiny face before him. "I would never have taken you for a mystery fan. More the modern novel type, I should say."

"Why?"

"You have a zest for life indicative of the modern world, a sense of urgency that seems to pervade our society. Gory murders don't fit the image you project."

"Like plants and silicon chips?" she said teasingly.

A slow smile widened his mouth. "Your point is well taken."

Mrs. Beaton rolled the wooden tea cart onto the enclosed miniterrace, the captivating aromas preceding her. In the middle of the table, she placed a large casserole with steam rising from the decorative slits in the flaky pie crust on top, then set down a bowl of salad for each of them. A large pitcher of lemonade completed their repast and was left on the tea cart for them to serve themselves from as Mrs. Beaton scurried back to the kitchen.

"Pass me your plate," said Jason, and Nicole complied. "Mrs. Beaton makes no attempt to hide her passion in life."

"Television soap operas," responded Nicole.

"Oh? How did you find out?" he asked, spooning a generous portion of the casserole onto her plate and handing it back to her before filling his own.

"She made it quite clear when I stayed here those three days."

"You made quite an impression on her. I see she has made her prizewinning chicken pie especially for you today."

"Prizewinning?"

"At the county fair that's held every fall."

Throughout the meal, as a result of Jason's gentle probing, Nicole spoke freely of her childhood in Lowville and her college years at Cornell University. He was an ardent listener and seemed to be hoarding her every word for future reference.

Suddenly realizing that her voice was dominating the conversation, she raised her eyes to meet his. "Enough of me. What was your childhood like?"

"Quite ordinary. Nothing spectacular. Would you care for some more chicken pie?" he asked, brushing aside any further comment on his background.

"No, thank you." She put her empty salad bowl on her empty plate and moved them aside to pursue her questions. "Surely there must be something in your childhood that was extraordinary."

"Is the past all that important to you, Dr. Winters?" he asked stiffly.

"I thought—"

"I never look back," he interrupted. "It is the future one must consider and be concerned with." There was a finality in his tone that indicated the topic was closed. "Some dessert?" he asked, then added, "It looks like rhubarb-pineapple pie."

Nicole decided to let the subject drop. Jason McBride was not a man to be questioned. She had the suspicion he did all the asking and would only submit to interrogation if the mood was on him. At the moment it was evidently not. The time would come when he would talk freely about his past, and it would be best not to pursue it right now. But his reticence only served to pique her curiosity and brought into sharp focus the musings of Steve Baker as to his possibly shady background.

"I couldn't eat another thing. The chicken pie was delicious. No wonder Mrs. Beaton won prizes for it," she said, giving her flat stomach a little pat of contentment.

"Why don't I show you the house? Then we can take a walk outside and come back later for the pie and coffee," he suggested.

"I'd like that. Jake said your farm encompasses a thousand acres or so."

He rose from his seat and gallantly assisted Nicole in moving back the heavy iron chair. They went through the wide french doors that connected the main part of the house to the patio and which opened into the dining room.

"As you can see, this is the dining room, where twelve guests can easily be accommodated for a formal dinner. The paintings you see are originals by artists of the nineteenth-century Hudson River school. You'll notice a working fireplace in every room, made possible by a massive center chimney—comes in handy during a really bad winter. Once the bricks heat up, the chimney holds the heat and keeps the house quite warm, lessening the strain on the furnace," explained Jason, his eyes scanning the room before coming back to Nicole.

"Lovely," she remarked, folding her arms over her chest, her body and head twisting to take it all in.

He gave her several minutes to absorb it all before leading her through another set of french doors and across the spacious foyer, which housed the staircase to the upper floor she remembered so well.

Jason motioned her into a room where the rich patina of wood glistened invitingly. One wall held a floor-to-ceiling bookcase. Two large chairs of deep maroon leather faced each other in front of an ornate fireplace, and a massive mahogany desk squatted regally before a set of long windows.

"What an impressive room!" exclaimed Nicole, crossing the red-toned Oriental carpet to the middle of the room for an all-encompassing view.

"The library," said Jason. "My grandfather was a collector of brass, as you can see. Over the years he picked up some unusual pieces."

Nicole went to finger some of the odder objects of brass. "They're exquisite." She lifted one. "And heavy."

"He went for the solid brass, not the hollowed-out pieces. I think you'll find the living room most remarkable," said Jason, gently cupping her elbow and steering her through another door.

Nicole gasped audibly in admiration.

"It takes your breath away, doesn't it?" asked Jason, his eyes glowing with pride and devotion.

"It certainly does," said Nicole as her eyes drank in the spacious, light, airy room that ran the length of the house.

Above the pale cream wainscotting, the walls were covered with a silk-screened Chinese print displaying exotic flowers and birds, wispy and delicate. For the most part the intricate brocade of the furniture was neutral, lending the room an aura of sheer tranquillity. An occasional piece of Japanned furniture bestowed a hint of the mysterious Orient. The seductive allure and grace of the room defied description.

Breaking the spell the room had cast on her, she turned to look at Jason. Catching him in an unguarded moment, she saw the deep emotion on his face and realized how much the man treasured his home. He turned to look down at her.

"Well . . . what do you think?"

"I'm at a loss for words. It's truly beautiful. I love the Oriental accents." She smiled broadly at him.

"All the pieces are genuine. My father was in the import-export business in Boston, dealing mainly with the Orient."

"I'm glad you showed me your home. I'll never forget what I've seen. It's just beautiful." She felt the warmth of his hand leave her elbow, and an intangible essence drained from her.

"Thank you for calling it a home. Most people refer to it as a house, their tone intimating *museum.*" His lips curled into a kindly smile, and there was a softening in his dark eyes. "Well . . . shall we take a small tour of the outside?"

Nicole nodded, her heart floating into her throat at Jason's warm glance, then followed his lead outside toward the horse barn and past it to pick up a dirt road that continued beyond. It was a deeply rutted road worn by the twin paths of wheels. Rough stone walls rose on either side like pebbles thrown by some long-ago giant. Large gaps in the walls permitted entrance to the well-husbanded fields that stretched between them.

"Are all these hay fields?" asked Nicole.

"No. Jake has been planting more and more corn for silage. I suspect he'll plow up a few more acres this year for corn. But I doubt if he'll give up on hay altogether. He's always saying there's nothing like good alfalfa and clover hay to make milk." Jason shoved his hands in his back pockets, his elbows crooking outward as he lessened his pace.

"He's right. As with all creatures on the face of the earth, the proper diet can make all the difference." Nicole glanced over the large greening fields protected by the manmade stone walls. "Were all these walls here before you came?"

"Yes. They're part of the landscape now. Jake has suggested I have them all bulldozed and buried to create more open land, thus gaining planting acreage. But to me they exude the serene charm of yesteryear, so for the time being they stay." He stopped and looked down at Nicole somberly, perusing her face with studied intensity. "Why do you wear your hair like that?"

Her feet halted in their tracks and her neck craned back to gaze up at the tall man beside her. "I beg your pardon." She had been thinking about green fields and stone walls when the question had come at her. What did her hair have to do with anything?

He took his right hand from his pocket, pushed his fingers through his unruly mass of raven hair, then returned the hand to its former resting place. "Nothing, Dr. Winters. Nothing at all." He raised his head, and his eyes left hers to squint protectively against the sun as he carefully scanned the surrounding fields.

Something told Nicole not to press him regarding what he had been about to say regarding her hair. His craggy face had a set and pensive look, as if the man was struggling with forces known only to him. An inner voice told her it was not the time to speak, not the time to intrude on his private thoughts as he resumed walking down the well-worn dirt road.

Stopping where the rutted road was intersected by a narrow dirt lane where one path led to more fields, the other to a ribbon of budding trees, thickets and evergreens, Jason veered down the lane to the trees with a surety of purpose.

With the air of an intrepid adventurer, Nicole followed him, the veins in her temples and wrists throbbing with apprehension, a sensation new and peculiar to her. She was painfully conscious of the man beside her and of the emotions he was stirring within her. She matched his stride, heedless of where he might be leading her. Whether it be the Stygian crossing or the yellow brick road to Oz, Nicole was in the grasp of an ominous compulsion.

CHAPTER 4

Reaching the outer edges where the thickets stood in attendance, a screen for the stately oaks, maples, firs and birches, the narrow lane shrank to a footpath. Nicole trailed behind Jason with hurried steps until they emerged from the density of woody growth to a spacious glade where erupting blades of grass were interspersed among velvety green moss.

Nicole's eyes widened in wonder at the sizable pond in which crystal-clear water winked with sporadic sparkles as the sun's rays danced over it. This is what Eden must have been like, she thought.

"My grandfather had this done. He had the stream diverted, then dug an immense deep hole, lined it with sand and white stone, put a dam at one end and then had the stream return to its normal course. As you can see, it makes a perfect swimming hole," Jason informed her.

"It's so clear," exclaimed Nicole, still drinking in the beauty and serenity of the glade.

"It is the same brook you unfortunately fell into, only much further up the line. Its clarity stems from the fact that the natural springs creating the flow are on my property and have in no way been contaminated by industrial or human wastes. There is a small waterfall at the emptying rim of the pond." He moved down along the bank, Nicole trotting behind him, her eyes fixed on the shimmering water.

A quiet smile spread over her oval face as she beheld the waterfall that cascaded some four feet down to splash against the rocky bed waiting to greet it before reverting to a streaming brook once again.

"It's all quite breathtaking, Mr. McBride. It's like a private haven away from the outside world. Consider me thoroughly enchanted," she said.

"I want you to know you are welcome to use it anytime you wish during the hot summer months."

"Oh, I wouldn't intrude on your privacy like that. Besides, there is a gigantic public pool in town."

"Which, during the summer months, is teeming with children. One cannot swim in it without running into one of them after two strokes. And the noise is not conducive to the serenity one should have while swimming. I insist you avail yourself of my offer."

She looked up at him, to find his coal black eyes boring into her with inflexible determination. A knot formed in the pit of her stomach as his gaze held her captive. Bizarre sensations bubbled under the surface of her skin. The place was indeed enchanted; she had never in her life felt this sense of otherworldliness washing through her with reckless abandon. Was it really the setting or the man that was bewitching her? The sharp cry of a vexatious blue jay pierced the cloak of sorcery, and she turned from him to stare at the miniature cataract.

"Well?" There was a taut edge to his voice.

"I'd be delighted to take advantage of your generous offer whenever time permits." Nicole knew he had made the offer after a considerable debate with himself. It would have been callous of her to flatly refuse him and it would have wounded his pride. Besides, with her heavy schedule, she doubted very much if she would have the time to use the tempting swimming pond.

"Good. That's settled. I wouldn't advise driving your car up these lanes, though. You can leave it near the horse barn," Jason said, staring at her with a peculiar expression on his face before he suddenly turned away. "I've often thought of making the dam higher so there would be a more spectacular waterfall. What do you think?"

"I think it is perfect the way it is," she replied, glancing furtively at him and seeing a feathery smile form on his lips as if he heartily approved of her reply. When he smiled, even imperceptibly, it eased the starkness of his visage. She wondered how a full-blown, open-mouth smile would affect his countenance. There was an invisible wall around the man, but he wasn't as aloof as the townspeople would have him. At least with her he seemed to be making an effort to make contact, which seemed to come to him with great difficulty.

She looked around the glade and found it was beginning to unsettle her, especially with Jason McBride so near. An eerie weakness was starting to gnaw at her, and she didn't like it. "Well, I'd better get back."

"I thought you had the afternoon off," said Jason in an accusing tone.

"I do. But I want to drop in on Jake's wife, Milly, while I'm out this way. Then I have some shopping to do."

"I see." His eyes clouded as he looked down at her. "Then we'll go back. But you must try some of Mrs. Beaton's pie or her feelings would be hurt."

They walked back to the house in silence. The kitchen was still deserted when they returned, but the pie was on the kitchen table, covered with a white linen cloth, and the electric coffee pot was sending signals that its contents were perked and ready to be poured. The table had been set neatly for two.

"Do you mind eating in the kitchen?" asked Jason.

"Not at all. I do it all the time," replied Nicole with a shade of laughter in her voice.

"I understand you are rooming at the Widow Thompson's place," he observed as he poured the coffee into their cups.

"Yes. It's quite comfortable there."

"Would you mind cutting the pie? I tend to make quite a mess of it." Without replying, Nicole cut and put a slice of pie on each plate. "Coming from a large farmhouse, don't you feel cooped up in three small rooms?" he asked.

"No. I'm really not there that often. I spend most of my time at the hospital or on the road. Besides, I couldn't afford anything much larger at the moment and I don't have the time to keep up with the housework a larger place would entail. It's quite cozy. Don't you feel lost in this huge house all by yourself?" Though she couldn't read those inky eyes, she thought she saw a trace of humor in them.

"I never feel lost anywhere, Dr. Winters. I spend a good deal of my time in the laboratory or, like you, on the road. The house is merely a place to eat and sleep and, when the occasion arises, to entertain," he replied.

"Do you entertain frequently?" She was a bit astonished. She found it difficult to picture Jason McBride entertaining a group of people.

"Only when necessary."

"When is that?" The notion intrigued her.

"You are a very inquisitive young lady. Perhaps the law should have been your vocation. You have a gift for persistent interrogation."

"I didn't mean to pry. I just never thought of you holding parties or galas." She washed down the pie with some coffee.

"Dinners, Dr. Winters. No parties or galas, as you put it. It is sometimes necessary to demonstrate and sell an idea of how and why one of my creations would be indispensable to a potential customer's business. A dinner can be a very persuasive factor," he informed her.

"You mean they come all this way?"

"This is the aerospace age, Dr. Winters. Small private jets can eliminate time-consuming travel. And my laboratory has a few specially designed pieces of equipment that are not available to the general consumer as yet. So the large house has its advantages at times." His pie and coffee finished, he leaned back in the chair and folded his thick arms over his chest. "How was the pie?"

"Excellent. Please tell Mrs. Beaton that for me. And I thank you for a nice lunch and a lovely day," said Nicole, rising.

"I'm glad to see you back on your feet." He stood, and they left the house.

Jason opened the car door for her when they reached the barn.

"Thanks again," she said, sliding into the car seat.

"You're welcome here anytime, Dr. Winters." He closed the car door, nodded a good-bye and stalked off toward the laboratory.

Nicole reached for the ignition key and sighed. Jason McBride wasn't the easiest man to know, yet she felt drawn to him in an odd way. Before turning on the ignition, she glanced quickly at the seat next to her and did an old-fashioned double take. Her medical bag wasn't there. It wasn't like her to forget it; it had become part of her hand. Where could she have left it? Certainly not down at Jake's cow barn. No. She had had it when she wrapped the leg of McBride's horse. The horse barn! That was where it was.

She scampered out of the car and into the horse barn. She expected it to be on the floor, but there was no sign of it. Her eyes searched every place the bag could be. Nothing. She raised her arms and let them drop at her sides in a gesture of hopelessness.

The chestnut mare poked its head over the stall door and gave a low whinny. Nicole smiled and went to fondle the mare's nose.

"If only you could talk . . ." she said aloud, then sighed deeply while nuzzling her cheek against the silken smooth hide of the well-groomed horse's cheek. "But then if I don't know what I did with my bag, how could you?" She stood back and studied the huge brown eyes of the mare. "You know, I could become quite fond of you, even though you can't help me out."

It all came back to her as she started to leave the horse barn. The laboratory! She had set it down there when Jason McBride had placed the microchip in her hand. She dashed out of the barn, to the loud and persistent whinnying of the protesting mare.

She rushed down the side of the long white barn, and as she briskly turned the corner, she collided with a wall of iron, literally knocking the wind from her. Her legs buckled, but strong hands gripped her upper arms, holding her steady.

She raised her head cautiously, almost fearfully, for the hands on her arms were electrifying her flesh in a manner totally alien to her. Her body leaning into his was being racked with small spurts of heated blood. She felt oddly giddy as dark eyes sought entrance to her soul. Her body relaxed as Jason McBride's head began to lower imperceptibly toward hers. Her eyes closed; her lips trembled like rose petals in the breeze. Acute awareness of the precarious situation rushed in on her when Jason's hands fell to his sides and her eyes flew open as she struggled to regain composure.

Jason drew in a sharp breath, straightened to his full height and stepped back. "I heard Charm whinny. Is something wrong with the horses?" His voice was deep and husky.

"No . . ." She cleared her throat. Her vocal cords didn't want to function properly. "I was looking for my medical bag and thought I had left it in the horse barn, then remembered I had left it in your laboratory."

He moved aside and with a sweeping gesture of his hand signaled the way to the laboratory. He unlocked the door for her and leaned in the door frame while she retrieved the bag.

Brushing past him, she murmured her thanks, then made her way back to her car, her legs imbued with a peculiar frailty. What was wrong with her? Why this bizarre beating of her heart? Jason McBride was only a man, and in her profession she had come in contact with a good many. But something in her subconscious told her this man was different from all the others she had known.

Her visit with Milly was briefer than she had intended. There was a restlessness in her that couldn't be quelled. Leaving Milly's, she went into town and picked up a few groceries. She had just enough time to shower and make herself a quick dinner before it was time to get ready for the usual Friday night meeting of the Young Women's League.

The next several days were uneventful: a cow down with milk fever, some infected hooves, a sow that refused to let her milk down for her brood of young ones, a group of calves to dehorn and some easy surgery at the hospital. Whether it was intentional or not, Nicole found herself driving down the road where McBride's house was located. She decided it might be a good idea to stop in and see how the black stallion's leg was coming along.

Thinking it best to announce her arrival, Nicole parked her car at the horse barn and walked to the rear door of the stately old house. As if expecting her, Mrs. Beaton opened the door before Nicole could press the buzzer. The older woman's rotund face beamed merrily amid a mass of graying, short, curly hair, which she fluffed with the palms of her hands as she smiled at Nicole.

"I thought that was your station wagon that pulled up by the barn," said Mrs. Beaton.

"Being in the neighborhood, I thought I'd take a look at the stallion," explained Nicole. "Is Mr. McBride at home?"

"No. He's in Boston. But young Tommy is in the barn. He comes

over most every day to feed, groom and exercise the horses. Come in
for a spell, won't you? I made a chocolate fudge cake and a fresh pot of
coffee."

"For a minute. I could use a break about now, and that cake sounds
too tempting to pass up," said Nicole, forcing a smile and hoping the
disappointment raging within her didn't show. She had been looking
forward to seeing Jason McBride.

They sat at the kitchen table, and Nicole devoured the cake as if it
were her last meal while the coffee hit the spot after a long afternoon.
Mrs. Beaton was full of the latest gossip, which she had heard while
getting her hair cut and permanented at one of the local beauty parlors.

". . . and I hear you've been out with that nice Dr. Baker again.
What's that? The second or third time?" asked Mrs. Beaton, conclud-
ing her long narrative.

"The second time."

"Does it look serious?" Mrs. Beaton's eyes widened in anticipation of
the answer.

The question and expression on Mrs. Beaton's face caused Nicole to
give a small laugh before replying. "Hardly. Two dates don't constitute
a permanent arrangement. We're just friends."

A look of frustration passed over Mrs. Beaton's face, as though she
had been cheated of some classified information. "More cake? Coffee?"

"No, thank you. It was delicious, but I'd better tend to the horse
now."

"You stop in whenever you get the chance, you hear? There's always
a sweet or two and coffee," said Mrs. Beaton as she walked Nicole to
the door.

"I will."

In the barn the young boy was sprinkling fresh straw in the stalls
after removing the old bedding. He greeted Nicole cheerfully when she
entered the barn. On her instructions, he led the stallion from the stall
with a capable hand.

Nicole squatted on her haunches and removed the tape and the roll
of cotton without a flinch from the dark horse. She ran her hand over
the tendon lightly at first, then increased the pressure. When there was
no reaction from the animal, she had the boy walk him around. There
was no indication that the horse was favoring the leg, so she pro-
nounced him fit to ride. After a brief chat with Tommy, she paid her

respects to the chestnut mare with caressing strokes, then left feeling a little empty at not having seen Jason McBride.

"You'd better get into Burlington and buy yourself a new dress or two," she warned herself as she rummaged through her closet for a suitable dress to wear for her date with Stephan Baker. The nights were becoming warmer, so she settled for a beige linen suit and a ruffled cocoa brown blouse. She tossed them on her bed, then went into the steamy bathroom, where her hot tub was waiting with its heady herbal scent from the crystals she had liberally sprinkled in. Dealing with animals and being on farms for the greater part of the day had made her very fastidious in her personal habits. She slipped into the tub, encasing her body in its luxurious warmth. After a soak and a scrub, she turned the shower on to wash her hair and rinse.

The brisk toweling made her skin tingle, and as she brushed her dry golden hair to a sheen, she decided to wear it in a soft coil atop her head. It was a change that added almost an inch to her five-foot-two frame. She applied light brown mascara to her lashes and used a pencil to play up her finely arched eyebrows. A dab of lipstick and she was ready to put her blouse and suit on. As she was about to slip into the high-heeled shoes, her doorbell buzzed.

"Well now, don't you look lovely," said Steve Baker as she opened the door, her feet devoid of shoes.

"Thank you. Come in while I get my shoes on." She closed the door behind him, then dashed into the bedroom.

"After dinner I committed us to a small house party. I hope you don't mind," Steve called as he sat on the sofa.

"Fine by me," she said, emerging from the bedroom, beige shoes gracing her feet. "Anyone I know?"

"I don't think so. A vice-president at Bitron Computers. He and his wife are patients of mine," replied Steve as he rose. "All set?"

"All set."

They went to the same steak house. Steve seemed to have a passion for the salad bar, where he loaded his plate with almost everything. They talked of the peculiarities of human and animal nature and found that their respective fields of medicine weren't all that far apart. It was almost two hours before they departed for the party.

The vice-president of Bitron had an ultramodern house with ultra-modern furniture and abstract paintings hung on the wall in profusion.

They were greeted with excessive obligatory salutations before being led into the living room, which was cluttered with convivial and curious guests to whom they were quickly introduced, Steve already knowing the majority of them.

Whenever Nicole was confronted with a small group of people and they learned of her profession, the conversation invariably circled on animals. It was a fact she found annoying, considering she was well versed in world and domestic events, politics and a host of other topics. She resented the tendency of people to believe it was the only topic she would be comfortable talking about. She looked across the room at Steve, who seemed to be undergoing the same experience as a rather portly man was holding onto his side as if he was indicating a problem area. She tossed Steve a weak, knowing smile when he glanced her way. He raised his glass in salute and gave her a sympathetic nod.

The group she stood with soon got tired of her cryptic replies regarding the animal kingdom and its relative maladies and drifted into a discussion of local politics. Nicole was listening intently when she caught the name McBride originating in the conversation of two women behind her.

"I saw him go into Vic's office the other day like a beast of prey. I can't make up my mind if he's devastatingly handsome or not," said one voice.

"Handsome or not, there's an aura, a magnetism about the man that has every single woman in Bitron—and some that aren't single—following him with her eyes every time he makes an appearance there," said the other female voice. "Being brilliant and rich helps."

"It helps, but I think he'd still have the same effect if he weren't. Six years at Bitron and still no one really knows the man." The voice sighed. "All he has to do is crook his finger and he could have any woman he wanted there, but he doesn't crook."

"I heard that new woman vet spent several days in his home under the guise of being sick. I should be so sick. Did you ask Steve Baker about it?"

"I tried, but he sidestepped the question. Mrs. Beaton was in the beauty parlor the other day but she's as tight-lipped as ever about Jason McBride. She can go on forever about anyone else, but when it comes to her employer her mouth goes on hold. She wouldn't even say what happened when the woman vet was there."

"You know, I have the sneaking suspicion that McBride has a wife hidden away somewhere." The voice became conspiratorial.

"What makes you think that?"

"Six years and no women about, at least none of the local ones. It's kind of fishy to me."

"Maybe he has lady friends stashed away in Boston or Montreal. He certainly spends a good deal of time in both cities. Just because he doesn't go with any of the women in Essex Junction doesn't mean he has a wife. I've seen him have a dance or two with some of our local belles when he decides to come out of hibernation and attend one of our social functions."

"Well, between you and me, I got curious about our dynamic Jason McBride and went to the personnel files to investigate his background. Do you know he is the only one at Bitron who doesn't have a file? There are absolutely no records at all on him. I find that a mite strange, don't you?"

"Maybe you overlooked it."

"I talked to Marge, Vic's secretary, when I couldn't find McBride's dossier, and she said when Vic got McBride's papers from Silicon Valley in California he read them, then immediately put them through the paper shredder. It's all pretty damn mysterious if you ask me." The voice paused. "Oh, they're putting out the hors d'oeuvres. Lucille makes the most delicious shrimp canapés you've ever tasted."

A slow fire of anger burned in Nicole at the woman's suggestion that she had feigned an illness to be in Jason's house. The woman had to have a screw loose even to think such a thing. Her first impulse was to set the woman straight. But on reflection Nicole realized that if she hadn't been eavesdropping she wouldn't have known about it. And this was really not the place to start an argument. As far as a Mrs. McBride went . . . well . . . hadn't Mrs. Beaton said there was no Mrs. McBride to her knowledge, and Mrs. Beaton's word was far more reliable than party gossip.

It was after midnight when Steve brought his car to a halt before the Widow Thompson's house.

"Well, how much free advice did they try to get out of you this evening?" he asked with a wily smile as he slipped his arm over the back of the seat and turned toward her.

"Oh, the usual. Fido isn't eating like he should, what can I do? My cat won't eat cat food, only food from the table, and so on. They invariably overfeed their pets but don't want to hear about it. They feed them prime cuts of meat, then wonder why their animals won't eat canned pet food. I've often toyed with the idea of writing a book on proper nutrition and exercise for pets."

"It would probably be a big commercial hit. If I were you, I'd do it—if only for laughs."

"Maybe you have a point. Then when they start with the questions, I could always sell them a copy of my book." She laughed.

"I have a set answer when they start describing their ailments. I tell them it sounds serious and they should come into the office for a complete physical. It usually stops them dead in their tracks."

"Oh . . . they seem to be good people on the whole. I don't think they mean any harm," observed Nicole.

"They are, I suppose. I guess it's only human nature to want something for nothing."

Without warning his arm slipped about her shoulders, drawing her quickly toward him, his lips pushing against hers with hard determination. As his ardor grew, Nicole became a trifle uncomfortable, and when her hands pressed against his chest, he released her.

"Something wrong?" he asked.

"No."

"Don't destroy my ego by telling me you don't go for me," said Steve with a wisp of a boyish grin under his mustache.

"I'd never be that cruel," she replied with vague laughter in her voice. "No. Let's chalk it up to a long day which has left me totally unromantic. Absolutely no reflection on you, Steve."

"Thank God. I'd hate to think I was losing my charm so early in life," he quipped, then took her hand in his, raised it to his lips and kissed it. "Good night, Nicole."

"Good night, Steve, and thanks for everything."

As Nicole got ready for bed she wondered about the excuse she had given Steve for not being receptive to his advances. She sighed aloud as she crawled into bed. Steve was a nice man, but . . . and there was a but. She didn't know quite what it was but it was there floating somewhere inside her. Funny, she thought, lying back in the bed. Ever since she had met Steve Baker she had wondered what it would be like to be embraced and kissed by him. Yet when the fantasy became fact, the reality did not hold the breathtaking, provocative promise she had thought it would.

Sleep came as various thoughts tripped through her head, making her rest fitful, her dreams disrupted and addled. When she awoke the next morning, it was an extreme effort for her to crawl out of bed. Even a tepid shower didn't bring her fully awake.

"You look a bit frazzled," commented Dr. Carey as she came into the office. He plucked a tissue from its cardboard box on his desk, removed his glasses and proceeded to wipe the lenses with vigor while his narrowed eyes continued to scrutinize Nicole.

"I was up later than I should have been last night," she confessed. "What's on the docket for today?"

"A couple of spayings, some skin problems and whatever else comes through the door," he replied as he replaced his glasses and threw the tissue in the wastebasket.

"No farms?"

"No. Not unless an emergency comes up."

"Well, that will give me a chance to catch up on some of the billing," stated Nicole, slipping into her white medical coat.

"Let's tackle the surgery first and get it out of the way. I love to watch you in surgery. You do such delicate stitching." He placed his hands on the arms of the oak chair and pushed himself out of it.

When both surgeries were completed and the skin problems had been treated, Nicole sat down at her small metal desk and got the record book out along with some blank billing sheets while Dr. Carey tended the hospitalized animals at the rear of the clinic.

She had half the billing finished when a distraught woman cradling a cinnamon dachshund entered the waiting room.

"Mrs. Welles, how are you?" greeted Nicole as she stood and came to the counter.

"It's Fritzy," said the woman, the tears in her voice beginning to reach her eyes. "He's dying."

Puzzlement and concern mixed on Nicole's face as she opened the door next to the counter and went out into the waiting room. Mrs. Welles was not the sort of person who gave way to unnecessary hysterics. Nicole looked hard at the limp dachshund in the woman's arms, then said, "What seems to be the trouble, Mrs. Welles?"

"He can't stand up. He keeps falling down and going into a coma," she explained with a quavering voice. "He's been like this for two days now."

Nicole knew dachshunds were subject to back disorders due to their elongated spines, but it usually affected the rear legs only. She took the small but heavy animal from the woman's arms and placed him on the tiled floor, where he slipped and stumbled as he tried to make his short, stubby legs move. He staggered around in circles, teetering one way then the next before giving up completely and lying on his side, oblivious to his surroundings.

"See!" exclaimed Mrs. Welles. "He's going to die. I just know it."

Without commenting, Nicole removed her stethoscope from the large pocket of her white coat and put the ends in her ears as she kneeled beside the inert animal, then listened to his heartbeat. Finished, she let the instrument dangle from her neck, removed a thermometer from her breast pocket and took the dog's temperature rectally, then carefully felt the animal's body.

"Well," she began as she rose to her feet. "His heart is sound and his temperature is normal. I'd like to keep him here a day or so and run a few tests if that's all right with you, Mrs. Welles."

"I had a feeling you'd say that, so I brought his blanket. It's out in the car."

When the woman left the waiting room, Nicole picked up the cinnamon-colored bundle, its coat sleek and shiny. The dog's eyes fluttered open at the touch of strange hands lifting him in the air, and the large brown eyes gazed languidly at her. For an instant Nicole had the eerie feeling that there was laughter in those eyes. Shaking her head as if to warn herself against seeing things, she cradled the soft body in one arm and gently stroked the animal's head with the other.

Mrs. Welles was quick in returning with the fleecy blue blanket, exclaiming, "Fritzy can't sleep without his blanket. Please make sure you keep it with him."

"I will, Mrs. Welles. We'll give you a call to let you know when you can take him home," said Nicole, thinking the dachshund didn't need any security blanket to sleep, for the doleful eyes had closed and the animal was breathing the even sounds of a deep sleep.

After murmuring a good-bye to the distraught woman, who was reluctant to leave, Nicole took her small charge to the rear of the clinic, where the inpatients were kept.

"Ah! What have we here?" asked Dr. Carey, shoving his hands into the pockets of his coat and peering at the sleeping animal in Nicole's arms.

"Mrs. Welles's dachshund, Fritzy. Complete with blanket," replied Nicole, the blanket draped over her arm.

"What seems to be the problem?"

"I wish I knew. There seems to be nothing wrong with him physically. His temperature is normal and his heartbeat good. But watch what happens when I put him down."

She placed the dog on the shiny floor and held him for a few minutes until he had his feet under him. It was a repetition of the same peculiar reeling followed by total collapse.

Dr. Carey squatted beside the little body and ran his probing hands over the animal. "You say no fever?"

Nicole shook her head. "It has me stumped. Do you have any ideas?"

"I'm as baffled as you are. We'd better get a blood sample and ship it off to the lab," he said, placing his hands on the floor to push himself up with a low grunt.

Nicole threw the blanket on the end of the stainless steel table, then picked up the dog and laid him next to the blanket. She quickly took a blood sample while Dr. Carey held the animal in case of a sudden reaction to the needle. But the creature was completely unmindful of what was happening to him.

She picked up the blue blanket draped over the edge of the steel table and took it to an empty stainless steel cubicle, where she folded it and placed it in one corner. The torpid dachshund lay in her arms with the sleep of innocence upon him as she carefully set him on the blanket. He curled up to continue his siesta as she shut the door of the cage.

The following morning Nicole could hardly wait to get to the hospital. The little dachshund had been on her mind all evening. Entering the one-story brick building, she gave a quick good morning to Dr. Carey, then went directly to the rear of the building with Dr. Carey sauntering behind her.

"Would you believe it?" Dr. Carey's eyes twinkled merrily as a wide-eyed Nicole stared at the yapping dachshund.

"It's incredible! I was beginning to think Mrs. Welles was right and there was no hope for him—that he had sleeping sickness or some such exotic disease that was incurable. But now . . . why, he's as healthy and lively as you or I," she stated as the dog's brown eyes flashed at her and he barked strong and clear.

"I think he's a bit indignant at being here," said Dr. Carey.

"It's either that or he's angry because his breakfast is late," said Nicole with a smile. "Have you fed them yet?"

"No. I had just walked in when the telephone rang. It was Mrs. Welles. She was relieved to learn her Fritzy hadn't died during the night and was his old self again," replied Dr. Carey.

"Is she coming to get him?"

"No. Not just yet. I told her I wanted to keep him for observation a little while longer. I had the blood sample shipped by overnight express after you left last night, requesting they call as soon as they have the results, which they said would probably be late this afternoon," he explained.

"I'll get the animals fed, then clean the cages. Do you have any thoughts about the type of ailment the dachshund could have had?"

A wry smile formed on the old doctor's rotund pink face. "A notion, Nicole. A notion. But I'm not saying a word until the test results are known."

"But—"

"Not a word . . . not a word." He threw his hands in the air defensively, a mischievous smile on his lips as he went back into the office.

Nicole set about feeding the animals and cleaning the cages and wondered what Dr. Carey had on his mind with regard to the dachshund. With all her expertise, she couldn't even scrounge up a vague idea as to the nature of the dog's illness or behavior. Dr. Carey must have known something she did not. If the results weren't back today, tonight she would hit the medical books and read until she had a clue. The morning flew by as routine chores and drop-in patients kept her busy, along with the unending ring of the telephone.

It was late afternoon when a lull gave the two vets a respite and they treated themselves to a coffee break. They were discussing some of the newer drugs on the market for animals when the phone shattered the peace of their breathing spell. With a loud sigh, Dr. Carey answered it. The conversation was brief.

"That was Jake Douglas. He has a calf down with the scours," he said, replacing the receiver and starting to rise.

"I'll go," said Nicole.

"I was hoping you'd say that. I'd like to be here if the report from the lab comes this afternoon," he admitted, slumping back into the chair.

"Won't you give me a hint?" she pleaded.

"Nope." He laced his fingers together and placed them behind his head, his eyes laughing at her.

Jake was anxiously waiting for her in the milk room. "This way, Doc." He led her into the main barn and down to the section where he kept the calves in small separate pens. "I paid extra to have the cow inseminated with a special high pedigreed bull. I'd hate to lose this one, Doc."

"We'll see what we can do," consoled Nicole, opening the pen and entering.

She looked at the droppings from the calf, dreading to see the black diarrhea that would signify that the calf had coccidiosis, a parasitic infection that it might be beyond her power to stop even with all the new drugs. She breathed more easily when she saw it was only simple diarrhea, which, with good husbandry, medicine and good luck, she could cure.

Opening her bag, she took out a hypodermic needle and a small vial of Aureomycin. She tipped the rubber-sealed vial up and plunged the needle in. She drained the contents of the vial, then injected the liquid into the animal.

"There . . . that should do it. I'll leave a bottle of tonic for you to give the calf later. Make sure all the feeding utensils are exceptionally clean and the milk you feed it is at body temperature. And don't let him get so hungry that he drinks too much in a short period of time. He should be fine in a day or so. Keep him isolated until he's back to normal. If he doesn't respond, call me," she advised, rubbing the spot on the animal's hide where the needle had gone in.

"My oldest feeds the calves. I guess I'll have to keep a closer watch on him," said Jake, scratching his sandy hair thoughtfully.

"How are things going otherwise?" she asked, snapping her medical bag shut.

"Pretty good. We'll be cutting first hay pretty quick, and I've almost finished plowing and harrowing the rest of the fields for planting," he announced with pride.

"Good for you, Jake."

"Well . . . it's that time again. I have to get the cows in for milking."

"Give my regards to Milly," she called as they went their separate ways.

Once in the milk room, Nicole hosed off her lightweight rubber boots, removed them, thoroughly washed her hands, picked up her boots and bag and went outside to come face to face with Jason McBride. Stunned by the unexpected encounter, her jaw sagged.

"Good afternoon, Dr. Winters." His voice was low and soft.

"Hello," she replied shakily. She took a deep breath in the hope that it would quell the flutter in her pulse. "Are . . ." She cleared her throat. "Are the horses all right?"

"In splendid form. I've been told you came and tended to Midnight's leg, pronouncing it fit for service."

"Yes. He no longer favored the leg, and all traces of tenderness had vanished. I saw no reason to restrict the animal any longer." My, aren't we being highly professional for someone who is quivering inside, she thought. "How was your trip to Boston?"

He shrugged. "Nothing spectacular. Pretty much routine."

Her light brown eyes met his squarely. "Well . . . I'd best be on my way."

"I am having a problem with Charm, though," he said.

"Oh? Want me to have a look at her?"

"Yes, but not in the way you think."

"I don't understand." Nicole's smooth brow crinkled in puzzlement.

"The lady is languishing for attention. I'm beginning to have pangs of guilt every time I take Midnight out for a good workout. She is desperate for someone to ride her. And that is where you come in, Dr. Winters." Jason looked down at her, an odd plea in his eyes.

"I'm afraid there is nothing in my black bag that would cure her of melancholy. I wish there were."

"There is always yourself. Tomorrow is Sunday. Surely even a busy vet like yourself has the Sabbath off. The mare would appreciate you coming out and riding her. Of course I would accompany you on Midnight. Shall we say about eleven o'clock? I'll have Mrs. Beaton pack a lunch for us."

"Tomorrow? I don't know. I don't think—"

"I thought you were an able rider," he interrupted.

"I am," protested Nicole. "But—"

"But what, Dr. Winters? Have you heard tales in town that make you wary of spending a day with me?" His dark eyes clouded.

"Of course not. What people in town do, say or think has no bearing on how I conduct my life or who I see. I make my own decisions, Mr.

McBride," she said quickly and firmly. Then she added, "I'd love to go riding tomorrow."

"Eleven o'clock?"

"Fine."

"I'll wait for you at the horse barn," he informed her. His eyes searched her face for a moment, then he strode off toward his ancestral home.

After climbing into the car, Nicole put her bag on the passenger seat and backed the car out of the barn's driveway, her mind in a whirl, her heart pumping erratically at the thought of spending the day with Jason McBride. She tried to convince herself that the idea of riding again was the main reason for the excitement she felt. It wasn't all due to the powerful man who had asked her. What possible harm could an afternoon of riding with him do? She was not making a lifelong commitment. But somewhere in her mind there was an answer to her doubts. When she tried to grasp it, it would wash back into the deep recesses of her brain, leaving her, as before, with unsorted emotions playing on an empty stage.

Dr. Carey was leaning back in his desk chair when she came into the office. A smug smile curled on his lips under his somewhat bulbous nose as he cleared his throat with a purposeful grunt.

Nicole glanced at him briefly as she put her medical bag down and opened it. She removed the hypodermic needle and was about to go into the surgery room when Dr. Carey spoke to her.

"Where are you going?"

"To put this in the sterilizer," she explained, waving the lethal-looking needle in the air.

"Aren't you the least bit curious?" he asked, his white, bushy eyebrows arching high over the rim of his glasses.

"Curious about what?"

"The dachshund, child, the dachshund."

"Oh, yes," she said anxiously. Her mind had been so full of Jason McBride and thoughts of riding with him the next day that she had forgotten all about the small animal. "Did the lab call?"

Dr. Carey nodded, then grinned. "And it confirmed my original diagnosis—high alcohol levels."

She put down the hypodermic needle and frowned in disbelief. "I don't understand. High levels of alcohol? It doesn't make any sense."

His face took on an impish aspect. "When I first saw the dog and the way he was behaving, the first thing that came into my mind was that he looked like someone who had been on a good toot for himself. You should see him now. Fit and frolicky! Doesn't even have a hang-over."

"But how? Why?" Nicole thought it incredible and unrealistic.

"If you knew Harry Welles you'd know the how and the why. He's a perennial practical joker. Probably thought it was hilarious to put a little schnapps in the pooch's drinking water."

"How terrible!" exclaimed Nicole.

"I'll have a talk with him privately. I'll throw a good scare into him and tell him he could be brought up on charges of inhumane treatment of an animal. When I finish with him, he'll confine his practical jokes to those who can fight back. By the way, we won't mention this to his wife. Although the thought of her wrath might cure him perma-nently," said Dr. Carey, his eyes narrowing as he toyed with the idea.

That night sleep eluded Nicole as she tossed and turned in bed. Every so often she would pick up her alarm clock and peer at the luminous dial, only to find ten minutes or so had gone by when it seemed she had been lying there for hours. Would morning never come? Would eleven o'clock ever come? And please . . . please . . . don't let it rain.

CHAPTER 5

Nicole's eyes flew open the minute the alarm sounded. Quickly shut-ting it off, she cast her legs from the bed to the floor and dashed to the window. She took a deep breath and smiled broadly. The bright sun was riding in a cloudless sky. It was a perfect day!

After a quick breakfast of scrambled eggs, toast and coffee, she stepped into the shower, where she scrubbed herself, then shampooed her long blond hair. Once dry, she wrapped the large towel around herself, tucking one end in at the cleft of her high, well-rounded breasts, then blow-dried her hair. When it was completely dry, she brushed it until it crackled with static electricity, the natural oils making it gleam with health. With a sideways toss of her head and an assisting arm, she brought the blond hair over her shoulder and began the single tight, thick braid which she deftly wound into a coil at the nape of her head, securing it with large plastic pins. A modicum of makeup, a sheath with a matching jacket and she was ready to head for nine o'clock services at church. As usual, Mrs. Thompson was already seated in the station wagon, waiting for her. Taking Mrs. Thompson to church on Sunday had become a ritual.

Throughout the service and though she tried to fight it, Nicole found her mind wandering with expectation toward the time she would be spending with Jason McBride. The last time she had felt like this was when they had handed her the diploma certifying her as a full-fledged veterinarian. It was a warm, bubbly feeling that consumed her very core.

After services, on the steps of the church, Nicole glanced at her watch anxiously as Mrs. Thompson extended her conversation with the minister. It was twenty after ten, and she would have just enough time to change and get to the McBride place if they left immediately.

It was after ten thirty when they arrived home. Nicole declined Mrs. Thompson's usual invitation for coffee and cake, explaining that she had a prior engagement, then dashed into her apartment.

Like a banshee on the loose, Nicole kicked off her shoes and shed her jacket and dress while at the same time managing to dig out her best pair of designer jeans and a light linen shirtwaist blouse of the palest yellow. Once her outfit was changed, she looked in the mirror to make sure everything was in place, then shoved her feet into a pair of dark blue sneakers. Though the day promised to be warm, she grabbed a sweater in case Mother Nature decided to be fickle. Seeing the time, she inhaled deeply, left the house in a run and started driving to the McBride place. If luck was with her, she would make it just in time.

Nicole's heart thudded heavily against her rib cage as she turned the station wagon into the driveway that led to the horse barn. Here she was a grown woman, feeling as excited as a schoolgirl on her first date.

Her first glimpse of Jason McBride knocked the wind from her lungs. He was leaning against the barn, watching her drive up. His tall, powerful form, though relaxed, suggested a tremendous, smoldering energy lying just beneath the surface, ready to erupt at the slightest provocation. The heavy muscles of his legs strained against the tight black jeans as if in a struggle to be free of them. His white shirt was open at the neck and the sleeves were carelessly rolled to the elbows, revealing sinewy forearms, the skin practically hidden by the mass of black hair covering them.

With a grace that belied his large, strong body, he eased himself from the slanting position and came to open the car door when she brought the vehicle to a halt.

"You're prompt," he said.

"One of my better traits," she replied with a nervous smile as she got out of the car.

"A commendable one." His eyes touched her face with a lingering glance as his fingers combed through his unruly black hair. "The horses are all saddled and literally champing at the bit."

"Let's not keep them waiting. I'm as eager as they are." Her heart did a little two-step when he cupped her elbow and led her to the entrance of the barn.

"Wait here. I'll bring them out."

A rare happiness swept over her as her eyes enveloped Jason McBride going into the barn. He was a fine figure of a man, and though she tried to deny it, she was deeply attracted to him.

Jason emerged from the barn flanked by the chestnut mare and the sleek black stallion. Nicole petted the chestnut's cheek, and her light brown eyes smiled into the large dark brown ones of the mare.

"Need help?" asked Jason, handing her the reins.

"No," she replied cheerfully as she held the reins loosely and went to the mare's side. Clutching the saddle, she put her foot in the stirrup. With a quick hoist of her lithe body, her other leg sweeping outward, she was astride the gentle mare.

"Well done," said Jason, already in the saddle, his bearing regal atop the black mount.

Nicole reached down to stroke the mare's neck. "Where to?"

"We'll go down the road we went along when I showed you the pond. Instead of veering off toward the woods, if we continue straight ahead, there are some fields where we can give the horses their head. All set?"

"Yes."

In unison they reined the horses to turn and in a slow, easy gait started along the dirt road that lay between the weathered stone walls.

"This is wonderful!" exclaimed Nicole happily. "It's been so long since I've ridden a horse. I didn't realize how much I missed it."

"Now you have no excuse not to go riding, Dr. Winters. Consider the mare yours—a small-enough gift for the way Midnight and I behaved at our first meeting," said Jason, his expression impenetrable as he stared at the road before them.

"I couldn't!" She looked at him with awe. "People don't go around giving away horses like that."

"I do, and I insist."

"You can insist all you like, Mr. McBride, but it's out of the question," Nicole stated emphatically.

"I don't see why."

"First and foremost, she wouldn't fit into my apartment and there is no place to keep her outside. Second, there are days when I wouldn't have the time to take care of her properly, and I wouldn't own an animal if I couldn't give it the care and attention it needed," explained Nicole, still somewhat stunned by Jason's unexpected gift.

"That doesn't constitute an obstacle to owning her, Dr. Winters. It was my intention that Charm remain here where she would be tended to and still be company for Midnight," he replied.

"Is that why you bought her? Company for Midnight?"

"One of the reasons."

"What other reasons did you have?" A strange series of thoughts entered Nicole's head. What if he did have a wife somewhere and the mare was really hers? Was this his way of obtaining revenge on an absent wife? Or did the mare belong to a former love he wanted to forget? She didn't want to think about such things and pushed the questions from her mind with a ruthless celerity. The day was beautiful, the riding was beautiful, the world was beautiful. She would not tarnish it all by letting phantom wives or loves intrude.

"I went to a nearby cattle auction with Jake in case he needed some financial assistance or a co-signer for a note. We were about to leave, as all the purebred holsteins had been auctioned off and Jake wasn't interested in anything else, when a most disreputable nag was led into the ring. She caught my interest because she was young and basically had good lines. Her previous owner should have been drawn and quartered for neglecting the animal in such a heinous manner." His face darkened with naked loathing. "I was going to leave and catch up with Jake when I noticed who was bidding on her—the owner of the local slaughter-house. I couldn't let a potentially fine animal like that be crudely butchered. I made a bid that brought the gavel down with a cry of sold from the auctioneer. I brought her home and called her Charm, for she certainly charmed me. She has been with me a year now."

"You must have been very determined to have her."

"I was."

"Do you always get what you want, Mr. McBride?"

"Usually." He gazed at her as though the answer was a foregone conclusion. As he reined the black steed to a halt, Nicole followed suit with the mare. Jason's grip on the reins loosened, and the stallion began to nuzzle the neck of the chestnut mare with forceful affection. "There are the meadows. Are you game for a good run?"

"Try and stop me," said Nicole with a broad smile.

They raced across the verdant carpet with abandon, the black stallion quickly taking the lead as the mare valiantly tried to keep up with him.

Nicole gloried in the sweet air winging over her face and the feel of a responsive horse beneath her. She felt like a child for whom tomorrows didn't exist. The sound of hooves beating against the earth was music she hadn't heard in a long time. It filled her with a rare jubilance, and her eyes shimmered with a fine freedom.

She saw Midnight paw at the air as Jason reined him in and spun him around to see if she and the mare were still behind him. Evidently satisfied of her presence, Jason once again sped over the meadows. With undaunted bravado, Nicole kept up the dizzying pace until she was spent and sensed that the horse was, too. She slowed the animal gradually to a trot before coming to a complete halt, her hands resting on the horn of the saddle. Admiration flowed from her face as she watched the tall man and magnificent horse move as one over the meadow, small puffs of earth spurting into the air in the wake of the thundering hooves. It was a sight she would always remember.

When Jason saw she had relinquished the race, he slowed the black steed to a gallop until he was beside her.

"Too much for you?" he asked.

"I think both of us could use a respite," she replied, patting the mare's neck fondly.

"I think now is the time for that picnic I promised you. What do you think?"

"Sounds perfect," she replied with a huge smile as she noticed his eyes skimming over her hair, which glittered like metallic gold as the sun's rays bounced over it.

"I left the basket at the pond earlier this morning. I thought that would be the best place for the picnic."

In tacit agreement Nicole turned the mare back in the direction of the pond. Jason and Midnight moved at a slow trot beside her until they came to the narrow lane piercing the line of trees. Jason nodded for her to precede him down the path where only one horse and rider could pass at a time.

When they reached the glade where the pond sparkled appealingly, Jason was off Midnight as Nicole was bringing Charm to a stop. He stood beside the quiet mare, his arms upstretched to assist Nicole to the ground.

She swung her leg over the horse's head and looked down at Jason. Her blood careened through constricted arteries like a wild roller coaster out of control, and she hesitated for a second. But his arms were inviting and tempted her beyond endurance. She began to slide from the saddle, her hands trembling as they reached out to rest on those wide shoulders.

Jason's hands almost completely encircled her small waist as he brought her body to slide down the length of his. The trees seemed to rustle from the voltage that dispersed into the air around the two of them as their bodies touched.

Nicole was unaware that her feet had touched the ground as their eyes met and locked with tangled emotions. His dark eyes searched hers with force as his large hands tightened on her waist with an urgency that weakened her. Her body went slack as his hardened. Her hands felt a minuscule tremor ripple across his shoulders as they slid to hold the rock-hard muscles of his upper arms. The very feel of him caused the pupils of her eyes to dilate as the heady contact began to sweep away any measure of reserve or latent inhibition she might have had. A warm delight seeped into her bones as Jason's head began to lower.

Midnight's strident whinny shattered the silence, startling birds to flight with heavily flapping wings. The mystical moment was lost, and Nicole's hands gave a slight push to Jason's arms, which instantly fell to his sides as he took a step backward.

"I'm famished," she managed to say with control. She was surprised she could even speak.

Jason's chest heaved in a silent sigh. "I'll see to the horses, then get the picnic basket."

A peculiar longing coiled inside her as she watched him pick up the reins of both horses and lead them to an area of lush grass, where they could nibble to their hearts' content. He tethered them loosely before retrieving the lunch basket and a well-worn quilt from atop a high flat rock.

"I thought it might be pleasant to sit near the waterfall while we eat," he said as Nicole trailed a step or two behind him. When they reached a level spot several feet from the tumbling waters, he stopped, put the basket down and extended a section of the quilt to her. "Here . . . help me spread this."

Nicole complied, and they promptly seated themselves on the quilt, the picnic basket between them.

"I don't know what Mrs. Beaton has packed to satisfy our palates," he remarked as he opened the basket, which was filled with plastic plates, cups, utensils and a thick stack of paper napkins.

"I'm sure whatever it is, it will be delicious. Mrs. Beaton is a skilled hand in the kitchen," said Nicole, peering into the basket, her appetite keenly honed by now.

Jason began to lift out insulated container after container and place them on the quilt. He passed her the necessary utensils, then drew out a large Thermos.

Nicole opened the containers, announcing the contents of each as she popped the lid off. "Potato salad, cole slaw, tomatoes, pickles . . . oh, a fruit compote."

"And last but not least, fried chicken with homemade biscuits," he added, putting the large plastic container holding the chicken between them.

They filled their plates like eager children, and Jason poured iced tea from the Thermos. As they ate greedily, only the sound of the gushing water splashing onto the worn-smooth rocks could be heard as it swirled and sprayed in its downward course.

Completely sated, Jason stretched his large frame along the quilt, the lower portion of his legs jutting onto the velvety moss as he rested on his side, his crooked arm supporting his head. Nicole wrapped her arms around her drawn-up legs, rested her chin on her knees and stared dreamily at the falling water.

"What are you thinking?" asked Jason in a low, quiet voice.

"That I could sit here forever and listen to the soothing music the waterfall makes. It's hypnotic. Magical."

"It must be."

"Why do you say that?" she asked, turning to look at him.

"My father proposed to my mother here and my grandfather to my grandmother in this glade," he replied, a fixed expression of sobriety on his face. She could sense an aura of gloom settling on him.

"Did . . ." She caught her lip between her teeth and turned away from him. She had almost asked him if he had ever proposed to anyone here. It was a question she didn't want to know the answer to—at least not now. Not when the day had been so perfect.

"What were you going to say?"

"Nothing important." In order to divert his attention, she related the story of Mrs. Welles and the dachshund. As the tale drew to a conclusion, she hoped she had lightened his sudden somber mood. She was disappointed. A frown spread across his rugged face.

"I agree with Dr. Carey. The man should be horsewhipped."

"You appear to be quite fond of animals. I'm surprised you don't have a dog or two about the place," she said.

"I've thought about it. But right now I'm away a good deal of the time, and it would only place another burden on Mrs. Beaton's shoulders. Perhaps someday when my schedule permits."

"She might like having an animal about the place. Have you ever asked her?"

"No."

"Maybe you should."

"Someday, perhaps."

Nicole lay back on the quilt and closed her eyes. "I think this is the first time since I came to Essex Junction that I have felt so totally relaxed and at peace with the world."

"Surely Dr. Carey gives you enough time off."

"Oh, yes. He's been more than generous and a dear to work for. What about you? From the way you talk, you don't seem to take much time for yourself."

"I have what I need," he replied tersely.

Nicole opened her eyes, and she could almost see him drawing a cloak of anonymity about himself. Whenever the conversation poked into his private life, Nicole could feel the resentment smoldering in him. Yet she persisted. "What do you do when you allow yourself some leisure time?"

"Have picnics with young women."

"Seriously. You must have other interests besides horses, plants and microchips," she said with a slight lift of her shoulders.

"Why should I? Is your life filled with hobbies or work, Dr. Winters?"

He had her there, and while she tried to think of a clever and witty retort, he continued.

"And why are you so curious about how I spend my free time?" He sat up, pulled up his wide-spread legs and rested his elbows on his knees, then tilted his head toward her. "Are you one of those women who can't stand to see a man idle away his time on frivolities? His nose should be constantly to the grindstone?"

"Of course not! If you don't want to talk about it, we won't." A hot anger was beginning to boil within her. She was only trying to make pleasant conversation. She got to her feet and walked to the widest expanse of the pond and gazed into its crystal depths, her emotions pulling at her in a futile tug-of-war. Suddenly she knew he was behind her, but she stubbornly refused to acknowledge it.

Silence hung in the air like a heavy death knell, occasionally disturbed by the swift trill of a bird or a leaf or two rustling in a chance breeze.

"There's an old sawmill several miles down the road. Would you care to see it?" asked Jason softly, as if the offer was in lieu of an apology he couldn't bring himself to make.

Nicole turned, a smile playing tentatively on her lips. "I've never seen a sawmill. Is it still in operation?"

"No. It ceased to function shortly after the turn of the century, due in part, I suppose, to the advent of electricity. Then, too, the land was probably logged out."

They repacked the picnic basket with the empty dishes and general debris of their lunch. Nicole refolded the quilt while Jason went to get the horses. At his request, Nicole handed him the basket and quilt once he was astride Midnight. She mounted Charm, who trotted behind the black steed, coming abreast of him when they reached the wider lane.

When they came to the rutted dirt road, Jason stopped and placed the quilt and the basket atop the stone wall, explaining, "We can pick them up on the way back."

In a loping gallop, the chestnut mare matched the stride of the stallion. Jason's majestic white house became invisible as they covered more and more distance.

The old mill stretched along the bank of the fast-running stream on a cleared parcel of land. The weathered boards of the long, one-story building were blackened with age, and a few were missing or broken. Nicole sat alert on the mare, one hand over the other on the horn of the saddle. It was an eerie sight, a ghostly shell from the past.

"I'll admit it's not much to look at, but it is authentic, not a rebuilt replica one sees in museums," observed Jason.

"Can we go inside?"

"Some of the boards are rotten. You might get hurt."

"I'll be careful," replied Nicole. At this point her curiosity overwhelmed any sense of danger. She slid quickly from the mare. She didn't trust herself if she were to be caught in Jason's arms again. The very thought of it sent waves of torrid excitement through her as she tethered the mare.

Flat stones acted as stairs to the extended, narrow structure, where one long side was unboarded and an occasional beam braced the roof. A large paddle wheel on the open side stood in decaying repose. Nicole glanced over the edge to see water rushing through the wheel. The paddles near the stream had long since succumbed to nature's instinct to erode that which has outlived its usefulness. A few of the paddles were struggling to remain part of the great wheel, but their hold on it seemed tenuous, as if they knew their time was short.

"Most of the iron has been removed, and of course the saw blades are gone. They fit into those long slots," said Jason, pointing to a heavy wooden table that was almost the length of the building.

"Water ran the saws?" she asked.

"Yes. The wheel was attached to a series of gears down in the pit next to the wheel. In turn, they powered more gears that turned the saw," he explained in simple terms.

Nicole moved gingerly over the rough, creaking wooden floor to get a glimpse of the pit. As her foot put pressure on a weakened board, it crumbled with a resounding crunch, startling her into a fast little backward jump.

Instantly Jason's large hands flattened over the front of her shoulders, drawing her back against his firm, taut body. The side of his clean-shaven cheek came down and pressed against the side of her head. Her lips parted and her eyes closed as dizziness invaded her; the heat from his body was flowing into hers with devastating effect. Her mind spun in an alien orbit, and her heart pumped in rapid, spasmodic explosions.

"I'd better get you out of here before you get hurt," he whispered, his lips brushing her ear lightly, his warm breath caressing her cheek, sending her senses spiraling to unbelievable heights. His deep voice echoing in his chest emitted vibrations that pulsed through her back and produced curious emotions deep within her. Her vocal cords became inoperable; her eyelids were leaden and refused to lift on command. His words had entered her brain, but she was no longer in the world of intellect. She had entered a universe where only the senses responded. It was only when Jason spun her around and held her at arm's length that she snapped back to reality.

"Are you all right?" he asked, his dark eyes clouding with uncertainty.

She nodded, her voice still out of commission.

"Let's get out of here," he commanded, gripping her arm with authority and steering her from the derelict, aged sawmill.

Outside Nicole rushed to the mare and laid her cheek against its silken hide as she stroked the horse's muzzle. It was an act of love, a release from the maze of her conflicting emotions.

"We'd better head back," said Jason, his sharp-boned face set with bleak resignation.

Astride the chestnut, her composure reasserted itself and she looked at Jason. "Must we? Couldn't we race through the field one more time?" She needed the exhilarating feeling of absolute freedom, of carefree abandon that riding to the wind would bring.

"Are you sure?"

"Yes." She smiled, a glow of vitality returning to her face.

His stern expression softened with the hint of a smile. He mounted the glistening steed with all the aplomb of Satan on horseback. "The fields it is, then."

Guiding the horses back to the spacious, treeless fields, Jason and Nicole were silent. Reaching their objective, Nicole dashed ahead with impish glee, only to be passed by a hard-riding Jason. When their haphazard chase was over, Jason brought the black stallion abreast of the mare and Nicole followed his lead with increasing curiosity.

"This isn't the way back to the house. Where are we going?" she asked as they proceeded to cross the field toward a string of maple and birch trees.

"You expressed some interest in how I spend my leisure time. I thought I'd show you," he replied, his face stony as he gazed ahead.

A wide gap in the line of trees soon presented itself. On passing through, a long stretch of flat, grassy land ran in front of them like a green ribbon.

When Nicole turned quizzically to look at Jason, her eyes caught a sizable structure fashioned from blue corrugated steel off to the side. She studied it for a moment, but before she could question him, he was riding toward it. She reined Charm's head aside and followed.

After tethering the horse to a low-hanging branch of a birch tree, Jason stood and waited for her to dismount. A mixture of relief and yearning filled Nicole as she alit from the horse without the strong arms of Jason to support her. At the same time she wondered why he had withheld his assistance. Had he felt the same surge of excitement when their bodies touched? Or did he feel that his aid was superfluous?

Producing a key from his pocket, Jason unlocked the side door of the structure, pushed it open and gestured for her to enter. Nicole's eyes brightened when she saw that the corrugated building housed a four-seater propeller-driven Cessna airplane. She walked up to it, then around it, her face glowing with wonder.

"I assume the plane is yours and you are the pilot," she said, returning to stand beside him.

"Your assumptions are correct. It comes in handy when I have business to take care of."

"Do you use it strictly for business?"

"No. It affords me pleasure, too. There is a sense of absolute serenity in soaring aloft, a detachment from earthly cares and reality. One can think up there in the clouds without mundane distractions." There was a calmness in his sonorous voice that gave credence to his words as his dark eyes took in the Cessna with obvious adoration.

"Have you ever gone cross country in it?" asked Nicole, noting that he could be quite attractive when his expression was suffused with tranquillity. She longed to reach up and trace her finger over his hard, square jaw.

"No. I use it for a radius of five hundred miles or so. If it is necessary to go to the West Coast, I use a commercial jet. It is easier and quicker," he replied, his attention reverting back to her. "Do you like to fly, Dr. Winters?"

"Would you believe I'm twenty-five years old and have never set foot in a plane, commercial or otherwise?" Her eyes sparkled merrily.

"Then we'll have to remedy that."

"Oh?"

"I'll be going to Montreal in the near future. If you can manage to take the day off, I'd like to have you come with me." His eyes moved back to the plane.

"If there isn't some major epidemic, I'm sure Dr. Carey wouldn't mind."

"You'd go?" His hands went into his back pockets as he continued to stare at the plane.

"I'd be delighted," replied Nicole enthusiastically. "You'd have to give me some notice, though, so I can arrange it with Dr. Carey."

"I'll see that you know well ahead of time." He took a deep breath. "Well . . . shall we head back?"

She nodded in agreement, even though she hated to see the day come to an end. There was something about being with Jason McBride that gave her a sense of completion, of wholeness. Once they were outside she pushed aside her mental musings to ask a more practical question. "How do you get gasoline for the plane up here?"

"If you'll look to your right you'll see I have my own pump. There is a thousand-gallon tank buried in the ground."

"However do you get it filled?" she asked, thinking how difficult, if not impossible, it would be for a truck to follow the circuitous route that had brought them to the hangar.

"There is a gravel road leading directly to the hangar. Actually we are only a half-mile from the house. Would you prefer to go back that way?"

"No. Not unless you are in a hurry." She wanted to get in all the riding she could. She didn't know when the opportunity would present itself again.

They cantered over the same route that had brought them to the secluded airstrip. Reaching the stone wall near the house, Jason scooped up the quilt and picnic basket with one sure swoop of his arm.

In the barn, Nicole began to undo the saddle cinch.

"I'll do that for you," said Jason as he lifted the black leather saddle from Midnight.

"If she is to be my horse, then I shall do for her when I am able. Or have you changed your mind?"

"You'll find, Dr. Winters, that I seldom change my mind."

After removing saddle, blanket, reins and bit, Nicole opened the wooden door to Charm's stall. The docile animal obediently entered, then turned for a stroking on the nose as Nicole shut the door.

Jason walked alongside her as she strolled toward her car. Reaching it, she looked up at him, smiling. "Thank you for a lovely day. And Charm." She couldn't bear those dark eyes burning into her any longer. She faced the car and stretched her hand to the door. Before she could grasp the handle, a staying hand came down on her arm.

"The pleasure was mine. Are you free for dinner tonight?" the resonant voice asked.

"Yes," she murmured, keeping her eyes glued to the car.

"I'll pick you up at seven."

"Fine." There was a slight crack in her voice, which she hoped he hadn't noticed. Her heart was tripping like a jack hammer, and her flesh was burning under the touch of his hand.

"I'll see you later, then," he said, letting his hand drop back to his side as Nicole swung the door open and hopped inside.

She tossed him a quick, nervous smile, started the car, then drove off, her entire being flooding with elation.

By the time she reached home, her thoughts had become a little more utilitarian. Jason McBride had a day of leisure on his hands and had wanted some company while riding. The dinner was his way of thanking her for providing companionship. As far as the mare went, well, that was only a gesture to signify she could ride the animal anytime she wished, not actual ownership. She would have to stem her own subliminal longings and stop projecting them upon the words or actions of Jason McBride.

A shower left her feeling clean and refreshed. She particularly loved the aroma the herbal shampoo gave to her squeaky clean hair. Her hair! She would have to do something different with it, something less severe. Definitely not a braid! She looked in the mirror and studied the blond hair that fell almost to her waist. She shook her head slowly, totally at a loss. She decided to select something to wear first.

Thumbing through the closet, she felt like kicking herself for not taking the time to buy some new dresses. Finally she grasped a hanger that held a cocoa brown silklike sleeveless dress. She tossed it over her head, thrust her arms through the fine spaghetti straps, then zipped up the back. The tight bodice was flattering to the swell of her breasts, and the gored skirt lent an appearance of fullness to her otherwise slim hips. With delicate high heeled shoes on her feet, a gold locket about her neck and filigreed gold earrings, she turned her attention back to her long blond hair.

After several cursory attempts to find a suitable hairstyle, she settled on a soft, rolled crown on the top of her head. Once the roll was secure, she took a hot curling iron to the straight wisps of hair about her temples that weren't long enough to scoop into the roll. Satisfied with her new coiffure, she swiftly applied a little makeup. It was none too soon, for as she recapped the pale orange lipstick, her doorbell rang.

Dashing into the living room, she snatched her purse and dark brown velvet jacket, then went to open the door. There was a rare happiness shining in her amber eyes.

They stood appraising each other in the glow of the porch light.

Nicole couldn't read the thoughts behind those dark eyes of Jason McBride, but her own were more than pleasurable as her eyes feasted on the tall, powerfully built man before her. He wore a lightweight pale gray three-piece suit, the expert tailoring of which did justice to his broad-shouldered physique. His blue-black hair was well brushed yet had a casualness that gave him an appealing quality.

"You hardly look like a veterinarian tonight, Dr. Winters." His voice was low, almost seductive.

"Oh? What do you think I look like, then?" she asked, looking up at him and smiling warmly with her lips and her eyes.

"A very fragile china doll." His hand made a move toward her, and for a moment Nicole thought he was going to caress her cheek. Instead he said, "Let me help you with your jacket. Though summer is almost upon us, there is a slight chill in the air tonight."

Nicole flipped her envelope purse from one hand to the other as he helped her into the velvet jacket. His warm hands rested on her shoulders as she straightened the jacket. For a fleeting instant she had the desire to lean back against him in the hope of reliving that moment back in the sawmill. His hands left her shoulders, snapping her back to the present.

"All set," she announced brightly.

The red Pontiac Firebird roared to life under Jason's hands and began its course through the back roads of Essex Junction until it came to the outskirts of Burlington, where it turned left onto Route 7, heading south.

Jason brought the sporty car to a halt in the parking lot of an old, sprawling, disreputable-looking green wooden building. Nicole winced a little at the sight of it. It had the appearance of a nefarious roadside dive. A quick sidelong glance at Jason only served to reveal his calm, confident visage. He cupped her elbow as they strode across the pitted macadam of the parking lot. He opened the door, which was barely covered with peeling paint, and ushered her in.

Never judge a book by its cover, she scolded herself as she marveled at the rich red velour walls capped by scrolls of heavy golden hues, the warm patina of the mahogany trim and wainscotting, the gleam of polished brass decorative pieces and chandeliers. The grandeur overwhelmed her as the maitre d' guided them across the thick-piled red carpet to a secluded table with a candle in a glass-and-brass holder. A single red rose stood in a slender fluted vial.

"It's good to see you again, Mr. McBride," said the maitre d' as he handed them the menus and discreetly left.

"I'm impressed," said Nicole, looking around. "Do you come here often?"

"On occasion," he replied as he perused the menu. "Have you decided on anything yet?"

Her eyes moved from side to side, trying to read the variety of dishes offered. "It all looks so good, I don't know where to start."

"Would you prefer I order for you?"

"You know the cuisine here better than I do. I'm sure it would be simpler if you did." She closed the menu and put it aside.

Nicole was too busy taking in the decor to pay attention to the order Jason was giving the waiter. The place made her feel quite regal with its heavy touches of gilt flickering against the bright red.

"I think you'll be pleasantly surprised by my selections," said Jason as the waiter poured white wine into their delicately etched glasses.

"I'm sure I will. I don't think this place could serve anything that wasn't delicious," she observed, then took a sip of the wine. Its piquant warmth raced into her stomach. "Have you designed any new microchips lately?"

"Why do you ask?" His voice was harsh, and his eyes narrowed as they pierced into hers with distrust.

"No reason," she replied, startled by his sudden brusqueness.

A chilling silence settled over the table as the waiter brought their appetizer of lobster bits wrapped in bacon and swimming in a pool of melted butter and lemon sauce.

"These are marvelous," exclaimed Nicole, forking the succulent morsels into her mouth. "I'm glad I let you do the ordering." She smiled wanly at him, wondering why he had become so upset at the mention of microchips. He was probably the sort of man who did not like to discuss business while he ate, she told herself, grasping at straws to excuse his abrupt change of mood.

"The food here is beyond criticism," he said, visibly relaxing.

The meal was served leisurely. A purée of tomato soup laced with herbs, medallions of lean lamb in a savory brown sauce ringed by rich egg noodles, side dishes of green asparagus and baby carrots, home-made hot bread and rolls brought an audible sigh of admiration from Nicole. A miniature single serving of a raspberry torte topped with freshly whipped cream was the crowning finish to their meal.

Throughout the dinner Nicole related the more memorable moments in her life, with heavy emphasis on the trials, tribulations and questionable antics she had endured and participated in during her days at Cornell University. Jason responded by regaling her with similar tales of his college days. Yet no matter how hard she tried to get him to talk of his postuniversity days, he avoided the topic. She could almost see the iron mask slip over his face if she referred to or questioned him about his life after his schooling was completed. She soon gave up the attempt.

When all the dishes had been cleared, their coffee was served. A small snifter of brandy was placed near Jason's cup, while a dwarfish wineglass filled with white liquid was placed at Nicole's.

"What is this?" she asked, holding the vial in the air.

"A pony of anisette. Put it in your coffee instead of cream," he instructed her, then watched as she performed the task.

Warily she took a sip, then a deeper swallow. "Oh . . . that's good. It tastes like licorice."

"I thought you'd like it."

Strangely enough, Jason did most of the talking on the return trip. He gave a running history of his farm in Essex Junction. Once he had embarked on the subject, Nicole found him to be a captivating raconteur, and he was bringing the red car to a stop before her home before she knew it.

Automatic reflex caused her to open the car door, but it was wrenched from hand as Jason swung it wide for her, then escorted her onto the porch.

A coil of tension circled the two people in the dim light of the porch. Jason McBride stood tall and ominous as he hovered over Nicole's slight frame.

She had to say something and say it quickly to break the mesmerizing spell. Her throat was dry and tight. If she didn't get a word out now, she never would.

"Thank you," she croaked, then cleared her throat. "That was a lovely dinner. I shall always remember it. If I could cook I would reciprocate by cooking a meal for you. But I'm a total disaster in the kitchen. Why, I can't even boil an egg without—"

Her babbling was stopped by Jason's fine and strong hand cupping her chin and lifting her face to his lowering head. As she was about to surrender to him and her own desires, bells rang in her head, warning her of the possibility of a wife or a sweetheart lurking in his background. With that thought in her mind, her hands pushed against his barreled chest and a strong, mournful "No, don't" escaped her lips. She spun, retrieved her key, opened the door and slid into the house, shutting and locking the door behind her. Her breath came in short gasps as she leaned against the door until the blast of the Pontiac's motor shattered the night, then faded into the distance.

Her body went limp as she stood there, her mind spinning out of control as pure emotion held her in its grip. She had turned away the one kiss she really wanted, and now she couldn't understand why. Why was she fighting herself where Jason McBride was concerned? Was she afraid she might be falling in love with a man who could possibly belong to another? She would have to clear the air once and for all. She would have to ask him point-blank if there was another woman in his life. Yes, that was the only solution. She would do it as soon as the opportunity presented itself.

CHAPTER 6

"Milk fever," said Nicole to the concerned farmer. "We'll have her right in no time." She jabbed a needle into a vein in the cow's neck and waited to see blood bubbling up before attaching the long plastic tube to the end of the receptive needle. She held the bottle of calcium high in the air to enable it to flow into the animal's bloodstream.

"That's what I thought it was, Doc, but I wanted to make sure," said the farmer.

Nicole was aware that the American farmer was a keen observer of his animals and husbanded them well, far better than himself at times. He had to if he wanted to survive in modern farming.

She had two more farms to stop at before heading back to the animal clinic. As she drove down the macadamed country roads, her mind wandered back several nights to when Jason McBride had almost kissed her. She ran the tip of her tongue over her lips and chastised herself for stopping him. The opportunity would probably never come again. He was the kind of man who, once rebuffed, wouldn't place himself in the position of being turned down again. She was glad she was on night call for the entire week. It gave her little time to think about the man.

Her calls on the outlying farms completed, she steered the old station wagon back to the hospital. Entering through the back door, Nicole went directly to the washroom to scrub her arms, hands and face, then proceeded to what she lovingly called the wards. The animals were all nestled in their respective cubicles, and nothing seemed amiss. Her smooth brow creased in a baffled frown as she noticed a large white Persian cat laconically staring back at her, its luminous green eyes haughtily assessing her.

She found the surgery empty and went to find Dr. Carey in the office. "I see Muffins is back. What's wrong with her this time?" Nicole asked as Dr. Carey swung around to face her.

"She sneezed."

"Sneezed?"

"I know, I know." He threw his hands out, palms up. "That Norris woman is turning her cat into a hypochondriac. I sometimes think the cat is addicted to our cuisine and knows she'll be rushed here if she so much as blinks an eye."

Nicole had to laugh. She had a feeling there was more truth than fiction in what Dr. Carey said. That white Persian cat stayed at the hospital at least twice a month. "Perhaps Muffins is crazy about riding in cars."

"That cat is crazy about something, and I don't think it is her mistress. The silly woman said the cat hadn't smiled for three days and then commenced to sneeze. The only cat I ever knew could smile was the Cheshire cat in *Alice's Adventures in Wonderland*," he said with a grumble in his voice.

"Is she still sneezing?"

"Good lord no. The poor cat probably got a whiff of that strong perfume the Norris woman wears. I went over the animal thoroughly and there is absolutely nothing wrong with her." He braced his hands on his knees and started to chuckle. "When she brought the cat in and put it on the counter, she held the cat's head in her hands, peered into its little white face and cooed, 'Smile, Muffins. Smile for Mommie, Muffins.'" Dr. Carey mimicked her in a high falsetto voice.

"You should go on the stage, Dr. Carey. You're a natural," observed Nicole with a huge smile.

"How did things go in the outback?"

"Routine. Nothing catastrophic."

"Oh, by the way, before I forget, Stephan Baker has been trying to get a hold of you."

"Did he say why?"

"No. And I didn't ask. None of my business." He paused thoughtfully. "That young man would be quite a catch for a young woman. He's built up a substantial practice and is well liked in the community."

"Are you trying to tell me something?" There was amusement in her eyes. She couldn't picture Dr. Carey as a matchmaker.

"No," he said. "Just an observation."

A last-minute call to a farm made Nicole late arriving home. As her key slid into the lock, she could hear the telephone ringing persistently in the empty house. She hurried to answer it.

"Hello," she said into the receiver a little breathlessly.

"Isn't it a bit late for you to be getting home?"

"Steve?"

"Of course. Who else has my mellifluous voice?"

"Dr. Carey said you've been trying to get in touch with me. What's up?"

"Just wanted to take you to dinner tomorrow night."

"I'm afraid I'll have to take a raincheck. I'm on night call all this week," she explained.

"What about Wednesday of next week?"

"Fine."

"Good. I'll pick you up at seven. Till Wednesday, then. There is something I want to ask you."

"What?"

"It can wait till Wednesday. Good night."

The receiver went dead, and Nicole looked at it quizzically before replacing it in the cradle. What could he possibly want to ask her that couldn't be said over the phone? She hoped it was nothing serious. Stephan Baker was a nice man, handsome, pleasant company and a good catch for any woman, as Dr. Carey put it. But he wasn't the man for her. He was highly aware of his good looks and enjoyed his reputation as a ladies' man. She sensed a latent arrogance in Steve that made her wary of a deeper relationship with him, never mind a permanent commitment. She liked the casual arrangement they had.

When Sunday came she steeled her emotions and went to the McBride place to ride Charm. Horseback riding was a joy she had missed since coming to Essex Junction. Knowing the horse was there for her to ride whenever she chose was a temptation she couldn't resist, even though she wasn't sure how Jason McBride would react to her presence after she had denied him the kiss he sought.

Every muscle was taut with the expectation of seeing Jason as she turned into the driveway to the horse barn. Her breast heaved rapidly as she entered the barn, her mind spinning as she tried to make up clever little words and phrases to say to him. She dallied in the barn, taking a longer amount of time to saddle the mare than was necessary in the hope that he would see her car and come dashing out of the house or the laboratory. But her dawdling was to no avail. Jason Mc-Bride did not make an appearance.

She took Charm over the same route she had ridden with Jason. But his image rippled tauntingly before her with uncanny accuracy. Her system couldn't tolerate it. It startled her to learn that she ached for him to be by her side. She wondered if the chestnut mare felt the absence of the black stallion. She turned the horse around and sought out new fields, new pathways.

With Charm safely back in the stall, Nicole gathered her courage and went to the house, where she was welcomed by Mrs. Beaton insisting she have some coffee and pie. It didn't take her long to find out Jason was at the Bitron plant, as Mrs. Beaton explained that he preferred to go there on a Sunday when the majority of the employees were off and he could pursue his trials and tests undisturbed.

On Wednesday night Steve was prompt. As usual, he took her to the steak house. Nicole was beginning to think he was either part-owner of the place or had a sizable block of stock in the chain. Perhaps he was just unimaginative.

The waitress's timing was off. She brought their entrées as they seated themselves with their plates of salad from the salad bar.

"The service is terrible tonight," grumbled Steve.

"Maybe the girl had a bad day," said Nicole with a shrug.

"That's no excuse. I certainly don't let my personal problems affect my professional life, and I'm sure you don't," he argued.

"No. But you can't compare the medical profession with waitressing."

"Why not? A profession is a profession. It doesn't matter what the field is."

Nicole looked at him obliquely. It was an absurd argument which she didn't feel like pursuing. Besides, her steak was getting cold.

"I find it galling to receive poor service, then nine times out of ten the waitress will sneer at you if you leave a less-than-generous tip," Steve continued, a frown on his handsome features.

"You seem a bit testy tonight," remarked Nicole. "Something go wrong?"

"I didn't know it was so obvious." He paused and looked up at her. "I had a pleasant evening all planned. Then, shortly before I picked you up, I learned that I have to go to the hospital tonight. A patient of mine was in a car accident."

"Was he badly hurt?" asked Nicole with an expression of genuine concern.

"A broken leg, and I guess he is pretty shaken up."

"Shouldn't you be there now? You didn't have to take me to dinner. If anyone would have understood, I would."

"I talked to the doctor who admitted him. He said to take my time. The leg has been set, and the patient has been given a sedative to calm him down, but he still insists on seeing me tonight. I saw no reason to call off our dinner date, but any other plans I had for this evening will have to be set aside. I'm sorry."

"Don't be. I know what it's like. Was anyone else hurt? How did it happen?"

"He was going along Route 89 when he got a flat tire, lost control of the car and struck an abutment. Fortunately no one else was in the car." He paused again to down a few mouthfuls of steak. "I feel awful about ruining your evening."

"You're not spoiling my evening at all. Don't give it a second thought. By the way, there was something you wanted to ask me."

"Oh, yes. There's going to be a dinner dance at the country club on Saturday night and I was wondering if you'd like to go with me," said Steve.

"I hope you're not asking me because tonight has been aborted," said Nicole, smiling.

"Asking you to the country club dance on Saturday was the main reason for taking you out this evening. I wanted to soften you up so you wouldn't say no," he admitted, pushing his empty steak plate aside and resuming his attack on the platter of salad.

"In that case, I'd be delighted."

"It's formal. You'll need a long dress," he informed her.

"No problem." She finished her steak and baked potato but, being quite full by now, only picked at her salad. They left the restaurant shortly after.

Steve did not get out of the car when they arrived at her home. After a swift peck on the cheek before she got out, he was off.

The next two days were hectic and entailed long hours either in the hospital itself or out on the farms. Nicole remembered how breezily she had told Steve an evening gown would be no problem, yet in fact it was rapidly becoming one. She had two from her college days but they were outmoded and a little tacky. She certainly couldn't wear either of them to the country club. She had intended to buy something new, but Saturday was drawing closer and she hadn't had the time to shop. Luckily, Saturday afternoon proved to be slack at the hospital, and after explaining her predicament to Dr. Carey, she managed to take a few hours to look for a suitable gown.

Nicole careened through the stores like a whirlwind gone berserk. After dumping the packages at her home, she was back at the hospital by three o'clock in the afternoon. Things were still slow, and Nicole took advantage of the lull to tackle the billing while Dr. Carey tended to the toenail clipping of a parakeet and a slight tear in a beagle's ear, minor in-and-out patients requiring minimum attention.

With a sigh of relief and a sense of accomplishment, she put a stamp on the last envelope and tamped the stack of bills into a neat pile, then went into the surgery, where Dr. Carey was sterilizing instruments.

"So you're going to the country club with young Baker tonight," said Dr. Carey, a pixielike grin on his face.

"Yes. At the Young Women's League meeting, the dinner dance was all they could talk about. It seems everyone has bought a new outfit for it."

"By tomorrow you'll be the talk of the town when they see you with Stephan Baker. I wouldn't be surprised if they had you engaged to the good doctor by morning. I can picture all the mothers of eligible young women tearing their hair out by the roots at the thought of it," he said with glee.

"Well, they'd be working themselves up over nothing," said Nicole firmly.

"Don't tell me that young Adonis hasn't captured your heart?" He moved his glasses down to the tip of his nose and peered at her earnestly.

"He has only captured my friendship," she replied lightly.

"And how does he feel about you?"

"Who knows?" She shrugged. "It's a subject that has never come up."

"You don't seem to care."

"I don't."

"I'll never understand today's youth. In my day when a young man took a girl out on a frequent basis, he was courting her. Life-styles have certainly changed." He threw his hands in the air in a gesture of hopelessness and went into the office.

"Do you want me to take these bills to the post office? They're all set," she said, trailing behind him.

"Yes, if you don't mind," replied Dr. Carey, then studied his wristwatch. "It's almost quitting time, so after you drop them off you may as well head home. Have a good time tonight."

"Thank you." She removed her white coat, scooped up the bills and left, a knot of excitement beginning to form in her stomach as she wondered if Jason McBride would be there, for the country club membership consisted mainly of people working for Bitron.

Showered and her hair freshly shampooed, Nicole looked forward to donning her new evening gown. Brushing her hair until it crackled sharply, she arranged it the same way she had worn it when she went to dinner with Jason McBride, a softly rolled crown atop her head.

She picked up the queenly gown from the bed. It was a satin sheath of dark antique gold with an overlaid full tulle skirt of iridescent and transparent gold. She stepped into the gown and pulled it up her body, then drew the single braided strap around the nape of her neck, secured it to the front of the form-fitting bodice and closed the small zipper at the back. The burnished gilt gown was the most revealing Nicole had ever worn. The front came to a halt just over the swell of her breasts; her white shoulders and back were completely exposed. She looked in the mirror and swayed, the gown glittering with each movement of her body. The sheath itself was slit from the ankles to slightly above her knees, giving facility to any motion she cared to make. The iridescent overskirt cascaded in soft folds, giving that much needed addition to her hips. Her sheer stockings already on, she stepped into dainty, elegant gold shoes and fastened the threadlike straps. A touch of mascara to emphasize her long, curling lashes; a dab of lipstick; a spray of cologne and she was ready. She put what she thought might be necessary in a small gold-colored purse, then drew her grandmother's shawl of dark brown silk from the bureau drawer. This was the first opportunity she had had to wear it since coming to Essex Junction.

Stephan Baker must have told her how fantastic she looked a dozen times before they arrived at the country club. The first time her ego swelled with pride, but after a while the compliment wore thin.

White linen tablecloths graced the circular tables that arched around the parquet dance floor, at the head of which was a raised platform for the musicians. The room was three-quarters full as Nicole and Steve were shown to their table, which accommodated six people.

Their four dinner companions were already seated, and Steve introduced Nicole with a certain amount of pride in his voice. Nicole knew one of the women, Carol Hanes. She was a member of the Young Women's League. Conversation was lively and fortunately avoided any mention of the medical profession, human or animal.

The meal was nothing exceptional; canned fruit cup followed by chicken à la king in puff pastry, a salad followed by a dessert of fresh strawberries topped with artificial whipped cream. A pale Chablis was served with dinner. When the tables had been cleared of all dishes and coffee cups, the men went to purchase drinks at the bar that had been set up in an alcove at the far end of the spacious room. Nicole declined Steve's offer of a cocktail, deciding to stay with the Chablis.

"Where ever did you get that dress? It's gorgeous!" gushed Carol Hanes while the men waited their turn at the bar.

"Thank you. I got it at Germaine's in Burlington," replied Nicole, smiling at the young woman of twenty-eight or so.

"Now I know where to go if I'm desperate for something unusual to wear instead of making the arduous trip to Montreal," stated Fran, the other woman at the table.

"What does your husband do, Fran?" asked Nicole.

"He's a computer analyst for Bitron."

"Bitron is the biggest shot in the arm Essex Junction has had in centuries. It seems everyone works there," said Carol with high animation.

"How long have you worked there, Carol?" asked Nicole.

"Two years now."

"Every time I come to a country club function, all one ever hears is Bitron this and Bitron that," declared Fran.

"What's this about Bitron?" asked Fran's husband, Harry, placing her drink on the table and seating himself, rapidly followed by Steve and Carol's escort, Tom Stone.

"Nothing of importance, dear," said Fran.

"Well, I'll be damned!" her husband exclaimed, his eyes wide in disbelief.

"What is it, Harry?" asked Fran.

"The genius of Bitron just walked in. I never thought I'd live to see the day when McBride would attend one of our little social gatherings."

"I don't see him," said his wife, turning her head.

"Heading for the bar," he informed her.

Nicole's head swiveled slightly to the side, her eyes drinking in the tall man who looked so dashing in a richly tailored tuxedo that he wore with notable assurance. As he leaned against the bar, his appraising glance surveyed the room quickly until his eyes caught and held Nicole's. An invisible spear charged through the room to lance her heart. She smiled, but his dark look remained inflexible as his eyes swung from her to Steve, then back to her. As he turned to scoop up his drink, she forced her eyes down and stared fixedly at the glass of Chablis.

"Well, I might have known he'd head for old Simpson's table. Nothing like making points with the president of the company," said Harry, taking a hefty swallow of his drink.

"I don't think Jason McBride has to make points with anyone at Bitron. He can command a more than generous salary anywhere," commented Tom Stone.

"Who is that attractive woman he's sitting down next to? I haven't seen her around before," said Steve, studying the not-too-distant table.

"Simpson's newly divorced daughter," informed Carol, her voice imbued with a conspiratorial whisper. "She was married to a French count or duke or some such thing and has come home from France to recuperate from the trauma. I'll tell you, it wouldn't take me long to recover with the size settlement I heard she got."

"You seem to have an inside track on the gossip at Bitron, Carol," noted Fran.

"As secretary to one of the vice-presidents, I get to hear and see quite a bit," replied Carol smugly.

"I'll bet you don't have the lowdown on our mysterious Jason McBride," said Harry with a challenging look.

"I heard his wife will be here in the fall," declared Carol with triumph.

Nicole's hand tightened on her glass. Carol seemed so sure, so certain—but Jason McBride did not act like a married man. She couldn't bring herself to believe it. It was rumor, gossip, hearsay. Yet her heart was throbbing erratically.

"Jason McBride married? I don't believe it," stated Harry flatly.

"You'll see this fall." Carol exuded confidence.

"Then where has she been for six years? I've never seen or heard of her," said Fran.

"There's some sort of cover-up as to her whereabouts, but believe me, she exists," said Carol.

Harry grunted his continued skepticism. Tom Stone stared at Carol, while Steve's eyes were still focused on the divorcée. The band began to play the first dance of the evening, and Tom asked Carol to dance. She was quick to assent.

"Let's dance, Nicole," said Steve. He stood and held back her chair for her as she rose.

Nicole was a little stunned and confused by Carol's revelation. Nobody at the table seemed to believe her. It made Jason McBride as mysterious as ever to her. She pushed it from her mind as Steve whirled her about the floor with the skill of an expert and she relaxed in his arms.

As they continued to traverse the dance floor and the band slipped into its second musical presentation, Nicole tensed as she saw Jason offer his hand to the lovely divorcée and glide her onto the dance floor.

"Something wrong?" asked Steve.

"No . . . nothing. I haven't danced since my college days, and I hope I'm not too rusty for you. You're very adept."

"Why, thank you, Doctor. But you're doing fine . . . just fine. By the way, when I went to the bar, several men asked me where I've been hiding you. You made quite an impression on the male population here."

"That's nice to hear."

"You're really a knockout in that gown."

"I confess I went all out in buying it. In my line of work I don't often have the opportunity to wear an evening gown. Denim and chambray are not the most feminine of outfits, and manure clinging to one's boots doesn't help, either," said Nicole with a grin.

"But you wouldn't give it up for the world. Right?"

"Right! I love it."

When they returned to the table, Carol's escort asked Nicole to attempt a rather fast disco number that the band had embarked upon, while Carol talked the handsome Dr. Baker onto the dance floor with her. It seemed the fast-tempoed music was never going to end. When it finally did, the four young people came back to the table, their breath short and gasping. For the next half hour animated conversation was more appreciated than dancing.

The trumpet player, who acted as emcee and general host, announced twenty minutes of uninterrupted music from the big-band era of the forties, in deference to the older members of the club. A ripple of applause trickled through the room, only to die before it fully bloomed.

"Now that's my kind of music," claimed Harry.

"You're not that old, Harry," said Fran.

"Not in age, only in body," quipped Harry. "I can manage the slow ones without missing a beat. Would you care to give it a try, Nicole?"

"I'd be delighted," replied Nicole.

Oddly enough, Harry was light on his feet for a rather corpulent man and he stepped to the music with rhythmic ease. But he was silent. It was as if he couldn't concentrate on his feet and voice at the same time. Nicole was glad for the respite. She found it difficult at best to converse with twisting thoughts of Jason McBride scrambling through her head.

When the tune was over Harry began to steer her through the maze of dancers and back to the table when a strong hand encircled her wrist.

"May I?" said the deep voice in a half-whisper.

Harry nodded and left while Nicole turned, praying her tangled emotions didn't gleam in her eyes like a revealing beacon. She didn't speak as his strong hand made its way to the small of her back, his other hand holding hers in a firm grip. She rested her hand on his upper arm and thrilled to the feel of the taut bicep as he tightened his hold on her.

The music began, slow and sentimental. A mood of long-ago romantic idylls cloaked the atmosphere. Its effect was not lost on Nicole. The soft music became a roaring symphony in her brain, a rhapsodic symphony of soaring emotions as his touch, his scent and the proximity of his body were almost more than she could bear. Her heart was beating furiously, and she had all she could do not to lean into him and lay her head against his chest. She wanted to stop dancing and just cling to him, letting the warmth of him flow into her.

"I understand you were out at the farm the other day riding Charm," he said.

"Yes." Now was her chance to ask him about a so-called wife. No, not here, she thought. Not in a crowd. She would wait until she was alone with him. Suppose she never was alone with him again? Then it wouldn't much matter whether he was married or not. Stop talking to yourself, Nicole.

"You should have let me know in advance. I would have stayed home and gone with you." Jason looked down at her, his expression inscrutable.

"I seldom know in advance when I'm going to have some free time. Besides, I really didn't expect you to go with me. I realize you have other things to do." She met his gaze evenly.

"Anyway, I'm glad you took me at my word about riding the horse whenever the spirit moves you. Though next time do try and let me know. I would enjoy riding with you."

"I wouldn't want to disturb you."

"You can't disturb me more than you have already." He continued to gaze at her, but his face masked any deeper meaning in his words.

Nicole let the remark pass, for his heavy, well-formed thigh was brushing against her, driving her to a point just past distraction. Words and emotions were tumbling in her head like a kaleidoscope gone mad. The physical contact was having a far more delirious effect on her than she could have imagined. Her blood seemed to swirl and separate, only to reform with tiny explosions.

"I hear you and Dr. Baker have become a twosome around town," said Jason solemnly.

She cleared her throat inadvertently and tilted her head back. Even though she was wearing heels, the top of her head barely reached his chin. "We go out on occasion. I see nothing wrong in that."

"I didn't say there was anything wrong with it," Jason objected.

"It was the way you said it. Your tone seemed to imply something." She was becoming angry, and she didn't know why.

"I wasn't aware of implying anything. You're a little quick to take offense, aren't you?"

"I don't like my personal life being examined by someone who refuses to discuss his own personal life." There . . . she had made an opening for him.

"I wasn't examining your personal life, Dr. Winters, only making an observation. Forgive me if I touched a nerve."

"You haven't touched a nerve. Dr. Baker and I are merely friends, nothing more," she replied sharply.

"Friends?" His mouth broadened in a slightly sardonic smile.

"Is that so unusual?"

"In this day and age, I would say it is most unusual."

"Well . . . it is your privilege to think whatever you wish." She turned her head and glanced at the band. Why did she care what he thought about her and Steve.

The palm of his hand exerted a force that molded her to him. His cheek came down to meet hers with ardent, tender pressure as the hand that held hers brought the back of her hand to rest against his shoulder. Like a single entity, they glided around the dance floor as the soft, mellow music pulsed through the room.

This is what heaven must be like, she thought. She could feel his heartbeat throbbing against her breast with strong regularity, and her own heart began to match the rhythm. His brawny, solid arm around her was holding her to his robust physique with fierce tenacity. The tuxedo couldn't camouflage the potent energy that lay beneath it, and Nicole trembled inwardly at the thought of that power being unleashed.

When the band concluded, Jason eased his grip but did not loosen it. Nicole looked up at him; their lips were inches apart. Her lips and mouth felt intolerably dry, and she ran the tip of her tongue over the outer edges of her lips. His hand moved back and forth over the small of her back lazily. Nicole started to step back, but his hold on her remained firm.

"Would it be too much of a strain on you to have another dance with me?" he asked in a low, quiet voice, his eyes daring her to deny him.

"No," she whispered. She felt a peculiar gauziness when his warm breath feathered over her lips in an invisible, nonexistent kiss.

As the musicians resumed their set of nostalgic love songs, Jason's head once again lowered to her, and she felt his lips brush the tip of her ear. It couldn't have been her imagination, for it set off a raging fire in her that sheer imaginative powers couldn't have produced. She relaxed in his arms and was glad he couldn't see the smile of contentment on her face. These were moments she would lock in her treasure chest of memories, to be taken out at will in the years ahead and delight in as she turned them over, fondled and cherished them in her mind's eye. She would hold them in loving hands, to be put back and carefully stored until she had the need to savor them again.

This time when the song was over Jason released her but kept his hand on her waist as he began to lead her back to her table.

"I'm going to Montreal next Thursday. I'll pick you up at nine in the morning," he stated confidently and matter-of-factly as they approached her table.

She turned to look at him. "I don't know if—"

"I won't take no for an answer. It's time you went up in a plane, and this will be an excellent opportunity," he countered as they reached the table, where Harry sat alone.

Harry rose and extended his hand. "Well, McBride, we meet at last. I'm Harry Butler, systems analyst for Bitron." Harry pumped Jason's hand as if he were shaking a cocktail. "We hear a lot about you at the company—wonder man of the silicone chip and all that."

"Happy to know you, Mr. Butler." Jason looked anything but happy. There was a pained expression on his face as he tried to extricate his hand. It was plain Jason McBride abhorred impromptu introductions. He was a private man who liked to choose the time and place for making new acquaintances. "You'll have to excuse me." He withdrew his hand quickly, gave Nicole a piercing look, then strode back to his table.

"He's an odd duck, if you ask me," muttered Harry as his wife and Carol's escort returned to the table, followed by Steve and Carol.

"Well, Nicole, I see you are the one to consult concerning Jason McBride. Actually dancing with the formidable man. And Steve tells me you were a guest in his home for three days," erupted Carol with a wickedly curious gleam in her eye as she sat in the chair Steve held for her.

Nicole's glance shifted from Carol to Steve, then back to Carol. "I know as much about Mr. McBride as the rest of you. I was not a guest in his home in the social sense. I met with an accident on his property, and he was kind enough to let me recuperate there, as my *doctor* wanted me to stay in bed and not move. I saw very little of Mr. McBride," she replied curtly to set the record straight once and for all, then cast an irate look at Steve.

"Carol, Tom is an absolute whiz on the dance floor. He made me feel like Ginger Rogers," said Fran with a calculating smile as she broke the incipient tension at the table.

Outwardly everyone relaxed, but Nicole felt small knots form in the pit of her stomach. She felt defensive about Jason, especially when they all seemed intent on putting him down. The tautness in her diminished as the conversation lightened and no one brought up the subject of Jason McBride again.

The drive home was inordinately quiet. Steve appeared to be locked in some inner thoughts of his own, and Nicole was busy inculcating the images and sensations of the memorable evening in the recesses of her brain.

While she was getting ready for bed, she recalled that Steve hadn't kissed her good night, a customary habit. At first those kisses had been ardent and eager. But as her response was always lukewarm at best, the good-night kiss had become perfunctory, lacking in any real desire on either part. Nicole shrugged and dismissed it from her mind. Anyway, she thought, it was probably time for Steve to move on to new conquests. The thought didn't disturb her in the least. She was still under the spell of being in Jason's arms. She went to sleep reveling in a dream that allowed her to nestle cozily in those arms.

CHAPTER 7

Summer fell on the land like a hammer swiftly striking an anvil. The heat swept through the air, proudly announcing that the cool and tepid temperatures of spring were banished for another year.

Nicole reached a lazy arm out and shut off the alarm moments before it was due to give its six A.M. signal. She had been awake since five-thirty, her heart pounding with excitement now that Thursday had finally arrived.

Getting Thursday off had proved to be no problem for Nicole. Dr. Carey was always eager to trade days off. She would have to handle things alone on Friday while he went fishing.

She went into the kitchen with a verve that belied the fact that she had just gotten out of bed. She prepared the coffee maker, then went to take her shower. With her shower and breakfast behind her, she completed any routine tasks. There was no problem about what to wear; she had been planning the exact ensemble all week. Her powder blue sleeveless linen dress was cool and comfortable and had a matching jacket that might come in handy if the weather turned chilly.

She took a chiffon scarf the same color as the dress and banded it about her head, pulling the trailing gauzy ends to the side, where they could casually drape over her shoulder as her long blond hair danced free, ending in soft curls. Pearl earrings, a single-strand pearl choker and light blue shoes completed her outfit. Makeup was minimal, as always.

Looking in the mirror, she became uncertain about her hairstyle; she was afraid it might look too girlish. She began to toy with the idea of putting it in her customary braided chignon. But it was too late; her doorbell had sounded.

Draping the jacket over the arm that held her purse, she took a deep breath to still her fluttering heart, then opened the door, her eyes bright, her smile wide.

"Good morning. I must say you are prompt, Mr. McBride," she said, her brain dazzled as she gathered in the sight of the tall man impeccably dressed in a lightweight three-piece suit of light blue. They looked like a matched set, Nicole thought with some amusement. As his dark eyes skimmed over her appreciatively, her eyes glowed and her smile broadened and the surface of her skin tingled with life.

"I'm always prompt, like you, Dr. Winters." He waited while she locked her door, then escorted her to his fire-red car.

"You really didn't have to pick me up. I could have met you at the barn," said Nicole, sitting in the bucket seat next to him as he steered the sleek machine toward the outskirts of the small town.

"I prefer it this way."

It wasn't long before he was driving past the driveway to his house and the road to the horse barn. He took a sharp corner, then, after a few hundred yards, veered off onto a dirt road. Within five minutes they were coming to a halt before the corrugated steel hangar. The single-engine Cessna looked expectant as it sat poised on the green grass outside the hangar.

"That was quick," commented Nicole.

"I think I told you there was a shorter route," said Jason in a soft, sonorous voice as he looked at her fondly. "Shall we get airborne?"

Nicole nodded and jumped out of the car before Jason had a chance to open the door for her. Her pace was brisk as she went toward the blue and white plane.

"Around the other side," instructed Jason, cupping her elbow. He reached up, gripped the chrome handle and pulled it down, then helped her into the seat of the cockpit, shutting the door firmly behind her. With the loping ease of a man who is very sure of himself, he went around the plane, opened the door and climbed into the pilot's seat. He glanced at her. "All set?"

"As ready as I'll ever be." She smiled, her eyes sparkling with anticipation.

Jason turned the ignition on. As the propeller began picking up revolutions, Jason taxied to the far end of the green velvet ribbon of land. Pausing while he revved the mighty engine to the necessary power for pretakeoff, he then began the dazzling run to be airborne.

Nicole watched the moving ground as if it were a treadmill whose momentum was running rampant. Her stomach slipped to her toes when the bumping of wheels against the uneven earth ceased and the plane nosed into the air above the trees, above the ground, above the earth.

After she had absorbed the initial thrill, she exclaimed, "Look! There's all of Lake Champlain! I never realized it was so big."

"In the air one gets a different perspective on the world. There is a unique beauty to it, an objectivity that is created in the soul rather than the mind."

"That sounds profound."

"Wasn't meant to be. It's a gut feeling, and after you've been up awhile and the newness wears off, I think you'll see what I mean."

"I don't think the newness will ever wear off," she claimed as the plane climbed higher into the heavens and banked northward. "Oh, look—the Adirondacks!"

Jason glanced at her briefly. "That's where they've always been."

The minor witticism caught her off guard and she turned to look at him, positive he would be grinning. But he wasn't. Her eyes took in the unyielding, razor-sharp profile with consummate fascination. He exuded total command over the machine, over himself, over the air around them as he maneuvered the plane with masterful precision just under the cumulus clouds. Not only was Jason physically powerful, but Nicole sensed an inner strength in the man that was a rarity in the strained convolutions of modern society. It filled her with calm serenity and security whenever she was near him. She knew he could lead her into the sulfurous pits of hell and she would have no fear.

"Don't you ever laugh out loud, Mr. McBride?" she asked, wondering what it would take for him to flash a toothy smile.

Jason's dark eyes moved slowly over her face. "My sense of humor has had its fine layers peeled away strip by strip over the years, Dr. Winters. But I'm not a totally humorless man. I do have my moments."

"I can't believe you're all that somber. A dulled sense of humor makes for a very grim world. I think it is an act you put on to keep people at a distance."

"I thought you were a veterinarian, or did you start out to be a psychiatrist?" He stared obliquely out the cockpit window. Then, before Nicole could reply, he said, "There's the St. Lawrence River, and you can see Montreal now."

Nicole craned her neck to peer at the fast-approaching river and city while Jason conversed on the plane's radio.

The landing was smooth. A rental car waited for them at the airport, and Jason drove with ease to the heart of the city, parked, then led Nicole to a small park where colorful flowers trembled every now and then as a breeze brushed their tender stems.

"I shouldn't be more than an hour and a half," said Jason. "I'll meet you at that tourist information booth over there. You don't mind if I tend to some business first, do you?"

"Of course not. The plane ride alone made my day. Anyway, I'm a great people watcher," she said, the corners of her lips lifting saucily.

"For a change of pace you ought to go through the Cathédrale Marie-Reine-du-Monde. It is an exact replica of St. Peter's in Rome, scaled down to one-third the size of the original," suggested Jason.

"I'm afraid I'll get lost."

"It's right next to the park here," he explained, his hand on her shoulder turning her to face the magnificent gray structure. "I don't think you'll get lost."

Nicole watched the tall, well-built man stride away from her, and her heart swelled with pride and with an awareness of totality within herself. She smiled and walked toward the church.

Before entering, she gazed up at the large central dome that dominated the smaller domes. Great paired columns projecting like but-

tresses flanked the windows on the exterior as they circled in a cylindri-
cal drum. Marching above them were gray stone panels with sculptured
garlands that formed a pedestal for the sweeping, lofty crown of the
dome enthroned upon it. The lantern surmounting the dome had a
rich, complicated, graceful design and rose above the gray surface with
imperious grandeur, giving a finishing touch to the beauty of the stately
cathedral.

Inside, Nicole actually felt the awesome religious power of the great
basilica. It was like entering a world of a long-past century. She had
never been inside the original St. Peter's, but if this church was a third
the size of its counterpart, then the one in Rome must be overwhelm-
ing in grandeur and opulence. She took a deep breath and padded
through the church as though she were walking on fragile glass.

The ground plan, designed as a Greek cross, was a far cry from the
simple wooden structures she had known in upper New York State and
Vermont.

From the windows in the dome, light streamed in like a banner of
golden vapor across the chancel, bathing the great heart of the cathedral with its ethereal splendor. Looking up into the huge dome was like
gazing into a spacious firmament, so vast, so luminous, so lofty.

Once the initial awe receded, Nicole observed more closely the de-
tails of ornaments. Statues in surrounding niches fretted in tortured
and twisted stone draperies, while white marble cherubs in medallions
spotted the great pillars of the nave.

The experience was so glorious that Nicole almost forgot the time.
With minutes to go before the appointed time to meet Jason, she
dashed down the stairs of the impressive cathedral, crossed the street
and rapidly walked to the middle of Dominion Square, then down
toward the gaily decorated miniature house of the tourist information
center.

Jason was already waiting. She smiled warmly at him and quickened
her pace, a serene happiness shining in her eyes.

"Well, you certainly look as though you've been having a good
time," said Jason when she stood in front of him, his eyes displaying a
certain softness.

"I have. It was marvelous . . . the cathedral, I mean. I've never
seen anything like it. The thought that the real St. Peter's dome is
three times the size of this cathedral staggers my imagination," she said
breathlessly, her amber eyes gazing at him.

Jason drew her arm through his as they began to stroll out of the park. "If you're impressed by that cathedral, wait until you see Notre-Dame de Bonsecours."

"Are we going there now?"

"No. I thought we'd grab a bite to eat before I got the car and gave you a capsulized tour of the city," he replied.

Nicole's eyes greedily drank in the sights as they strolled up one street, then down another in a seemingly haphazard quest.

The restaurant was quite plain, with no heavy-handed mood or atmosphere. Plain wooden chairs edged square tables that wore red plaid cloths. To her embarrassment, the menu was in French and she had left her dubious mastery of that language somewhere back in high school.

"I think I'll let you order for me, Mr. McBride. You did so well the last time," she said with pointed confidence.

"I'd be delighted. I think we should keep it fairly light, though, for I have a more sumptuous meal in mind for this evening."

"Dinner? I thought we'd be heading home before dark."

"I have tickets for the Place des Arts this evening. I hope you like Brahms," he said, laying his menu on top of hers.

"Place des Arts?" She hadn't expected to spend the entire day and evening in Montreal. The man surprised and mystified her. Did he intend to stay overnight? The thought wormed its way into her brain and hung there.

"It's a complex of three theaters. We will be in the Concert Hall, where the Montreal Symphony is giving a program devoted entirely to Brahms. I hope you don't have an aversion to classical music. I never thought to ask."

"I do have a preference for classical music." She was about to question him on the problem of getting home when the waiter came to take their order. When he left, Nicole continued her previous train of thought. "If we stay in Montreal until dark, how will you see to land the plane?"

"Do you doubt my abilities?"

"No. But I thought one had to have lights to land in the dark." She slowly twirled the glass of wine the waiter had brought when he took their order.

"Set your mind at ease, Dr. Winters. The entire strip is lined with floodlights. I'm surprised you didn't notice them. They go on by automatic relay, which I set before we left. Does that lessen your misgivings?"

"Yes." But a question remained in her eyes.

"Don't tell me you believe I brought you up here for a shameless clandestine affair in some hotel room," he prodded her, his eyes staring directly into hers.

She winced at his directness, then said calmly, "It had crossed my mind."

"But you came anyway."

"I came because I was under the impression it was only a quick business trip and I was only along for the brief plane ride. I didn't realize you intended to spend the evening here, too."

"If you knew I had deeper designs, would you have come?" he asked, a dark eyebrow arching querulously.

"No."

"Why?"

"I don't like being duped into spending an evening with a married man." There . . . she had said it. She had brought it out in the open. Every inch of her body tensed as she waited for his reply. But at least she would know one way or the other.

Jason leaned back in his chair, took a sip of wine, then closely studied her for several seconds before speaking. "And what gave you the idea I might be married?"

"I heard it from what I consider a fairly reliable source." She thrust her chin out in a small gesture of defiance.

He set his wineglass down on the table and leaned forward intimately. "If I were to tell you I had no wife, who would you believe— me or your source?"

"You, of course," she replied a little too eagerly, knowing it was the answer she wanted to hear, but with more decisiveness.

"Then let's hear no more about it."

"But you haven't answered my question yet. Are you married?" The question was asked with slow deliberation.

"As far as I'm concerned, Dr. Winters, I've given you my answer and the matter is settled. I would appreciate it if you would find another topic to pursue."

"I think this is as good a topic as any." Her annoyance at his evasiveness was becoming evident.

"Look, I have a pleasant day planned and would hate to see it go sour because you insist on discussing a subject I consider closed." His voice had a hard, flat tone.

"If you feel that way, perhaps it would be best if you took me home right now," she said stormily, starting to rise from the chair.

"Sit down," he ordered gently. "I shouldn't have been so gruff. I apologize. Perhaps I wanted the day to be too perfect. I'm sorry. I can understand your feelings about being played for a fool by a married man. Please set your mind at ease, Dr. Winters. . . . Shall we pretend the day has just started?"

With a sigh Nicole resumed her seat. Maybe she had hoped for a perfect day also, and her innate curiosity was bent on destroying it. "You're right. I shouldn't have questioned you, then doubted your answer. As you say, Mr. McBride, we'll start the day over." She smiled, and he returned it.

The waiter brought their entrées, removing any possibility of renewed tension.

The aroma emanating from the dish placed before her tempted her salivary glands beyond endurance, and Nicole attacked her food with relish. The dish half consumed, she buttered a piece of the crusty bread and exclaimed as pleasantly as possible, "I knew I could rely on your judgment when it comes to food. It's delicious—but what is it?"

"Veal kidneys sautéed with bits of ham in a cognac-mushroom sauce," he replied easily, his mask of severity slipping away.

"I never thought I'd be enjoying kidneys."

"Wait until dessert."

She grinned at him impishly. For some reason she couldn't stay angry with him for any length of time. "I thought you said this was going to be a light lunch."

"Dessert will slide down." The edges of his mouth curved upward, deepening the furrows along his cheeks.

Nicole grabbed another piece of bread before the waiter cleared the table of their empty dishes. She munched on it while Jason related some of the historical background of Montreal. She listened attentively until he paused.

"If you hadn't told me you were born in Boston, I would have taken you for a native Montrealer. Your French is superb," she remarked.

"In my line of business it pays to know the other fellow's language. Otherwise one is subject to the whims of others, placed in their hands like an innocent, vulnerable babe. I'm surprised you don't speak French or some other language."

"Learning the obtuse language of medicine was enough for me," she countered as the waiter placed the dessert and coffee on the table. "This looks delectable and full of calories."

"Tarte au sucre," he announced. "A pastry made of maple sugar, eggs and cream. Rich beyond belief."

As soon as they finished the dessert and coffee, they left the restaurant to browse through the myriad shops conglomerated like a miniature city beneath the Place Ville-Marie as shiny, towering skyscrapers soared into the heavens above them.

Retrieving the rented car from the parking garage, Jason headed for the tree-clothed mountain that rose above the gray asphalt city like an omnipotent guardian. Halfway up he stopped and parked the car amid a host of other cars and buses on Mount Royal. Opening the car door, he extended his hand and helped her out. They walked up the grass-coated ground to stand away from the general crowd.

"It's unreal! I've never stood and looked down on an entire city before," said Nicole.

"It is an impressive panorama. I thought you might enjoy it."

"I have always thought of Montreal as a quaint old city. I'm surprised to see how ultramodern it is," she remarked, gazing over the sprawling metropolis below.

"The new hotels, malls, offices, street widening, the Metro—a complete renovation of the city was spurred by Expo 67 coming to Montreal. See those two small islands to the east in the St. Lawrence River . . ." He lifted a directional hand. "That's where all the exhibitions were housed."

Nicole studied the islands and the city for several seconds, then turned around and looked at the rest of the mountain looming above them. "Why didn't we go all the way to the top?"

"This is as far as motor vehicles are allowed. One has to walk the rest of the way or take a horse-drawn carriage. It would take too much time, and I want to show you Old Montreal, the one you have pictured in your mind." He gazed down at her with warmth glinting in his dark eyes, the slight breeze ruffling his raven hair.

Nicole wanted to reach up and smooth it down. She felt on top of the world in more ways than one.

"Well . . ." He sighed and looked off into the distance. "If you've seen enough, we'll take in the Old Quarter."

She nodded, and they went back to the car.

With the car once more in a parking garage, Nicole walked alongside Jason as they entered Montreal's Old Quarter, where the cobblestone streets still prevailed and three-story town houses of yesteryear huddled together, displaying their various hues as the sun's rays caressed their surfaces. Wrought-iron staircases curled, angled or plunged straight upward to the second floors of the eclectic edifices, giving the residents direct access to the street.

"This is more like I expected Montreal to be," said Nicole, her head angled, taking in the picturesque scene of a bygone era. "Those staircases are really splendid, especially the circular ones."

"And dangerous," commented Jason.

"Oh? How come?"

"They ice up in the winter and can be extremely hazardous. For the sake of authenticity, the city has allowed the existing ones to remain but bans the building of new ones," Jason explained.

"Well, dangerous or not, they add a certain flair I find quite charming."

As he gave a running commentary on the Old Quarter, his hands were thrust deep in his pants pockets, and Nicole impulsively slipped her hand through the crook of his arm. He looked at her, and when she thought he was about to smile his approval, he averted his eyes to the street. But he didn't seem to mind, and she liked the feel of his strong arm as he adjusted his gait to match hers.

"Here we are," said Jason. "Notre Dame. Prepare yourself for an experience beyond the norm. It will dazzle you with its beauty."

As Jason led her into the church, Nicole stood awestruck at the foot of the nave. Jason was right. But dazzle was a gross understatement of the effect the cathedral had on her. Absolute wonder overcame her as the rich gleam of gold filled her eyes. It took several minutes for her vision to become more discerning and notice the splendor of the woodcarver's art profoundly displayed in the interior of the edifice. They walked down the nave toward the chancel and altar, both of which seemed to have been dipped in molten gold to form a semicircle of pinnacled niches enshrining saints and apostles, arched in regal, golden silence around the altar.

Finally drawing her gaze from the mesmerizing altar, Nicole glanced upward, her mouth agape, at the soaring Gothic vaulting. Captured between the lofty wood ribs of the vaulting were diamond-shaped areas of a vibrant blue studded with golden stars. She wouldn't have believed anything like it could have existed if she hadn't seen it with her own eyes. The highly crafted wood with its glowing patina, the deep tones of blue and so much gold assailed her sensibilities with gargantuan distinction.

"Well?" Jason's voice was low as they stood at the side of the chancel.

"I don't think there are enough words in the dictionary to describe it all." Her face had a gamin look of innocence as she turned to gaze at him.

"I hope I haven't rendered you speechless for the day," he said, a wry smile in his eyes.

Nicole grinned. "I'll admit I'm impressed. But as you've probably gathered, I doubt if I'll lose my powers of speech."

They continued to walk through the church until their senses were sated. After leaving Notre Dame, they strolled through the warm streets of the Old Quarter, stopping every so often to browse in a curio or antiques shop or to contemplate the artifacts in the small museums that were scattered about the area. They ended up meandering along the busy harbor, the sights, sounds and smells inscribing themselves as if in indelible ink on Nicole's memory. Throughout the day their conversation had been light, impersonal but affable.

"I'm famished," exclaimed Nicole as they trekked back to the heart of the city.

Jason glanced at his wristwatch. "We have time for a leisurely dinner before the concert. You can eat to your heart's content."

The restaurant was the exact opposite of the one where they had had lunch—faultlessly elegant, richly appointed, a regal aura, in short, a dining establishment where only the very rich would dare to pick up a menu. The impeccably clad waiter was proper to the point of being stiff. Even though the menu was in both French and English, Nicole let Jason order for her. He seemed to derive a certain pleasure from it, and she didn't care one way or the other. Jason gave their order in French, and the waiter disappeared, only to return swiftly with a bottle of Pouilly-Fumé. He displayed the label for Jason, who nodded his approval, then poured it.

"To an interesting and pleasant day," said Jason, raising his glass to clink with hers. He swirled the liquid in the glass, inhaled its aroma, then took a sip. "Hope you approve of the wine."

She followed suit before taking a sip of the slightly green white wine with its distinctive smoky taste. "Excellent." She paused and looked directly at him. "You must have seen Montreal a thousand times. I hope you weren't bored showing it to me."

"Not at all. It is always different, especially when you are with someone who has never seen it before. It gives one a new perspective, a fresh appreciation of old, familiar sights. I must admit your enthusiasm rubbed off on me."

"I can't get over the churches," said Nicole with a sigh, "the magnificence and splendor of them. There's a craftsmanship to them that modern architecture seems to lack."

"Each era has its distinguishing characteristics," said Jason as the waiter served their appetizers. "I wish I could have introduced you to Malpeques, but they are only available from September through December. However, I'm sure you'll find the Canapés Sangroniz to your liking."

"Malpeques?"

"Sweet, juicy oysters from Malpeque Bay on Prince Edward Island. They are extremely delicate and light, with hardly a trace of the iodine that so many oysters have. A very special treat, I assure you." Jason plopped a one-inch square of the toasted bread laden with a mixture of Roquefort cheese and butter topped with Beluga caviar into his mouth.

"The substitution is superb." There were four of the squares on her plate, and she ate all of them with zest. When the small crock of steaming soup was served, Nicole tried to recognize the contents from the aroma, then announced with pride, "Shrimp bisque!"

"Your sense of smell is acute and accurate, Dr. Winters."

She spooned some into her mouth. "The flavor is a little different from the bisque I've had in the past, though."

"It is laced with a special combination of brandy and wine."

"You seem to live the life of an epicure," said Nicole.

"Not really. I enjoy good food that is well prepared. A steak on an outdoor grill, freshly picked corn on the cob—in fact, my tastes are quite pedestrian. However, if I'm going to dine in a restaurant, I only select those that still have chefs who know how to cook. Unfortunately, they are becoming few and far between. Most restaurants have deteriorated into little more than fast-food outlets where the entrées are prepackaged and frozen, then shoved into a microwave oven before they are served to the customer. That is not my idea of dining out."

"I like your philosophy, Mr. McBride. My mother could never understand why people bought frozen dinners. I'm afraid she'd have a fit if she knew how many of them I consume. They come in quite handy for the working woman, especially one who is not too skilled in the kitchen to begin with."

"I take it you are not the domestic type." He swirled the wine in his glass, his soup finished.

"My mother tried to instruct me in the fine art of cooking, but I never paid much attention. I was always too eager to get out of the house and tend to the animals. I do what is necessary around the house, but my heart and mind aren't really in it," she replied honestly.

The waiter cleared the table, his movements measured and precise. Their wineglasses were unobtrusively refilled and their entrées were served with gracious restraint: Steak Charles, a thin, tender steak that was the specialty of the house, in a bed of savory wild rice.

"Fiddleheads!" exclaimed Nicole. "I love them. I didn't know restaurants served them."

"I'm surprised you know what they are. Most people don't," remarked Jason, one eyebrow arched.

"When we were small my brothers and I used to pick the budding ferns, and my mother would cook them in butter so they would keep their woodsy flavor and texture of asparagus."

"I have a fondness for them, too." A hint of a smile played on Jason's wide lips.

The cherries jubilee was the crowning touch to their dinner, a light, tasty dessert that blazed its way to their table.

The Place des Arts was a short walk from the restaurant. As they entered the red-carpeted main lobby, Nicole felt as though she had walked into a world of science fiction. After spending the better part of the day in churches of another era and in the cobblestone streets of the Old Quarter, the Place des Arts was an architectural shock to her senses. The modernity jolted her as she gazed at the high white ceiling with its fanciful sculptured lights blazing in a golden glow. Metal sculptures on one vast wall struggled with their own abstraction. Circular walls of royal blue encased the two floors, the second of which had balconies holding square white tables and subtly curved red chairs. It was like traversing a time warp. Jason's warm hand on the small of her back brought her back to reality.

"Acoustically, this concert hall is one of the most nearly perfect in the world," he whispered in her ear as he guided her through the open doors to the orchestra and their seats.

The lights went down, voices ebbed to a murmur, the conductor mounted the podium and Brahms soon filled the concert hall.

As they left, Nicole regretted leaving her jacket in the car, for there was a chill in the late-night Montreal air. Her shoulders hunched involuntarily.

"Cold?" asked Jason.

"I should have brought my jacket."

Jason promptly removed his suit jacket and placed it over her shoulders along with his arm. "The car isn't too far away."

Nicole hugged the jacket to her as if she were embracing the man himself. His arm around her shoulders and the feel of his body alongside hers were sending sparks into her bloodstream, warming her with a special kind of heat and a dizzying sense of elation that no other man had ever caused in her.

Reaching the car, she returned the jacket to Jason and slipped on her own. It was fast approaching midnight when the single-engine Cessna soared off the runway of Montreal's airport. Nicole looked back at the receding city squatting on an anvil-shaped island at the juncture of the Ottawa and St. Lawrence rivers. The metropolis sparkled like diamonds scattered on indigo velvet. A huge illuminated cross atop Mount Royal caught Nicole's eye.

"That cross down there . . . what's it for?" she asked, swiveling her head toward Jason.

"It was erected to commemorate the day in 1642 when Maisonneuve, the founder of Montreal, carried a wooden cross on his shoulders to the crest of Mount Royal. It's more impressive when viewed from the ground at night."

Nicole leaned back in the co-pilot's seat, closed her eyes and sighed.

"Tired?" asked Jason.

"A little. But in a pleasant way."

"I take it you enjoyed yourself, then."

"Enjoy is the understatement of the century. I was enchanted," she replied with a purr in her voice.

"Have you been to Nova Scotia or Prince Edward Island?"

"No. The most spectacular sight I have ever seen is Niagara Falls. After a particularly grueling exam, a group of us decided to drive out there and have a carefree weekend. Other than that, I had little time for touring the country. Veterinarian medicine is a hard taskmaster."

In the dimness of the cockpit, Nicole knew Jason was staring at her, studying her with a rapacious look, and tremors of delight danced along her spine. She gazed out the window into the night, where lights flickered below like multifaceted gems. Soon she saw the parallel string of white lights as the plane banked into an approach to Jason's grassy airstrip.

Though it was a bit bumpy, the landing was perfect. Nicole felt like a flying veteran as she slid out the cockpit door, but soon learned she wasn't as she heard the hem of her dress tear with a sickening rip. "Oh, dear."

"What's the matter?" asked Jason, coming to her side.

"I've torn my dress. Here I thought I was being so clever getting out of the plane on my own," she replied, twisting and reaching backward with her hand to pick up the torn section in an attempt to estimate the damage. In the dark she couldn't quite see, but her sense of touch told her the rent wasn't as bad as it had sounded.

"You should have waited for me to help you," said Jason sternly. "Come over into the light and we'll see how bad it is." His hand closed over her upper arm and guided her to the well-lit hangar. "Turn around."

She complied and tried to turn her head enough to see the hem but couldn't quite make it. "Is it beyond repair?"

"I don't think so. Perhaps you can have it rewoven," he suggested.

There was an uneasy silence in the car as Jason drove down the darkened country roads to Nicole's place. The atmosphere in the sporty vehicle was charged with the peculiar tension that often develops between a man and a woman when they sense a subtle change in a heretofore reserved relationship.

When he stopped the car in front of her house, she was about to give a quick thanks and say good night, but Jason had leaped from the car and was opening the door for her before she could coordinate her thoughts. Without a word he escorted her up the porch steps.

"I had a marvelous time and I truly thank you," she said, fumbling in her purse for her key.

Quietly, with his index finger crooked, he lifted her chin, bringing her to face him. "We've had some scorching weather lately, and you haven't taken advantage of my offer to use the pond. A cool swim on a hot day can be very refreshing. Promise me you'll come out for a swim when you have a free day," he said in a subdued, husky voice.

The muscles of her throat tightened and her stomach rolled as she tried to stem the growing desire to be kissed by Jason McBride. "I promise," she finally whispered.

His dark eyes probed hers as his finger released her chin and his curled hand caressed her cheek, his knuckles moving lightly over the fair skin.

"Good night, Dr. Winters." His hand dropped to his side, and he left.

She watched the red Firebird dissolve into the darkness, her nerves splintered by his gentle touch.

CHAPTER 8

Color showered through the sky like exploding stars, miniature novas bursting to scatter dazzling gems on the dark canopy of the sky. The whining eruptions dispersed brilliant hues of color as dinning booms echoed lazily over the vast expanse of water. Burst after burst—reds, blues, yellows, whites—phosphorescent pigments illuminated the sky with their intense glittering tones. It was the Fourth of July over Lake Champlain.

Nicole, Steve, Carol and Tom Stone sat at a picnic table in one of Burlington's parks that edged Lake Champlain and watched the spectacular pyrotechnics of the fireworks specialists as the latter practiced their craft with skilled knowledge.

"Oh . . . did you see that one?" exclaimed Carol with a kittenish giggle meant to attract the attention of the handsome doctor.

All evening Nicole had had the impression that Carol was far more interested in Stephan Baker than she was in her own companion. And she wasn't being very subtle about it. There was a shrewdness about Carol that was masked by an angelic face, a charming voice and discerning mannerisms—none of which was lost on Steve, who had a gleam in his eye and whose smile was calculated to make female hearts flutter. Nicole had seen that look before and knew it well. He had looked and smiled at her that way the first time she met him in Jason McBride's home. At first she had thought it quite attractive. Now she only found it amusing.

A wry smile touched her lips as she watched Carol maneuver Steve into taking a stroll by the edge of the lake, leaving Tom to his own devices. She felt the vibrations under her elbows caused by Tom's constant strumming of his fingers on the wooden table. He was obviously trying to keep a tight rein on his temper.

"What do you do exactly at Bitron, Tom?" asked Nicole, hoping to stem his rising anger.

"I'm a programmer. One of many," he replied glumly, his eyes following Steve and Carol with acid resentment.

"It seems that everyone who doesn't farm around here works for Bitron." It was an inane and often repeated statement, but Nicole was trying to divert Tom's attention.

"It's a big outfit," he said in a manner that indicated he really didn't care. "Doesn't it bother you that Steve has gone off and left you sitting here with me?" he asked, his annoyance bubbling to the surface.

"Why should it? He's a big boy and can take care of himself," she replied.

"Are you and him . . . well . . ." He groped for words.

"Steve and I are friends, nothing more. We've been going out together for several months but there is nothing serious between us." Nicole had the feeling that that was why Steve continued to see her. He felt safe with her, since she obviously wanted no pressing commitment from him. "What about you and Carol?"

"I take it seriously but she doesn't," he admitted grudgingly, then turned to face Nicole as his fingers stopped the steady drumming.

"How long have you known each other?"

"Two years. Since she came to work there. But we've only been going out a few months. I thought I knew her pretty well, but I guess I don't."

"Two months is hardly enough time to know anyone. I sometimes wonder if we can really know another person," said Nicole, thoughts of

Jason McBride floating into her mind. Would she ever come to know him the way she wanted to—his whims, his moods, his laughter. More than anything she would like to see him laugh heartily.

"Well, I have a sneaking suspicion Carol isn't going to grant me the time to get to know her," said Tom. He stood suddenly as the wandering couple returned, Carol's arm possessively through Steve's.

"I guess the finale is coming up at any moment," observed Steve. "When it's over, why don't we treat ourselves to a pizza? Or are you on duty tomorrow, Nicole?"

"No, I have the entire weekend off."

The sky lit up in a frenzy of colors exploding one after another in a clamor of blasts, rumbles and booms. A scattering of applause sounded as the gleeful observers expressed their appreciation for the brilliant and exciting display of fireworks.

At the restaurant, the pizza was hot, bubbling with cheese and toppings. Carol was a shade more attentive to Tom, which eased a potentially awkward situation. It was fairly late when Steve drew his car up in front of Nicole's house.

"Would you care to come in for some coffee?" asked Nicole.

"I'll take a raincheck, if you don't mind. I'm coffeed to death. Besides, I have early hospital rounds tomorrow." He paused thoughtfully. "That Carol is quite a woman, don't you think?"

"Yes, she is. Brains and beauty. I also think she fancies you," said Nicole with a mischievous smile.

"She fancies a lot of people, I'm afraid. I heard she even tried to blow down the walls of Jericho and capture the elusive Jason McBride a year or so ago. Tried to get him to take her up in that plane of his," said Steve.

"Did she succeed?" Her lips were trembling as the words spilled from her mouth.

"Who knows? Carol never mentions it, and McBride is as impenetrable as stone." Steve leaned over and kissed her on the cheek. "Maybe I'll see you over the weekend."

"Thanks for the lovely evening, Steve."

"It's always my pleasure."

She left the car and walked onto the porch like an automaton, her mind whirling with thoughts of Jason and Carol. By the time she was ready for bed she had rationalized that Jason couldn't have taken Carol for a ride in his plane or Carol would have been the first to announce the fact with haughty pride.

Though she had convinced herself that Jason had never succumbed to Carol's wiles, incoherent and eerie dreams darted through her sleep. She was in a maze, with panic flooding her as she tried to find the way out. Every time she thought the opening was in sight, the solid form of Jason McBride blocked her exit, causing her to flee in another direction, only to come up against the iron sinews of his body once again, halting her frantic search for an escape. Whenever she looked up there was the vague face of a mysterious woman disdainfully smiling down at her, a hint of triumph in her cruel eyes. The dream repeated itself throughout the night in different colors, different mazes, but always with Jason and a veiled woman.

Finally dawn trickled through the window, and her eyes flew open in relief. By the time she had had breakfast and had gotten dressed, she had decided to stop at the hospital and make sure no emergency had arisen. She secretly hoped for one, for she needed to work to erase Jason McBride from her thoughts altogether.

"What are you doing here?" asked Dr. Carey, his bushy white eyebrows arching like wings about to take off.

"I thought I'd drop in and make sure you weren't deluged with work," she said cheerily.

"I thought I told you to take the weekend off. I'm not bashful, you know. If I had needed you I would have called. Fourth of July weekend is always dull around here. I'll probably close up shop early."

"No farm calls?"

"No. And I doubt if there'll be any." He took his glasses off and stared at them as though they were some alien object.

"Well, as long as I'm here, I'll do the animals for you."

"I've done them already. Them? There's only one. I'll give you three guesses who it is and the first two don't count." He grinned wickedly and put his glasses back on.

"Muffins."

"You're too shrewd. Want to know why?"

"She won't stop smiling?"

He chuckled. "That's good. Very good. But it seems the poor cat was upset by all the fireworks last night. Went about meowing all night and by morning had almost torn the house apart. Mrs. Norris thinks the undue noise of the firecrackers has induced distemper in her Muffins."

"Muffins has had her shots, hasn't she?"

"Of course she has. I've tended to that cat since it was a kitten. Why, that cat has had more and better medical attention than some humans I know. The diagnosis was pure and simple. The cat's in heat. She wanted out of the house to search for a mate."

"Did you tell Mrs. Norris that?" Nicole's eyes twinkled.

"Yes, I did. Rather bluntly, as a matter of fact." The round, pink cherubic face cracked in a smile.

"Well?" Nicole could hardly keep the laughter back.

"The woman looked at me as though I were a fiendish, lecherous monster even to suggest such a thing about her angelic cat. She hesitated about leaving the animal with me. She was positive I would let the cat loose to prove a point, I suppose. But when Muffins began that low, growling meow, she thought it was the cry of agonizing death and begged me to cure the imaginary distemper. So . . ." He paused and peered at Nicole over the rim of his glasses. "Back to you. It looks like it's going to be a scorcher today. Why don't you find somewhere cool to hide and enjoy an idle moment? I think I'll go fishing or some such thing."

The words "somewhere cool" rang a bell in her head: Jason's pond. She had promised she would avail herself of its refreshing water, and today was perfect for it. "Thanks," she said to Dr. Carey.

"What for?"

"Giving me an idea. I know just the place to be cool and idle."

"Where?"

"Riding," she replied quickly, remembering her promise to Jason not to mention the pond to anyone.

"Oh, that chestnut of McBride's. You love that horse, don't you? A fine animal. Now, anyway. I saw the creature when McBride brought it back from the auction. He called me over to give it a thorough examination. What a sight! But he's done wonders with the animal. And that stallion of his. A superb beast!"

"Well, if you need me for anything, that's where I'll be," stated Nicole, eager to get on her way.

At home she slipped into an emerald green bikini that was conservative compared to some on the market, then covered it with a pair of yellow shorts and a yellow tank top. After quickly tieing her sneakers, she set about making some ham and cheese sandwiches. She put oranges, apples and bananas in a plastic bag, wrapped the sandwiches and packed them in a large, long-handled tote bag along with a tall Thermos of lemonade, some towels and sundries.

Her stomach fluttered as she drove to the McBride farm, then up the road to the horse barn. Braking the station wagon, she grabbed the tote bag, swung her slim legs out the car door and drew a sharp breath before proceeding to the barn.

Charm whinnied, shook her head and snorted in recognition, while Midnight surveyed Nicole with a calm eye. Setting the tote bag down, Nicole immediately threw her arms around the mare's neck, hugging and nuzzling her. The stallion lumbered to the edge of his stall and poked his head over the door, shaking his large, shiny black head, his mane flouncing like a swirl of black dust about him.

"Oh, all right. Can't leave you out, can we, Midnight?" she said aloud and embraced the black animal fervently before lovingly caressing his nose. "Sorry, old boy. I'll have to leave you here. I can't ride the two of you at once. I wish I could. I hate leaving you all by your lonesome like this." She rubbed his cheek with her hand, then led Charm out of her stall.

Nicole bridled and saddled the chestnut mare, then led her outside, where she slung the handles of the tote bag over the horn of the saddle before mounting. The horse's gait was slow and steady. It was too hot and sticky to race. As Nicole looped the reins to turn the mare down the small lane to the pond, she saw two men loading hay onto a big stake truck in the field adjacent to the lane. That blue-black hair glistening in the sun could only belong to one man—Jason McBride.

Her gaze riveted on the tall, well-built man clad in denim shorts, his bronzed torso and legs bare to the blazing sun. He tossed the baled hay up onto the truck for Jake to stack. With each motion the big muscles of his back and arms slid under his skin with potent ease; his thigh and leg muscles bulged with power hardly tapped as he swooped the bales upward. Mesmerized by the undeniable strength of Jason's physique, Nicole folded one hand over the other, resting them on the horn of the saddle as she stared at the moving form in wonder. She had always been drawn to him, but seeing him in the field, his virility so strong and blatant, fascinated her.

Her face flushed when he caught sight of her sitting astride the gentle mare. The bale in his hands stopped in mid-air on its journey to the truck. To hide her chagrin at being caught staring at him, she smiled broadly and waved to them, then nudged Charm to continue down the lane.

The glade wherein lay the pond was as enchanting as she had remembered it. She placed her tote bag near an old, tilting birch tree that rose skyward from a bed of spongy moss. After she removed the saddle from the mare, she tethered her loosely under the shade of a leafy maple tree where the grass was tender and succulent. She slipped her sneakers off, then her shorts and tank top. Unpinning and uncoiling the blond braid of hair at the nape of her neck, she put the plastic pins in the pocket of her shorts, letting the thick plait, secured by a rubber band at the end, hang down her back.

She walked to the rim of the pond and tested the water with her toes. It was delightfully cool and inviting to the touch. It held a promise of relief from the heat and humidity that were tormenting her small, well-rounded body.

The white sand and rocks that lined the pond made it appear deceptively shallow as she waded in, no longer able to resist the temptation. Her body tingled as the cool, clear water enveloped it, and she was soon swimming like a duck who had been deprived of its natural habitat for a long period of time. She soon learned the true depth of the pond. It was well over her head and dropped off sharply only a few feet from the edge.

Her surge of energy momentarily spent, she left the water and stretched out on a carpet of moss, her blond braid tossed to one side. The sun filtering through the trees rippled over her skin like elusive butterflies, landing for a second, then flitting off to rest upon another spot. It was a delicious feeling, and she gave herself up to total relaxation without hesitation.

Almost an hour had gone by, and the warm, sticky air began to make itself felt once again. She rose lazily and walked to the very edge of the pond. As she braced herself for a dive, a cold, wet muzzle thrust against her back, swiftly tumbling her ungracefully into the water.

Sputtering and coughing, she came to the surface to see Midnight bobbing his head up and down in approval as Jason stood beside him in his very brief shorts.

She watched Jason unsaddle and tether the stallion beside Charm as she treaded water. In a flying leap Jason dove into the crystal waters a short distance from her. When his head bobbed up, she gave him a vengeful splash for letting Midnight shove her in so unceremoniously.

He returned the splash twofold. She turned her head to avoid the onslaught, only to have Jason sneak up behind her and playfully push her under.

Quickly coming up, she swam around as if nothing had happened, waiting for the moment she would catch him off guard. When the opportunity presented itself, she gathered her strength and shoved Jason's head underwater, then swam for the shore with the speed of a dolphin. She was giddy with triumph and laughed freely as she stood on the comparative safety of the ground.

He stalked from the water and drew himself to his full height as his feet touched the mossy bank. Combing the fingers of one hand through the mass of wet, black hair to smooth it back from his face, he caught Nicole giggling at him with gleeful abandon. His expression softened and he released a deep-throated laugh that increased in intensity each second.

The blinding glint of his even, white teeth against his darkly tanned face dazzled Nicole, and the mirth slowly slipped from her lips. The usual stern visage had been transformed into an astonishingly handsome Greek god descended from Mount Olympus. A profusion of curled, wet, black hair burnished by the sun to a deep henna scattered thickly across his expansive chest before trailing down to a V at the top of his shorts. The laughter rumbled deep within him, and the lines that ran from his cheeks to his jaw became furrowed like etched crevices, enhancing his rugged, dark good looks.

As he approached her, she swallowed hard, for her stomach seemed to be rising to her throat. When he stood directly in front of her, she looked up at him with an ingenuous smile. His smile vanished as they communed with unspoken words, drawing her into the deep, bottomless pools of his black eyes. Her breathing became shallow, and her heart pumped furiously. She was on the edge of a precipice, about to cast herself headlong into the unknown.

His arms reached out and his hands circled her waist, inching her toward him. With a hunger neither could deny any longer, their arms enfolded each other, pressing flesh against flesh, soul against soul. They stood clinging to one another in quiet desperation, with a binding tenacity that attempted to mold their bodies into one entity. His head shifted downward as his cheek pressed against the top of her head.

"Nicole . . . Nicole," he whispered in a low, heavy voice as the side of her face nestled in the damp down of his broad chest.

"Oh, Jason." Her hands moved over the taut sinews of his back, memorizing every nuance of the wide shoulders, the hard ribs.

He took her head in his hands and gently tilted it upward to meet his. With slow deliberation his lips touched hers tenderly again and again until her lips were moving in rhythm with his. When the moment was right, his mouth covered hers with a knowing mastery, and her limp body leaned into his in total surrender. His well-muscled thighs flexed as the weight of her bare legs rested on them. His kiss slid over her neck to taste the soft sweetness at the base of her throat, while her fingers laced their way through the coarse hair of his head, her eyes closed, her mind tripping through the elysian fields of the gods. His hands made her skin feel alive as it never had before. Her flesh was pliant under his skillful touch, and like the oncoming tide that inundates the helpless shore, she relinquished any hold she might have had on propriety. His lips traced the throbbing vein in her neck, then once again captured her mouth with relentless desire. The kiss widened and deepened, then raged with an unquenchable fire as pent-up passions were discharged into the realm of enchantment.

The trees arched high like flying buttresses of a living cathedral. The sun poked long, shimmering fingers through the leaves like glowing wisps of angels bestowing their beatific blessings on the two people lost in an embrace below them. Encased in nature's temple, they were oblivious to the song of the birds the music of the breeze blowing its way through rustling leaves, the fugues played by the water as it spilled over the barrier to the profusion of rocks below. Time itself lost meaning for Jason and Nicole as they immersed themselves in new revelations of emotion and wandered into a divine limbo.

The idyll was later shattered by the concerted whinnying of the two horses. Instinctively Nicole pulled herself from Jason's arms to see what had disturbed them.

"Nicole," said Jason hoarsely, putting a staying hand on her shoulder. "There's nothing wrong with the horses."

"I'll check to make sure." She needed time to collect herself, to recoup from the impact of being in Jason's arms. It had had a heady effect on her and had erased her sense of reality. When she returned, her face was still aglow, her step light. She kneeled beside him, sitting back on her legs, her hands on her thighs as Jason lay sprawled on the mossy ground. She smiled down at him lovingly.

"Would you like something to eat? I have sandwiches, fruit and lemonade. What would you like?"

"You." His long arms reached out and drew her to his reposing form. He held her against him as his lips sought hers with renewed fervor. The warmth of his body flooded her, and a sweet joy consumed her. But before she became lost in that dizzying whirl that only Jason could induce, she placed her hand on his chest and pushed herself from him while an atom of self-control remained.

"Some lunch . . . remember?" she asked.

Taking a deep breath, Jason sat up, a slow smile playing over his wide lips. "You have a one-track mind, don't you?"

"So do you." She laughed. "Besides, it's way past noon."

"Are you on a time schedule?" There was a glow in his dark eyes that reflected shards of amber as his hand moved up to caress her face.

"My stomach is."

Jason scrambled to his feet, then offered her his hand in assistance. With a quick jerk of his strong arm, she was on her feet, Jason catching her by the waist. Her hands were gently braced on his shoulders when he bent and kissed her lightly on the forehead.

"You get out those sandwiches of yours while I see that the horses have a drink of water and move them to a new feeding spot," said Jason as he released her.

Nicole went for the tote bag, but she wasn't aware of her feet touching the ground. She thought she was floating. Somewhere in the back of her mind she had the feeling she would awake at any moment to find it was all a dream. Being with Jason was only a figment of her imagination. The idea that it was all an illusion was so vivid that she turned, expecting to see only Charm. But there was Jason standing tall between the two horses drinking at the edge of the pond. It was real; very real.

A radiance settled on her as she emptied the contents of her tote bag on one of her clean towels that she had spread on the verdant ground. She was thankful she had packed three sandwiches and plenty of fruit. She had done so thinking it would do for both her lunch and supper if she decided to stay the entire day.

Nicole sat, her legs drawn up with her arms around them, her head tilted in Jason's direction, watching him with loving tenderness as he moved the horses to fresher grazing.

Finished with the horses, he smiled warmly, almost seductively at her as his long, muscular legs brought him to the minor feast she had laid out for them. He bent over, his fingers reaching out to touch her cheek, before placing his hulking frame in a sitting position across from her.

"Not exactly pheasant under glass, but it will help to forestall any gnawing hunger pangs," she said, handing him a plastic-wrapped sandwich.

"I'll consider it a banquet." He unwrapped it and took a hefty bite. When he had finished half of the sandwich, he looked at her with wry amusement. "Not bad. Not bad at all. And here I thought you said you couldn't cook."

"Ham and cheese sandwiches don't exactly require the skill of a French chef. It's when I get near a stove and have to use several different burners at a time that I bring death to whatever food I'm preparing. Meat, raw. Vegetables, mushy. Potatoes, burned. I can say with authority that I've disproved the old adage, Practice makes perfect. There's an old Pennsylvania Dutch saying, The hurrier I go, the behinder I get. Somehow I always think of it when I attempt to prepare a full-course meal."

"Does it bother you?"

Nicole laughed. "Not in the least. Should it?"

Jason reached over, took her hand, turned it palm up and kissed it. "I have the feeling the only thing in the world that bothers you is seeing animals in pain."

"You're very perceptive, Mr. McBride," she said, letting her gaze be drawn into the dark, liquid pools of his eyes. Of course, she couldn't let him know how very much *he* bothered her—and so very pleasantly.

"Have any more sandwiches there?" he asked.

She passed him another ham and cheese sandwich, then placed the Thermos nearer him as she peeled a banana.

Sandwiches, fruit and drink gone, Jason stretched out, his hands laced behind his head. After picking up the remnants of their lunch and cramming them into her tote bag, she lay down beside him, her head in her hand propped by a bent elbow while her finger drew abstract designs through the thick mat of curled hair covering his chest.

"Jason, would you answer a question?" She had to find out if there was any truth to Carol's statement about him. His fuzzy answer when they were in Montreal hadn't satisfied her. Yet she wondered if the answer really mattered to her now.

Jason pulled a hand from under his head and laid his forefinger over her lips. "No questions. No answers. No words. There is only now. There is no past, no future, only the moment. Now is the reality, Nicole, tomorrow an intangible. All else is lost in a dream . . . a dream that may never come or has fled before we can touch it. The only actuality is you and me, here and now."

His large hand sought the back of her head and lowered it to his own, their lips grazing at first, then surrendering once more to the deeper passions that stirred within them as the sun glided over the heavens, marking the passage of time.

With his hands laced under his head, Jason stretched his muscular body to its former position. Nicole lay on her back beside him with quiet joy. It wasn't too long before she heard his steady breathing, and when she gazed over at him, he was sound asleep. She sighed, closed her eyes and was soon oblivious to the world around her.

When her eyes finally fluttered open, they beheld Jason gazing down at her, a broad smile on his face.

"Well . . . finally decided to join the realm of the living," he said.

"I think you were the first to slip away to never-never land," she replied, sitting up, her eyes blinking to wash the sleep from them.

"I suppose I was," he admitted. "Perhaps we both could use another dip in the pond. I'm sure that would bring us back to life." He stood and offered her his hand.

She took his hand and sprung to her feet. "As a doctor, I was just about to suggest that."

"When I went back to get Midnight, I told Mrs. Beaton to prepare dinner for us at about six o'clock, after which we can ride the horses in the cool of the evening, then return to play a game of chess. How does that sound to you?" he asked as they strolled to the edge of the pond hand in hand.

"Sounds great to me," she agreed, smiling.

"Tomorrow we'll fly to Rhinebeck."

"Aren't you getting a bit ahead of yourself?" Her eyes sparkled with vitality spurred by her growing feelings for the man next to her.

"Am I? Do you have other plans?" His face clouded as his eyes skimmed over her upturned face.

"No. But I would like to be asked, not told."

Jason grinned slyly. "I didn't realize I was being so presumptuous. Will you fly with me to Rhinebeck?"

"I'd be happy to, Jason," said Nicole, a twinkle of merriment in her warm eyes. "By the way, what's at Rhinebeck?"

"World War One vintage planes and a demonstration of the art of flying those relics," he explained, then dove into the water with Nicole close behind.

The rest of the afternoon melted away as they swam. Nicole lost count of the number of times Jason held her in his arms and kissed her with a rare and deepening passion. As their stomachs growled with hunger, they agreed it was time to resaddle the horses and head back. Her bikini dry, Nicole slipped into her shorts, tank top and sneakers, with Jason fondly following her every move.

Mrs. Beaton seemed extraordinarily pleased by Nicole's presence. After a superb dinner she served them coffee on the patio, where screens let the breezes dance in and out. Jason was describing Rhinebeck to Nicole when Mrs. Beaton came rushing in.

"There's a phone call for you, Dr. Winters. It's Dr. Carey," the older woman said breathlessly.

"You can take it in the living room," said Jason, rising and going to the french doors and opening them for her. He followed behind as she padded over the luscious carpets and rooms to the living room.

She lifted the receiver and proceeded with an almost one-way conversation in which Dr. Carey did most of the talking. When she placed the receiver back in the cradle, she turned to Jason with an expression of mixed worry and disappointment.

"I have to go back to the hospital. There is an emergency and Dr. Carey needs me. I'm sorry."

"Will you come back later?" asked Jason, the fingers of his hand stroking her neck with enticing tenderness.

"I don't think so. From the sound of it, I'll be some time."

"Tomorrow, then?"

"Yes. I'll meet you at the hangar. What time?"

"Eleven."

As his arms flew to encircle her, her hands found the thick cords of his neck and his head lowered to hers, his lips straining against hers, working their magic and honing her senses to a sharp edge as she responded fully to the blazing probe of his kiss.

"Oh, Jason, I—"

"You'd better go before I refuse to let you," he said in husky tones.

She took a deep breath. "I think you're right." She dashed into the hall, then to the back foyer and out the door, her heart bursting with rapture. Was this love? Was this what she had waited for all her life? It was so different from all the crushes she had had in the past or all the times she had felt attracted to a particular man. This was a blinding force that consumed every pore of her body, every cell of her brain. She was filled with sensations that transported her beyond the realm of the known into an unknown that gave every indication of being sheer heaven.

She drove the old station wagon without thinking as her hands automatically steered it to the hospital. By the time she reached the clinic, she knew she was irrevocably in love with Jason McBride regardless of the consequences, regardless of his past.

CHAPTER 9

"I'm sorry I had to call you in from your day off. But you have a finer hand than I when it comes to delicate surgery," said Dr. Carey.

"What happened?" asked Nicole, slipping into her white coat, her eyes studying the emaciated German shepherd on the stainless steel operating table.

"It's John Sherwood's dog. The animal's about three years old and for the last year has been quite sick."

"I remember now. He came in when I first started. Severe vomiting, wasn't it?"

"Yes," replied Dr. Carey. "The animal got hit by a car about a year ago. Nothing seemed too wrong at the time, and the dog appeared to get over it in fine mettle. Anyway, it began having these bouts of vomiting, and John thought it was probably something the animal ate while roaming about the farm. He didn't pay too much attention to it until the dog began losing a lot of weight. That's when you saw the dog in here. It seems this time the vomiting became intense and the animal would no longer eat anything and appeared to be in great pain. He hated to bring it in on the holiday weekend but couldn't bear to see the animal suffer any longer. I told him to bring him here right away, holiday or no holiday."

"Cancer?" asked Nicole as she thoroughly scrubbed her hands.

"I don't think so. I can't feel any carcenomas. I have him heavily sedated and want you to do an exploratory on him."

"I think that would be the best course right now." She pursed her lips in thought. "I'll get the anesthetic ready and prepare the instruments while you shave him."

"Good enough."

With a sure, steady hand Nicole began the operation with Dr. Carey's assistance. It wasn't long before she discovered the crux of the animal's problem. Though a resulting hernia from the accident had healed, the dog's gall bladder had remained pushed up into his chest and the scar tissue around the tract leading from his stomach to his small intestine was causing the pain and vomiting.

Fingers moving swiftly and unhesitatingly, Nicole removed the dog's gall bladder and reconstructed the gastric outflow, then closed the incision.

"That was remarkable, Nicole," said Dr. Carey. "You have a gift for this work. I'm glad I have always trusted my first impressions of people."

She smiled, pleased that Dr. Carey had expressed his admiration for her work. She stripped off her surgical gloves and began to unstrap the animal on one side while Dr. Carey attended to the other.

"I'll put him in the back for now. He'll be out for some time. Well, I think a celebration is in order. While I see to the dog's comfort, why don't you clean up in here, then I'll make some coffee. I think I saw a box of doughnuts around somewhere," said Dr. Carey, lifting the sleeping animal from the table.

After placing the instruments in the sterilizer and making sure all surfaces were scrubbed down, Nicole removed her white coat and tossed it into the hamper. She went into the office, where Dr. Carey already had his cup of coffee and was munching on a sugary doughnut.

"I'm glad it turned out to be something we could fix. That shepherd is a fine animal. Sometimes surgery breaks my heart when I open them up and find there is nothing I can do to save them," said Nicole, pouring herself some hot coffee.

"Sherwood loves that dog. He'd be lost without him. That reconstruction you did was a superior piece of work," said Dr. Carey.

"Thank you. Coming from you, I consider that high praise indeed."

He finished his doughnut, took a sip of coffee, then removed his glasses and proceeded to clean them with a tissue. He squinted and looked at his glasses thoughtfully.

"I've been thinking, Nicole. Now that I have some fresh blood in here, maybe we ought to try some of the newer, more experimental methods."

"What did you have in mind?" She looked over the doughnuts and decided to skip them, Mrs. Beaton's dinner having fully sated her appetite.

"I've been reading about this new method of acupuncture for veterinary use."

"Acupuncture? Sounds a little far afield to me."

"No, I don't think so. It has proved quite useful in some cases." Dr. Carey rummaged through the papers cluttering his desk. "Ah! Here it is. Quite an article. You should read it." He handed her the pamphlet-like journal on veterinary medicine. "It's in there somewhere."

"Sticking needles is an art form," said Nicole, thumbing through the journal. "It would require special training."

"It isn't done with needles. It's acupuncture with a cold laser beam."

Nicole's eyebrows shot up. "A laser beam? Now I am intrigued."

"Read the article. It's something to keep in mind for the future. I'm sure you could pick up the technique in no time." He put his glasses back on and reached for another doughnut. "Sorry I had to pull you away from the McBride place. Hope you got some riding in."

"I had a marvelous afternoon, and Mrs. Beaton served a fine dinner."

"I've had some of her pies and cakes. She's always a winner at the county fair." He paused and stared at the doughnut pensively. "I have a feeling something more than the horse is attracting you to that place. Or am I prying into things that are none of my business?"

"I'll admit I find Jason McBride a pleasant and companionable man," she replied openly, then thought, my God, what am I saying? I'm in love with him and always have been. The realization struck her with the force of a thunderbolt. Love had been lying in her heart like a bud ready to burst forth ever since the day she had first opened her eyes to see him standing at the foot of the bed when she had met with the accident and he had taken her into his home. That was why Steve had never stirred her or become anything more than a friend.

"From the look on your face, I'd say Jason McBride means more to you than that. Be careful, Nicole. I wouldn't want to see you get hurt," said Dr. Carey somberly.

"What do you mean? How could I possibly get hurt seeing Jason McBride?"

"There are things in his background that might prove to be . . . how can I put it . . . well, perhaps detrimental to any relationship other than a moderate friendship," said Dr. Carey with quiet hesitation.

"What things?" she asked, immediately on the defensive.

He shrugged. "It's all hearsay and I wouldn't want to be the one to pass on rumors unjustly. Forget I said anything. I have no right to interfere."

"You're not being fair, Dr. Carey. First you warn me, then you refuse to tell me why. I've heard all sorts of rumors about Jason and find none of them valid. He's not the ominous mystery man everyone makes him out to be."

"Then you won't find my misgivings valid, either." He took in a deep breath and let it out slowly. "Maybe it's an old man's fear of you running off and leaving me to contend with the practice on my own again."

"I don't think you have anything to fear on that account. I love my work and especially love working with you. The fates were with me the day I applied for a position here. I've never been happier," said Nicole, a ring of finality in her tone.

"Why don't you run along? There's no sense in the two of us being here," said Dr. Carey, a strange look of relief rushing onto his face.

"I wouldn't dream of going home now. I want to wait until the shepherd comes around and check him over."

"In that case I think I'll go along and get some dinner. Those doughnuts have awakened my appetite." He rose, removed his white coat, then stretched. He patted Nicole fondly on the arm and smiled. "I'll be back later to see how the patient is doing."

Nicole poured herself another cup of coffee as she heard the back door close and Dr. Carey's car drive away. She then turned her attention to reading the article on acupuncture with laser beams.

Dressed in a brand new turquoise sun dress, Nicole stopped at the hospital before keeping her appointment with Jason at the airplane hangar. She breathed a sigh of relief to see the shepherd up, his eyes bright and alert, a far cry from the animal that had been brought in the day before. A balanced diet would soon have him a fine specimen of canine breeding.

When she told Dr. Carey where she would be for the day, he gave her a rueful glance but said nothing. They discussed the shepherd and the laser beam article over a cup of coffee; then Nicole was on her way.

As she approached the McBride farm, the thought of seeing Jason filled her with elation. She wondered if he would see the love she felt for him in her eyes. Would it matter if he did? Would it alter his attitude toward her? Would it put him on guard against becoming involved? She sighed and clutched the wheel tighter. As she rounded the corner, the road to the hangar became clearly visible. She veered onto it and was at the hangar in minutes. There were two kinds of excitement spinning webs around her. One was a thrilling sense of joy at seeing and being with Jason again. The other was a nervous throbbing in her veins that he might have regretted the tender moments in the glade and slipped back into his shell of reserve.

He was standing in the road, arms folded over his chest, when she brought the car to a halt. He wore tight black jeans and a white polo shirt. To Nicole's eyes, he was handsome beyond belief. When she saw him smile, she grabbed her purse and quickly got out of the car. She began to walk toward him, but when he held out his arms, she dashed into them, heedless of warnings, doubts and rumors. For her, there was only Jason and she was in his arms.

He pressed her body close to his, kissed the top of her head, then brought his cheek to hers and whispered, "I'd like a warmer welcome than that."

Nicole tilted her head back to look up at him, her lips parted in a doting smile. "I can make it as warm as you like."

Jason kissed the tip of her upturned nose before his lips playfully nibbled over hers with taunting pleasure. In moments the initial sportiveness vanished, to leave in its wake a rapacious, penetrating kiss. Nicole clung to him, happiness surging through her veins. Nothing had changed since yesterday.

"I wish I hadn't filed a flight plan," said Jason as he held her from him. "Spending the day in the glade would be far more to my liking." He sighed heavily. "We'd better get going before I change my mind."

With his arm firmly around her, they crossed the velvet ground to the waiting plane. Nicole felt a swell of excitement when they became airborne and marveled as she watched the earth change formation below her in eerie slow motion. With an overview of the Adirondacks on one side and the Green Mountains on the other, the small Cessna headed south with the ease of a condor riding the wind currents. Jason explained the mechanics of flying the craft and the use of the various instruments. When the course was set, he let her take the wheel, verbally guiding her every move.

When they began approaching Rhinebeck, Jason once again took control of the plane. He circled, then banked for a landing on the long, grassy runway. Reaching the end of a somewhat bumpy airstrip, he turned and taxied the plane to a clear area off to the side of the landing strip where a number of other small private planes stood in quiet repose.

"Here we are," said Jason as he helped Nicole down from the blue and white plane.

"There are quite a few people here," she commented, looking across the airstrip to a number of buildings and a large spectator stand.

Jason slid his arm around her waist and led her over the airstrip to join the milling crowd. "It's usually fairly crowded. Some of them are habitués who come every Sunday."

"Do you come down frequently?"

"Not too often anymore. My work seems to bite more and more into my time. Shall we have a look at the planes?"

Nicole gazed up at him with a smile and nodded.

He took her from hangar to hangar, where prototypes of early flying machines were exhibited along with vintage World War I planes. Nicole found it difficult to believe that some of the machines were capable of getting off the ground, much less flying in the air. Wood, tin, even paper constituted the construction of many of the planes. Jason gave her a detailed running commentary with enthusiasm as they walked from hangar to hangar and from old barn to old barn.

"Would you care for something to eat before they start the show?" asked Jason when they returned to the airstrip.

"I thought you'd never ask. I'm starved," she said with an air of levity.

"Have a seat and I'll get us something," he said, leading her to a group of picnic tables where geese and ducks strutted unmindful of the people passing by as they searched for morsels of cast-off food.

Nicole watched the feathered creatures with the fascination of a psychological behaviorist. She imagined they were looking at her with the same keen interest before they wobbled off to find someone who had more to offer than empty stares. When Jason finally returned from the small, crowded food stand, he was carrying a cardboard tray laden with hot dogs, french fries and soda.

"The menu was limited," he announced, placing the tray on the well-worn picnic table and taking a seat opposite her.

"At this point, food is food." She took a hot dog and a paper napkin. "Are they really going to fly those old planes?"

"Why shouldn't they?"

"They look a little flimsy." Her face registered concern as her eyes raked over the old planes lining the airstrip.

"The men who fly them are very capable pilots and quite experienced. They wouldn't go up in them if they weren't safe. Those planes are as sound mechanically as my Cessna."

As they ate, Jason went on to describe the types of planes she would be seeing. Nicole noticed how his eyes sparkled with a dark light as he spoke, and there was a boyish eagerness animating his bronzed face. He was an intense man who became fiercely caught up in any topic that interested him. She smiled at him fondly as she sucked the chilled soda through the straw.

"I have been going on, haven't I?" His lips spread in a wide smile as he reached for her free hand and held it.

"When I first met you, you seemed to be a man of few words. In fact, you seemed reluctant to talk at all. Now you're a veritable fountain of information."

"Disappointed?" He squeezed her hand warmly.

"No. I love listening to you." She squeezed back.

"It's been a long time since I've been this candid with a woman. You've started turning things around for me, Nicole. I'm beginning to look at the world a bit differently now that I know you're in it."

"Oh, Jason, you've led me through doors I never thought existed. I can't tell you how much I—"

"Hush. I don't want you to say anything you might regret later. Let's take what moments we can."

There was a plea in Jason's eyes that Nicole couldn't ignore, and it disturbed her. It gnawed at her innate curiosity, and she was on the verge of questioning him again when a look of quiet foreboding swept over his face. She would have to be patient, for she knew the time would come when Jason would open up to her and reveal the mystery of his past. He wouldn't deceive her.

People were beginning to move toward what passed for a viewing stand in hurried determination, causing the wandering geese and ducks to honk and quack with disgruntled annoyance.

"Hadn't we better see what is going on?" asked Nicole, her mood disrupted by the din.

Jason released her hand and swung his long legs over the picnic bench as he scooped up the debris of their lunch and tossed it into a rusted barrel with accuracy. When Nicole rose and came to his side, his arm slipped around her as if it were second nature to both of them. Then he steered her to the spectator area.

Tiers of weathered wooden planks were held off the ground by cinder blocks. Finding some empty seats, they sat down, Jason drawing her close to him with a sure arm. A brass band began the festivities with a medley of early twentieth century songs and marches as pilots with caps, goggles and white scarfs undulating in the breeze started to wander onto the field.

A thrilling pulse of blood went through Nicole as the flying machines came down the runway with a roar of engines and then took off. The antique planes soared into the air—two wingers, three wingers dancing aloft in mock battle. When one of them began to throw smoke out of its tail and went into a tailspin, Nicole clutched at Jason's thigh as the plane nosed closer to the ground. He gave her a comforting hug when a gasp escaped her lips as the plane pulled out of the dive only a few feet from the ground and rejoined the others in the air. She swallowed hard as Jason smiled at her.

"Thought he was going to crash, didn't you?" he asked with mild amusement.

She put a hand on her chest. "I never thought he'd make it. Do they do that often?"

Jason's arm tightened around her. "Often enough to give everyone a vicarious thrill. Look there . . . Watch them now."

One of the biplanes began looping around and around, then rapidly lost altitude as it swooped downward toward the narrow but long landing strip. The pilot instantly straightened out and flew only several feet from the ground, past the stands, dipping his wings victoriously. The planes cut in and out dangerously close to one another, and Nicole was sure there would be a head-on collision in the air or that at the least a wing or two would be taken off. No horror movie had ever had her so knotted with tension and excitement. When the aerial acrobatics were over, she stood with the rest of the crowd and applauded with gusto.

"Enjoy it?" asked Jason as they slowly moved with the dispersing crowd.

"It was the thrill of a lifetime. I hope you don't do stunts like that in the air."

"On occasion. Perhaps on the way home I'll treat you to a few rolls and loops," he taunted.

She gave him a pixieish look. "You might have one very sick lady on your hands if you do."

"Anyone who does what you do for a living I'm sure has a very strong stomach."

"Jason, you wouldn't."

He gave her a mischievous grin and lightly kissed her on the forehead.

They spent another hour wandering around the aerodrome, with Nicole particularly interested in getting a closer look at the planes that had been flying in the mock battle and were now on the ground. It was some time before they were airborne again.

On the trip back to Essex Junction, Jason did roll and loop the Cessna, and to her surprise Nicole found herself enjoying it. It gave her the sensation of being a free-flying bird whose mastery of aerial acrobatics was unsurpassed. From the air she quickly recognized the landing strip on Jason's farm, and in minutes he was bringing the aircraft to touch its wheels on the grassy ribbon, then taxiing to the hangar.

With the plane secured in its nest, they took the long route back to Jason's house, going across the fields hand in hand as though a life force was flowing from one to the other through those hands.

"You'll stay for dinner?" asked Jason.

"If Mrs. Beaton doesn't mind."

"I think you know the answer to that. Would you care to do some riding either before or after dinner?"

"I'm not dressed for it. But I would like to stop in and see the horses," she replied.

"We'll see the horses, then get to that chess game we had to postpone last night. By the way, what was the emergency?"

"A German shepherd was in a pretty bad way. We had to operate."

"Everything all right now?"

"He came through it with flying colors."

After paying their respects to the mare and the stallion, Jason escorted her into the house, where Mrs. Beaton had the table on the patio all set for their dinner. When they had finished and the table was cleared, Jason set up the chessboard and Nicole demonstrated her newly acquired skill at the game. She didn't tell Jason she had taken some books on the art of playing chess from the library and, with the aid of a small set she had purchased for herself, had practiced and studied the game.

It was almost eleven when Nicole announced it was time for her to leave.

"I'll walk you to your car. There's a path from the house to the hangar which I don't think you know about," said Jason.

"Thank Mrs. Beaton for me."

"I will."

A brilliant full moon illuminated the night, making the fields and trees shimmer with silvery shadows in which an occasional firefly twinkled its fleeting golden light as the song of crickets and other tireless insects joined in the eerie chorus and mingled with the steady croakings of near and distant frogs. Night birds, with their own peculiar melodies that distinguished them from the avian songs of day, warbled and hooted unseen. It was the music of night threaded with its own idiosyncratic cadence. The woodsy smell of newborn and decaying vegetation permeated the air with a pungent aroma that was somehow pleasing to the nostrils.

Jason's arm was carelessly draped over Nicole's shoulders as they slowly walked through the busy enchantment around them. He didn't speak, nor did she. It was as if the imminent parting was painful to both of them. At her car they turned to stare at one another.

"It's been a fantastic day, Jason. I'm glad you took me to Rhinebeck," she said, breaking the quietude and smiling up at him.

"You're quite lovely in the moonlight. Your hair is like spun filaments of gold, your skin like fine opalescent silk." His fingers caressed her cheek and trailed over her neck lingeringly.

Sparks ran down her back at his touch. She felt weak and strong at the same time as his eyes skimmed over her. His arms circled her and drew her close as his lips moved over hers with determined desire. Her hands worked their way up to his shoulders with equal passion. His mouth moved over hers with increasing ardor, and she met that ardor with a driving force of her own as tiny explosions went off within her like roman candles firing a blazing burst of incandescent light into the night sky. She went beyond rapture into a realm where deep, unsuspected passions were aroused, tossing her like a rubber boat in a raging sea. Jason's lips found their way along her throat, and her heart began to beat with such ferocity that she thought it would jump through her skin. Every muscle in her body tensed as she strained against him, waiting for his lips to find their way back to hers. When they did, the energy poured from him like a blazing furnace that was on the verge of exploding with overactivated heat. Unable to tolerate the deep, prolonged kiss without total submission, Nicole pulled away.

"Jason . . ."

"I know . . . I know," he said. His hand pressed her head to his heaving chest and cradled it there as he held her body firmly with his other hand.

She could have remained like that for an eternity, but a voice of reason made itself heard and she said, "I think I'd better go now."

His hold on her loosened. "When will I see you again?"

"I don't know. I'm on night call next week, and next weekend doesn't look too promising, either," she replied, her voice tinged with regret.

"I can wait," said Jason, stepping aside so she could have access to the car door. "I'll call you."

"Do." She reached up and ran a finger over the gray strands lacing at his temples and made silvery by the cast of the moonlight.

He gripped her hand and kissed her fingertips. "Good night, Nicole."

She drove home in an almost catatonic state, lost in a dream that was real. She didn't know how long it would last, but at the moment she didn't care. She loved Jason McBride and was beginning to feel he loved her, too. She knew there was nothing that could shatter her love for him or her belief in him. No matter what lay in his past, she was committed. There never could or would be another man for her like Jason McBride.

The summer proved to be an extremely busy one not only at the hospital but also out on the farms. A multitude of skin problems due to the heat and a variety of insects were high on the list, along with viral infections that thrived in the humid warmth. Nicole found her free time rigorously curtailed and the telephone becoming the main link between her and Jason. But there were the shining days when they were together swimming, horseback riding and flying, and the gentle nights playing chess, exploring new restaurants or sitting in the cool breezes of the evening just talking.

Jason's penchant for surprising her with little gifts delighted her and gave her a feeling of exultation whenever he presented her with one. Her small abode was becoming filled with a variety of potted plants from African violets to flowering cacti, each grown and nurtured by Jason himself. He showered her with books dealing with the intricate mysteries of Josephine Tey and Margery Allingham. He had an instinct for knowing the things she liked, and his generosity seemed endless. She was deeply touched when he gave her one of the fruits of his labor in perfecting the art of bonsai, a miniature juniper shaped to appear wildly windblown in a flat, blue-glazed clay container. She treasured it.

The red Firebird became a frequent sight traveling to and from her residence, just as her old station wagon was often seen parked at the horse barn or near the airplane hangar. Nicole had never been happier as the summer began to draw its hot mantle from the earth.

The long Labor Day weekend had only provided her with one full day to be with Jason, which they spent once again in Montreal, where she finally got her first taste of Malpeque oysters.

Over a week had gone by since their last day in Montreal, and Nicole was confounded when she realized that she hadn't heard from Jason in all that time—no calls, no little presents. Not that she cared about receiving presents from him. It was the absence of the man who presented them that disturbed and confused her. It wasn't like Jason. They had grown close over the summer months, and she couldn't believe he would ignore her so out of hand. Something must have happened to him, and the thought filled her with dread. Had his past returned to seek revenge? She made innumerable phone calls to his house, only to hear the phone ring incessantly without anyone answering it. On two occasions she even drove out there, only to find no one around, not even Mrs. Beaton. Surely he would have let her know if he was taking an extended business trip. It was as if he had vanished from the face of the earth. Her distress and inattention to matters at hand were soon obvious to Dr. Carey.

"You're not yourself, Nicole. What's happened?" Dr. Carey asked as he watched her scrub after an operation.

"I don't know. That's the trouble," she replied, then sighed heavily. "McBride?"

"Yes. It's been two weeks since I've heard from him or seen him."

"Have you tried the house?"

"Yes. Nothing. I can't even raise Mrs. Beaton." She dried her arms and hands on the pristine white towel and turned to face Dr. Carey with an expression that verged on extreme pain.

"Have you tried calling Bitron? They might have an idea or two as to his whereabouts," suggested Dr. Carey.

"No. I never thought of that." She reflected as though the notion were rolling from one side of her brain to the other. "No, I couldn't do that. It would look as though I was checking up on him. If he wanted me to know where he was, I'm sure he would have let me know."

Dr. Carey rubbed his chin, his cherubic face screwed up in a frown. "I hate to say this, Nicole, but have you thought he might be tired of the . . . er . . . arrangement?"

Nicole's expression turned to ice. "Dr. Carey, I know you mean well, but it isn't like that between Jason and me. We respect each other enough to talk it out, and he's honest enough to tell me to my face that he no longer wants to see me. He is not the sort of man to run away and hide from a situation. Something is wrong. I can feel it."

"A couple of weeks is nothing to work yourself up about. He probably has his reasons. Perhaps some secret work for the government, something he couldn't tell you about," said Dr. Carey comfortingly as he tried to assuage her fears.

"There are three more surgeries scheduled for this afternoon, aren't there?" she asked. Performing surgery commanded all her attention and thought. Working and tending to the animals helped divert her from thinking about Jason. She was thankful the hospital was busy.

"Yes. Two minor and one a little more extensive. I'll get the next patient and we can prep her." Dr. Carey went into the back ward and soon emerged with a large female calico cat that was due to be spayed.

The operation was a simple one which Nicole could almost do in her sleep. When all three were completed, herself and the operating room cleaned, she went into the office and started a fresh pot of coffee. The aroma soon brought in Dr. Carey.

"Now don't get me wrong . . . I'm not prying, only curious, and you don't have to answer me if you don't want to. But was it because of McBride that you stopped seeing young Baker?" he asked, heading for the coffee maker.

"Yes, in a way. But I really think Steve had his eyes set in another direction anyway," she replied candidly. "Carol Hanes found him fascinating, and I guess Steve has been returning the interest, from what I've heard."

"Carol Hanes . . ." He poured himself a cup of coffee with a thoughtful expression. "Carol Hanes . . . I don't seem to recall anyone by that name."

"She's a secretary at Bitron."

"So many new people have moved in around here I can't keep track of them all unless they have a pet or two and bring them in for treatment. Used to be that everyone knew everyone else. Now everything is clustered and fractionalized—the Bitron group, the farmers, the suburbanites, the diehard townfolk. It just isn't the same anymore. Everything keeps shifting, and I don't seem to be shifting with it."

"I think you do marvelously. At least you're willing to move with modern medical techniques, which some of the older vets aren't," she said by way of consolation. The telephone rang, and Dr. Carey automatically reached for it.

"Hello." Silence. "I see." More silence. "All right. I'll have her out there right away." He hung up the phone and looked at Nicole, frowning in puzzlement.

"Well? Whose cow is down?" asked Nicole, sipping the hot coffee and wishing she had a doughnut or a piece of danish.

"Strange . . . that was the Keeler boy. The one who takes care of McBride's horses when he's not around."

"What's happened?" She was instantly alert. Her blood froze in her veins and her throat went dry as a disquieting fear clutched at her heart.

"That's what is so strange. I don't know. The boy mumbled something about the mare and said for you to come over right away."

Nicole almost dropped her cup as her hand began to tremble. "Didn't he give you a clue as to what it might be?"

"No. Only that you should come right away."

She immediately put the cup on her metal desk, whipped off her white coat, grabbed her medical bag and flew through the hospital and out the rear door.

She drove faster than she should have but excused herself as a multitude of horrifying visions of the mare in irreversible medical distress assailed her mind. She was far more attached to the horse than she had realized.

Her tires skidded as she turned onto the road leading to the horse barn, then spun in the loose gravel. She bounced forward in the seat as her foot hit the brake with inordinate force at the entrance to the barn. She hopped out of the car, grabbing her bag in one sweeping movement, and rushed into the barn.

The minute she entered, Charm had her head over the wooden half door and gave a whinny while shaking her head vigorously. At least she is standing and appears to be normal, Nicole thought as Tommy came out of Midnight's stall to greet her.

"Have you seen Charm yet, Doc?" asked the young boy.

"No. I just got here. She seems bright enough," said Nicole, caressing the animal's neck with relief.

"Take a look at her right flank, Doc." Tommy opened the stall door and gestured for Nicole to enter.

As she went into the newly cleaned stall, her hand gently skimmed over the mare's silken hide from the neck to the flank. Her stomach knotted when she saw the mass of welts rising on the mare's flank. Charm moved sideways when Nicole's hand lightly flicked over the ugly marks.

"There, there, girl. I'm not going to hurt you," she said softly to the mare, then turned to Tommy in anger. Her eyes were blazing with raw outrage. "How did this happen?"

He scuffed his feet, then stared at them. "Well . . . I hate to be the one . . ." He looked up, but something at the barn door caught his eye and he stopped in mid-sentence, his jaw sagging, his eyes wide.

Seeing the startled, almost frightened expression on the boy's face, Nicole came out of the stall to see what he could be staring at with such alarm.

Framed in the barn's doorway was a tall brunet whose narrow green eyes quickly surveyed Nicole with caustic intensity. She stood erect, encased in a sleek emerald green pantsuit with a black, satiny turtleneck blouse against her snowy complexion.

"Who are you? And what are you doing here?" The brunet's voice was sharp, controlled and chilling.

"I'm Dr. Winters, veterinarian to these horses, if it's any of your business," replied Nicole curtly. She didn't like the woman's manner. She had an air of superiority that was derived from scorn instead of self-confidence, and Nicole got the impression that this was just the sort of person who would take a whip to an animal. There was a coldness in the woman's eyes that was calculating and cruel.

"Everything that goes on here is my business. I'm Linda McBride—Jason McBride's wife."

CHAPTER 10

The blood seemed to drain from Nicole and seep out her toes. She felt like a rigid column of chalk, white and powdery. She was face to face with Jason's wife—not a ghost but a living reality. Curling her hands into fists, she dug her fingernails into the palms of her hands so the pain would jolt her senses and erase the sinking feeling in the pit of her stomach.

"If, as you say, everything here is your business, then perhaps you can tell me how the mare received those welts on her flank," said Nicole in a calm, steady voice.

"She's not a very responsive animal. She needed some reminders as to who was in control. That is why they invented the riding crop." Her tone was as icy as the green eyes that continued to rake over Nicole.

"No one puts a whip to my horse," said Nicole, her voice low and menacing.

"Your horse?"

"Yes. My horse."

"Then what is it doing here?" Linda McBride folded her arms at her waist, a sardonic smile on her lips, as though she were enjoying the inquisition.

"I board Charm here." Raw anger was gnawing at Nicole. It didn't matter that she was on someone else's property and confronting the owner's wife. She was made too distraught by the fact that the woman in front of her had severely whipped the mare.

"Charm . . . how quaint." She turned, took several steps, stopped and spun around. "By the way, I consider anything on this farm mine, and I shall ride the chestnut whenever I choose." White teeth flashed quickly between bright scarlet lips before Linda McBride stomped off toward the house.

Nicole felt like an overheated kettle, steaming and about to blow the lid. Her fists clenched tighter and her lips pursed as she stared at the space that had been vacated by Linda McBride. When Tommy suddenly spoke, she realized she wasn't alone.

"What are you going to do, Doc?" He sounded small and distant.

"Get Charm out of here, that's what I'm going to do."

"Mr. McBride won't like that," he warned.

"He'd like it even less if the mare had the hide whipped off her," she replied heatedly.

"Where will you keep her?"

"I don't know yet, but I'll have her out of here tonight." Nicole grabbed her medical bag, left the barn and gunned the old station wagon to life.

Her brakes squealed when she stomped on the pedal in the hospital's small parking lot. She slammed the car door shut, then the rear door of the hospital, then banged her medical bag on top of her metal desk. The sound caused Dr. Carey to spin in his oak swivel chair.

"Well, I hope your wrath doesn't mean we've lost a patient," said Dr. Carey, his bushy white eyebrows coming together in a frown.

"No. But I could have strangled her," spewed Nicole through clenched teeth.

"Strangle a horse? Come now, Nicole. It's not like you to become angry with an animal."

"Not the horse. That—that Linda!"

"Linda? Now I am confused. Who the devil is Linda?"

"Linda McBride. Jason's wife."

Gravity and compassion swirled on Dr. Carey's rotund face. "I was afraid something like this would happen. I warned you, Nicole, not to get involved with that man. I always had the feeling there was something wrong there." He sighed and slowly shook his head. "Ah well . . . you're young and time heals all."

"Whether he's married or not has nothing to do with the mare's condition. I'm furious with that woman for taking a riding crop to Charm's flank and raising such painful welts. That gentle creature positively cringed when I ran my hand over her. I'd like to put a riding crop to that woman's backside and give her a taste of her own medicine." Nicole went to the coffee maker and poured herself a cup of coffee. With a shaking hand she brought it to her lips and took a deep swallow. Then in a calmer voice she said, "I've got to get the mare out of there before that woman can do any more damage. Any suggestions as to where I could board her?"

Dr. Carey leaned back in his tilting chair. "I can understand how you feel, but McBride might have something to say about removing the animal from his property."

"He's not here to put any restraints on that woman, and I know he'd be as upset as I am about her using a riding crop on the horse with such a heavy hand, if at all. I have to get the mare out of there tonight."

"I still say you're exceeding your bounds by relocating the animal, but I can see there is no way I can talk you out of it." Dr. Carey pressed his lips together pensively. "Perhaps Jake Douglas has room for her. It would be close. Then when McBride comes back, he'll know where to find her."

"Perfect!" Nicole put down her empty coffee cup. "I'll go over there right after supper and see if it can be arranged."

As she came closer to the Douglas home, Nicole wondered if Jake had any idea as to where Jason could be. She had never thought to ask him before.

After a few raps on the door, Milly greeted her with eager warmth. Jake soon joined them in the kitchen, leaving the television blaring in the living room. Nicole explained the purpose of her visit, her feverish animation receiving sympathetic nods from both Milly and Jake.

"I have a spare calving stall we could put her in for the time being. I'm sure Mr. McBride would want it that way. He puts a lot of stock in those horses of his," said Jake. "When would you want to move her?"

"Tonight, if possible," replied Nicole.

"We'll go get her now, then," said Jake, and Nicole rose. "No. You stay here, Doc. The oldest boy and I will go fetch her. It'll be better that way."

Milly looked as if she could hardly wait for Jake and the boy to leave. When they did, she turned to Nicole like a ripened fruit ready to burst.

"I almost fell over when Mrs. Beaton came down and told me who had moved into the house. I haven't seen the woman yet. She's always taking off in the red Firebird. But Mrs. Beaton says she is very attractive. I'm wondering why she has suddenly turned up after six years," said Milly. "Mrs. Beaton didn't have any answers, either."

"Where is Mrs. Beaton?" asked Nicole, hoping some of the pieces of the puzzle would fall into place.

"Mrs. Beaton went out to California to visit with her daughter for a while. After three days with that woman she said she couldn't take it anymore. Why, she treated Mrs. Beaton like her personal servant. Had her running around like a chicken with its head cut off. And abusive! Mrs. Beaton couldn't do anything to please her," gushed Milly.

"Where is Ja—Mr. McBride?" asked Nicole as little tremors bounced through her.

"That's another funny thing. From what Mrs. Beaton said when she came to tell me good-bye, he brought that woman into the house, introduced her to Mrs. Beaton, then took off in that plane of his like the devil himself was after him. It's all very strange. I can't imagine why he'd do such a thing—dumping a total stranger on Mrs. Beaton like that. Mrs. Beaton said he looked like a man being chased by demons. It's a crying shame about the mare. You don't think she'd hurt the stallion, do you?"

"I don't think Midnight would let her get anywhere near him. Even though he is basically gentle, he can put on quite a show of fury when he wants. I think she'll stay away from him," Nicole replied with confidence.

"I'm surprised you didn't know she was there, Nicole. It's been the talk of the town for several days now. And you being so close to Mr. McBride and all, I'm surprised he didn't tell you."

So am I, thought Nicole, a sadness washing over her face for a second, then being replaced by a vague smile. "I've been pretty busy lately, and he might not have been able to get hold of me before he left." It was the only plausible excuse she could think of.

Milly chatted away, offering various fantasies concerning Jason's secrecy about the mysterious Mrs. McBride. By the time she had reverted to talking about the farm, Jake had returned.

"Did you have any trouble?" Nicole asked anxiously.

"None at all. There wasn't a soul around, not a light on in the house, and Mr. McBride's red car was gone," replied Jake as his boy scampered back into the living room with alacrity.

"Is the chestnut all right?" asked Nicole.

"Fine. Settling down real nice," said Jake.

"I'll pay you whatever you think is fair, Jake," asserted Nicole.

"I'll let you know after I figure the feed and time."

"I'll stop in tomorrow," called Nicole as Jake headed into the living room. She said good night to Milly and left, her emotions drained but her mind a little more at ease.

It wasn't until later that night that the fact sank in that Jason was indeed married. Seeing the mare in that condition had been like some horrible nightmare that had overshadowed everything else. At the time it hadn't occurred to her that she would never be in Jason's arms again, never have his lips caress hers, never have him touch her so knowingly, so tenderly, arousing her in a way she had never thought possible. She knew she would never stop loving him no matter how betrayed she felt. Why did he have to deceive her like that? Why couldn't he have trusted her enough to tell her he was indeed a married man? He had played a fraudulent game, and that she found hard to digest. She could have forgiven him anything if he had been open and honest with her. But now. . . . She knew tears would never resolve anything, but try and tell that to her heart.

The next day, finished with some outlying farms, Nicole swung by Jake's place and satisfied herself that Charm was doing all right. She gave the animal a warm hug before leaving, not the least bit embarrassed by her open display of affection for the animal.

Back at the hospital, Dr. Carey was busy working on a rabbit's infected ear while its young owner stood worriedly by. Nicole donned her white coat and mechanically went about tending to the patients in the back room of the hospital.

"Is the mare doing all right?" asked Dr. Carey, drying his hands on a large paper towel as he came up to Nicole, the rabbit and owner happily taken care of.

"Great," replied Nicole, giving him a quick little smile.

"I have some news that might cheer you up."

"Oh?" Her eyes were full of anxiety. Had Jason called? Was that woman an imposter?

"Stephan Baker called while you were frolicking about the countryside. Wanted me to have you call his office as soon as you came back." He sent the paper towel into a waste basket with the backhand toss of a basketball player. His aim was accurate.

As soon as she finished her chores, she went into the office and dialed Steve's number, wondering what could be on his mind. It was several minutes before he came on the line.

"You vets are as hard to get hold of as us people doctors," said Steve lightly.

"Some of our patients can't make it into the office," she said, then added, "I can just picture a herd of cows parading into the waiting room."

"I wish some of mine couldn't. But be that as it may, how about dinner tonight?"

"What happened to Carol?" she asked, a smile forming on her lips. She had the feeling Steve was on the run again.

"We'll talk about it at dinner. And I thought you might like a friendly shoulder to cry on."

"Oh? And what gave you that idea?"

"I heard about the unexpected arrival of one Mrs. Jason McBride. Dinner?"

"All right."

"I'll pick you up at seven. Will that give you enough time?"

"Yes." She replaced the receiver, then looked up to find Dr. Carey watching her. He appeared to be about to say something, then changed his mind and went back into the operating room.

The Steak House restaurant hadn't changed one iota since the last time she had been there. Returning to the booth with their salads, Steve nodded a greeting to an elderly couple seated at a table along their path.

"Did you see the look of surprise on the Bentons' faces?" Steve asked as they resumed their seats. "Maybe it will put an end to the rumors."

"What rumors?" asked Nicole, turning to look at the Bentons.

"One, that I was about to be entrapped by the luscious Carol Hanes.

Two, that you and McBride were inseparable. Did you know he was married?"

"No."

"You should have listened to Carol. I found out that she is a veritable Sherlock Holmes when it comes to obtaining information about people, and ninety-nine percent of the time she is right on the button. Yet it does seem strange for his wife to show up now, after an absence of six years or so. Do you know anything about it? Have you seen McBride? Talked to him about it?"

"Evidently he left Essex Junction shortly after bringing his wife to the house." His wife . . . it still sounded strange to her, as if it were a new word she couldn't quite comprehend the meaning of. "Other than that, I know nothing. Didn't Carol have an explanation?"

"No. But she did wallow in the glory that her information had proved to be correct. She flaunted it every chance she got."

"You sound a little bitter. What happened?"

He shook his head and pushed his empty salad plate to one side, then poured them each another glass of red wine from the carafe on the table. "Like all women—present company excluded, of course— she began to act as though she owned me. She's strong-willed and thought she could impose her desires on mine. When she began to take me for granted and assumed marriage was imminent, I knew the time had come to dissolve that little tête-à-tête."

"And I'm the drop of acid to melt her hold on you," said Nicole with wry amusement.

Steve sat silent, studying the wine in his glass. Suddenly his blue eyes met hers with a seriousness she had never seen before.

"Marry me, Nicole. We'd be good together." He continued to stare at her, searching her face with intensity.

Nicole lowered her eyes and fingered the stem of her wineglass. Steve's proposal had astonished her, and she almost laughed. But she knew he was serious—at the moment, anyway—and she would never hurt his feelings by seeming to take his offer lightly.

"You know, with all my education, all I can think of is the old cliché, This is so sudden," she finally managed to squeeze out.

"That doesn't sound like a very promising answer. What is it, Nicole? McBride?"

"Yes," she murmured softly. She wasn't the type to deceive or lead anyone on.

Steve took a deep breath, then let it out slowly. "I thought as much. But with him being a married man, I had the feeling it might have destroyed your liking for him and you might find room in your life for me. I am fond of you, you know."

Nicole reached across the table and put her hand on his. "And I'm fond of you, Steve."

"But?"

"But I don't want to marry you. I want your friendship, and that can be a very precious relationship in itself." She withdrew her hand and smiled at him warmly.

"Well, win a few, lose a few." He smiled wanly, then raised his glass to her in a salute that she imitated.

Nicole knew that despite his outward levity, Steve's pride had been wounded. From what she knew of him, he had never asked that question of anyone before, and for a handsome, charming man like Stephan Baker to be turned down the first time he proposed marriage must have been devastating to his ego. Her own vanity billowed, even though it was tempered by a twinge of regret. She didn't like undercutting someone else's self-esteem so curtly.

"You don't know how much I appreciate your offer, Steve. It gives my ego an enormous boost, especially from a man as attractive as you," said Nicole, hoping her words would nullify any damage her refusal might have caused.

"Nothing ventured, nothing gained." He laughed weakly. "My God! You have me talking in platitudes."

"Someday you'll fall deeply in love with someone and be thankful I didn't accept."

He shrugged. "Who knows?" He drained his wineglass as the waitress brought their entrées. When the waitress left, he said, "I'll never find another woman like you, Nicole. You understand me."

"Again, I'm flattered. But understanding is not a basis for marriage."

"Maybe you're right. I don't know." He cut into his steak, and for the rest of the evening the conversation became less personal and more general. On the drive home Steve seemed to be his old undaunted self again.

"Would you care to come in for some coffee?" asked Nicole as he brought his car to a halt in front of her place.

"I don't think so. I have early hospital rounds tomorrow. But how about dinner and a movie next Friday night?"

"I have the league meeting next Friday."

"Can you skip one?"

"It's the first one since May. They suspend the meetings during the summer months, and I'd hate to miss the first one," Nicole explained.

"Aren't you afraid to be subjected to an inquisition about McBride?" asked Steve. "They all know you've been seeing him on a social basis and they all know about his wife coming back. I have a feeling those women are going to tear you apart with their questions."

"They're not all ogres. Some of them are really very nice human beings. As for the few who aren't, I'm sure I can cut them down to size. I can be just as scathing as they when the occasion warrants it," replied Nicole with certainty.

"For your sake, I hope so." He took her hand and gave it a squeeze of camaraderie. "I have an even better idea. The county fair is next weekend. We could make a day of it on Sunday. What do you say?"

"Sunday sounds great. Dr. Carey will be one of the judges for the horse show, and I'd be interested in watching him," said Nicole.

"Who's going to mind the store?"

"The answering service will handle everything. Besides, I expect most everyone will be at the fair."

"See you Sunday then, around ten. We can gorge ourselves on junk food all day." Steve gave her a light kiss on the cheek before she got out of the car and went into the house.

It was a few days before Nicole could find the time to take Charm for a good workout. Wearing a dark brown turtleneck sweater, dark brown corduroy jeans and newly purchased boots, Nicole entered Jake's barn, her step zestful and sure as she headed directly toward the stall where Charm was housed. The horse recognized her instantly and gave a vigorous whinny and a fretful shaking of the head. Nicole smiled broadly and threw her arms around the horse's neck.

"I think the mare missed you," said Jake, coming up behind her.

"I wish I could spend more time with her," said Nicole. "Would you happen to have some old reins and a saddle kicking around, Jake?"

"Mr. McBride brought them down," he replied.

Nicole's heart lurched, and she held onto the horse to keep herself from trembling. "Mr. McBride is back?" she asked in a raspy voice.

"Yes. He came back the day before yesterday."

"Did he say anything about the mare being here?" She turned to look at Jake calmly even though her nerve endings were sputtering like small exploding firecrackers.

"Well . . ." He scratched the top of his head. "When he first came into the barn he was solemn. I couldn't tell if he was angry or not. When I explained what happened, I knew he was angry just from the expression on his face, but he didn't say anything. He stalked from the barn and was back in twenty minutes with the saddle and the reins."

Nicole remained silent. Visions of the man danced before her eyes and she couldn't make them go away. When she finally spoke, her voice sounded hollow and distant to her.

"Are there any fields on this side of the road where I could ride without harming anything?"

"Sure. The cornfields are empty now and they'll give you plenty of riding space. I'll get your stuff."

She stroked Charm's nose while she waited for Jake to return. It took every bit of self-control she had not to go running to Jason's house to see him, but the thought of seeing him with his wife served to reinforce that control.

With reins in hand, she went into the stall and put them on the chestnut, then saddled her. She led the animal out of the barn, then mounted her with ease. She walked the horse along the cow paths out to the edge of the cornfields, where stubs of lopped-off cornstalks stood in neat, evenly spaced rows. She could feel the eagerness of the mare to stretch her legs to the fullest, and she herself was impatient to feel the wind streaming over her face in the concerted movement of horse and rider. She loosened her grip on the reins and gave the chestnut mare her head, letting the hooves crash against the ground with increasing speed. When she thought the horse was exceeding the bounds of judicial exercise, she reined Charm in slowly until she had her in a comfortable canter.

As they approached the woodlands rimming the cornfields, Nicole brought the mare to a dead halt and stroked her neck in an effort to keep the chestnut absolutely quiet, for at the edge of the woods was a young deer absently nibbling at some newfound blades of tender grass. Nicole studied the animal in silence; it appeared to be totally oblivious to woman and horse as it munched its way over the grass, its short white tail pulsing like a speeding metronome. Suddenly it looked up, not at Nicole and Charm but off in another direction, its large brown eyes luminous as huge dark moons. Swiftly it wheeled and darted into the cover of the deeper part of the woods. Seconds later Nicole heard the pounding of hooves coming closer and closer. She turned in the saddle to see the black stallion and its powerful rider heading directly toward her. Her heartbeat grew stronger and her hands shook as she held the horn of the saddle. Jason!

He brought Midnight to a leaping halt alongside Nicole. Jason's black hair swirling about his head like a thunderous cloud, his dark eyes caressed her face as if he were seeing her for the first time.

"Nicole . . . I must talk to you," he said with an urgency that defied refusal.

"I was just about to head back to Jake's." She drew the reins to the side, turning the chestnut's head toward the expanse of the empty cornfield and starting to cross it.

"Let me explain, Nicole," he said as he followed her. It was more of a command than a request. There was no plea in his tone. It was hard, flat.

"There is nothing to explain, Jason. Like you said, we took what we could while we could and now it's over. No explanations, no regrets. All right?" Her insides were tied into little knots. If he so much as touched her, she would tumble into his arms, hysterical with her love for him, and that she could not allow herself to do. The stakes were too high.

"Can you really walk away from this summer so easily?"

"Summer romances have a way of cooling down when winter comes."

"A summer romance! Is that how you look at what we had?" He combed his fingers through his thick hair, which had been ruffled by the force of the wind when he charged across the field.

"Under the circumstances, I see no other way to view it," said Nicole, her head held high, her gaze remaining steadfastly straight ahead.

"What circumstances? Linda?" he growled.

"I do not wish to pry into your private affairs or to be a sounding board for whatever marital difficulties you may have. I am not a naive, pristine juvenile, Jason. I am a grown woman who has managed her life quite well, and I'm sure I can continue to do so without getting myself involved with a married man." The words cut deep into her and she despised herself for saying them with such frosty intensity. But she never would survive halfway measures with Jason. It had to be a clean and swift break. She knew how to cloak herself in professionalism in order to endure the sorrows of life as well as the joys.

"For God's sake, Nicole! It's Linda I want to talk to you about. You must let me explain!" Outrage was creeping into his voice.

She couldn't bear to hear another word about Linda, especially from Jason's lips. She didn't want to know what if any difficulties there were in his marriage. She wasn't going to let pity or compassion suck her into an adulterous affair with Jason McBride, regardless of the love she felt. She reined in the horse and looked Jason squarely in the eye.

"It's over, Jason. Over. Recognize it and do me the favor of leaving me alone." With that she nudged Charm, who sprinted over the field with graceful speed back toward the cow barn as the wind dried the salty drops that were coursing over Nicole's cheeks.

She spent more than an hour currying and fussing over the mare once the animal was back in the stall and the saddle and reins neatly returned to where Jake had stored them. The unexpected meeting with Jason had left her badly shaken. Tending to Charm had a soothing effect on her, calming her heart and reknitting her frayed nerve endings. She left as Jake was herding the cows in for the evening milking.

The hospital was unusually noisy for early evening when she returned. Cats were wallering, dogs were yipping and a new dimension in sound had been added—a parrot screeching obscenities.

Taking her white coat from the rack in the office, she slipped it on and went into the operating room.

"What's going on around here?" she asked Dr. Carey.

"Oh, am I glad you're back! I was sitting here having a nice cup of coffee and a doughnut when the floodgates opened. Madness! Sheer madness! I think they all knew you took a couple of hours off and decided to descend on me like the plague. By the way, how was your ride?"

"Fine." She grimaced. "Have I been hearing a parrot?"

"Yes. Feisty devil. Psittacosis. Parrot fever. I have him isolated in the rear. Wear a surgical mask if you go near him. I already gave him a shot of antibiotic that should bring the virus under control. We'll have to watch him for a few days, then take samples to see if he still retains the virus," said Dr. Carey.

"Did you warn the family?"

"Yes. I told them to watch for remittent fever, headaches, coughing —the usual—and if they have any of these symptoms to get to their doctor and have him call me for the diagnosis. People don't seem to realize that the health of their animals can affect their own health at times." He shook his head wearily. "I have a very recalcitrant tomcat out in the waiting room and I'm going to need your help with him. I think this will be a case that calls for the use of a heavy pair of gloves."

They worked until past eight in the evening, the cases varying from simple to demanding. When the waiting room was finally empty and the animals in the wards were bedded down for the night, Dr. Carey offered to buy Nicole a late dinner, and she gladly accepted.

They walked the few short streets to an old hotel that had been renovated and made into apartments but still sheltered the original ground floor restaurant, the latter also having been updated and refurbished.

Nicole quickly perused the menu and decided on the grilled pork chops with applesauce, whipped potatoes and peas, all of which was preceded by a large salad, while Dr. Carey chose the liver and onions, which he claimed were the best around.

"You're going to the county fair, aren't you?" he asked, his salad disappearing at a rapid rate.

"Wouldn't miss you judging the horses for the world."

"The judging is on Sunday, you know."

"I know." She tackled her salad with zest but couldn't compete with Dr. Carey's speed.

"Going alone? Or with some of your lady friends?"

"This may come as a shock to you, but I'm going with Steve Baker," she said with an impish smile.

"Ah! What about the Hanes woman? All over?"

"I don't know how she feels about it, but according to Steve, it's over," she replied.

"The women of this town seem to be having a devil of a time pinning that young man down," commented Dr. Carey, pushing his empty salad plate to one side.

"I don't think he wants to be pinned down really. He likes his life the way it is." She saw no reason to mention Steve's proposal of marriage. It would tarnish his image as a carefree, elusive bachelor. Besides, it would open doors for Dr. Carey she didn't wish to pursue.

"You sound defensive." His pale blue eyes widened behind his glasses.

"Didn't mean to. To some people mating isn't the end purpose in life. But then I shouldn't have to tell you that. You seem to have enjoyed your bachelorhood," she argued, grinning slightly.

"Came close once. A pretty little thing she was." He lifted his chin and gave it a quick, thoughtful scratch.

"What happened?" asked Nicole, suddenly quite interested.

"Don't really know. Too wrapped up in my work, I guess. I was young, full of ideals and goals. She wanted more attention than I had time to give. Eventually she found someone else."

"Ever regret it?"

"No. I've had a good life—hectic but good. A lot simpler since you've arrived. What with the influx of newcomers and their pets and the decrease in large-animal work, I'm even toying with the idea of taking on another vet. What do you think?" he asked as the waitress brought their dinners.

"There's more money in small animals, especially of the pet variety, and from the looks of the billing that goes out every month, I think the clinic could support another vet," said Nicole earnestly.

"It'll be a lot easier to get another vet now that I have you. Most of the new ones refuse to work on large animals. They don't like trotting about in the muck and mire on the farms and getting all filthy when they have to tackle a wary pig. When I first saw you I couldn't imagine a pretty little thing like you pitting yourself against cows and horses and getting all messed up. But now I gather you rather enjoy going out to the farms."

"My natural habitat." She smiled and cut into her second pork chop, dipping it in the applesauce before putting it into her mouth.

"I keep meaning to ask you—was anything said about you moving the chestnut mare down to Jake's barn?"

"No. In fact, Mr. McBride brought the saddle and gear down to the barn himself."

"He's back, then?"

"Yes."

"Have you seen him?"

"This afternoon, while I was riding."

"I see." Dr. Carey quietly began to work away at his liver and onions. "We'll have to give the idea of hiring another vet some serious thought, Nicole. When you get a chance, go over the books and give me an idea of where we stand. And while you're at it, make some allowances for some new equipment. I have my eye on some pretty fancy stuff for the operating room."

They sat over coffee for some time, discussing the types of new equipment that might serve their purposes best and what sort of vet would complement their own personalities.

CHAPTER 11

The fairgrounds were alive with people of all sizes, shapes and forms. The air was filled with the chattering of voices, peals of laughter and the tantalizing, divergent, pungent aromas emanating from various makeshift food concessions. It seemed as though everyone was walking around with a piece of fried dough in his or her hand, child and adult alike.

"What time does the horse show start?" asked Steve as they wove their way in and out of the crowd.

"At two," replied Nicole. Her long blond hair was pulled up into a ponytail. She wore crisp white slacks, her white sleeveless scoop-necked blouse glimmered like silk and her tanned feet nestled in white strapped sandals. For late September it was an exceptionally hot day as the sun beat down relentlessly.

"Shall we try our hand at some games or start sampling the tasty wares?" asked Steve, taking her arm as they plowed through the horde that seemed intent on separating them.

"Why don't we do both?" The smells were tickling her taste buds beyond endurance.

"Good thinking. I knew I brought you along for a reason," said Steve, giving her arm a squeeze. "What should we try first?"

"I don't know about you, but I'm dying for some hot, salty french fries," replied Nicole, her decision having been made long before they entered the fairgrounds.

With paper cups of the hot potatoes in their hands, they strolled toward the small-scale midway, where game booths of every description were strung out, each abutting the other like twin strips across a wide, grassy area that was well trodden while barkers hawked their games as the easiest to win with fabulous prizes to be gained. Nicole and Steve tried pitching dimes, tossing rings over shortened rods and shooting wooden ducks until the salty french fries created a thirst that had to be quenched.

The sun was high overhead, sending waves of heated air down to the people below. It seemed everyone was feeling the effects of the sun's rays and tempting offerings of food, for there were sizable lines in front of every cold drink stand. They searched for a stand where the lines weren't so staggering, but their attempts were futile. There was nothing to do but be patient and stand in line with the others.

They went back to the games, where Steve finally won a stuffed frog for knocking down the required number of wooden bowling pins with a ball.

They munched their way through hamburgers, corn on the cob and slices of pizza and sipped their way through colas, lemonade and orange crush. Steve bought himself a cowboy hat, which Nicole had to admit made him look quite dashing.

As two o'clock drew near they meandered toward the other end of the fairgrounds, where the horse ring was located along with the live animal exhibitions.

"After the horse show we'll have to see the animals," said Nicole, looking for a trash bin to throw her empty paper cup in.

"Don't you see enough of animals?" asked Steve with amusement.

"I never see enough of animals. I have a compulsive affinity for them," she replied, smiling.

"I must admit I envy your ability to perform surgery. It was never my strong point. Although I suppose most of your surgical work is really quite simple," remarked Steve with a teasing twinkle in his eyes.

Nicole gave him a playful jab on the shoulder. "You know damn well animal surgery can be as complicated as human. Last week alone I had to operate on three cows with twisted stomachs."

"Oh, come, Nicole. How can a stomach get twisted?" He grinned in total disbelief.

"Your knowledge of bovine anatomy is sadly lacking, my dear colleague. A cow has four stomachs, and occasionally the last coil of the stomach fills with gas and floats to the side. Then I come to the rescue by cutting into the abdomen and sewing that coil back to the underbelly while the cow is standing in her stall. At least you people doctors have more ideal surroundings in which to cut and suture. Sometimes the light is so bad in the barns, I work by touch and instinct," explained Nicole.

"How do you know when the stomach is twisted? They can't talk. Or are you another Dr. Dolittle who can talk to the animals?" asked Steve with interest mixed with a trace of mockery.

"Don't be smart," warned Nicole jokingly. "I can tell by the general symptoms and the surefire technique of plunking the cow's side. If it sounds like I'm tapping a basketball, it's a twisted stomach."

"It's a good thing people don't have four stomachs. My office wouldn't hold them all, and I'd never get a moment's rest. What's on the agenda after the horse show?"

"I told you I want to see the animals. Jake Douglas has a few of his cows here for the dairy judging. He hopes to win one of the prizes for best holstein. I'd like to see which cows he brought. And there are still all the other exhibits—produce, crafts and the like."

"Looks like we're going to have our dinner here, too," said Steve, his hand waving in a gesture of resignation.

"Dinner? How can you mention food?" Nicole laughed as they approached the tier of wooden seats that flanked one end of the show ring, where the horses were already beginning to enter.

The stand was quickly filling up, but Nicole and Steve managed to find two good seats from where they had an excellent view of the entire ring. The crowd settled down as the horses and riders came into the ring and began the intricate patterns that constituted the required movements the judges looked for.

Dr. Carey was in the middle of the ring, walking around, his clipboard and pencil in hand as he studied the performers with rapt concentration. His face displayed the same seriousness he demonstrated in the operating room when a delicate operation was being performed.

Nicole's eyes followed the horses and their appropriately dressed riders around and around the ring until her peripheral vision spied a raven-haired man, his elbows braced on the wooden railing of the ring as he leaned forward on it. It had never entered her mind that Jason McBride would be at the county fair.

She held her breath as his eyes caught hers, and she knew he must have been staring at her for some time from the other side of the ring. She couldn't pull her gaze from his as her heart squeezed tight. She was painfully conscious of the beating of her heart. A hollow feeling pervaded the pit of her stomach as her entire body ached with the love she felt for him. Raw emotion swelled in her and emanated from her eyes across the grassy show ring. For a fleeting moment she and Jason were no longer at the crowded county fair but alone in the serenity of the glade.

Jason stood erect, as if he understood all the turmoil that was boiling inside her. His dark eyes seemed to be returning the message she was sending him, and in that instant Nicole thought Jason had some feeling for her. A shudder ran through her, and she wanted to vault across the ring into his arms. But there was a foreboding glint in his eyes that warned her of the hopeless, impossible nature of any kind of relationship between them. Her heart shattered like delicate glass when he thrust his hands into his back pockets and walked away, staring at the ground beneath his feet. Her eyes continued to follow him until he vanished into the shuffling crowd.

The applause crashed in on her reverie like relentless waves pounding the shore to remind it of its tenuous hold on permanency. She swallowed hard while vowing to herself that she would not shed one single tear. She had to live in a world of reality, and that reality was life without the married Jason McBride. She had to accept that fact if her life was to continue along the path she had designated. She clapped with the others when the winner of a certain division of horsemanship was announced.

Though she moved through the rest of the day with the same vitality and stamina that were her trademarks, her natural, spontaneous gaiety had lost its edge.

Several days later Nicole received the opportunity she had waited for ever since she had received her degree.

"Think you can handle it, Nicole?" asked Dr. Carey, cleaning his glasses with religious fervor.

"I'm dying to do it. When did he call?"

"Ten minutes ago." He resettled his glasses on the bridge of his nose and smoothed the wire curves behind his ears.

"I'll get my medical bag packed," she said, then went into the operating room for the necessary instruments. When she came back into the office, Dr. Carey was packing his medical bag. "I thought I was going to take care of the Sargent cow. Or have you changed your mind?" she asked with a trace of disappointment.

"I've decided to close up shop for a few hours and come with you. I've never actually seen a cesarean section done in the field before. I can't resist the temptation. Just think of me as your scrub nurse," he replied, snapping his bag shut. "Shall we go? We'll take my van. I don't trust that old station wagon of yours."

The barn was ablaze with fluorescent lights. They were greeted in the milk room by an anxious farmer and immediately led to the ailing cow with the calving difficulties. The beast was down on her side, a distended stomach presenting itself to their view. Once the cow was anesthetized, Nicole scrubbed the area on the cow to be incised with soap and water, then shaved the surface quickly. With a sure, steady draw of the scalpel, she sliced through the hide of the abdomen, then proceeded to open the uterus. With the aid of Dr. Carey, she lifted the abnormally large calf from its mother's womb. Farmer Sargent and Dr. Carey held the fledgling animal while Nicole secured the umbilical cord and severed it, then removed all traces of afterbirth. She closed the incision, her stitches neat and precise.

"There . . . she'll be as good as new in a few hours, Mr. Sargent," declared Nicole, radiant with the elation that comes from a job well done.

"Fine work, Nicole," said Dr. Carey, obviously well satisfied with her performance.

"I wouldn't have believed it if I hadn't seen it with my own eyes," exclaimed the farmer, who was rubbing the calf down with a burlap bag.

"The miracles of modern science, Joe," said Dr. Carey brightly, his eyes beaming as they watched the calf struggle to its feet. "If there are any problems, just give us a call."

Nicole climbed into Dr. Carey's fairly new van, which contained not only the usual veterinarian equipment but also various types and designs of fishing gear.

"I don't think I'll ever get over the thrill that shoots through me whenever I bring a new creature into the world or heal one that might have left it," exclaimed Nicole as they headed back to the hospital. "I saw the cesarean done at Cornell several times but never actually did one myself. I feel like I have a high on."

"When I was in school, they used charts or dead animals. It really didn't have much meaning for me. Once I was in practice, I thought I'd have a chance to do one but soon found that the farmers were not only wary of the operation but refused to spend that kind of money. But now, with expensive registered stock and prize bulls to service the cows, attitudes have rapidly changed. To watch you perform the section on a living animal was thrilling and a fascinating experience for me. You have nimble fingers, Nicole."

"Thank you."

"I think a celebration is in order. I'll stop at the bakery and get some doughnuts. On second thought, seeing it is a truly festive occasion, I'll get jelly doughnuts covered with tons of powdered sugar."

When she wasn't on night call, it had become a habit for Nicole to go out to Jake's farm and ride Charm after she had her supper and if she had no other engagements. As she raced across the fields, it was always in the back of her mind that Jason would soon be thundering behind her. But the longing remained in her mind. Jason never came, and she knew she should have been grateful, but she wasn't. He lingered in her soul like a recurring dream. When their eyes had locked during the horse show at the fair, she had had the gnawing feeling that she would never see Jason McBride again unless it was in some passing crowd. She never asked Jake about him; it would only serve to stir and wrench her heart. Every day she had to reconvince herself that she wanted the break to be clean. The temptation to call him or see him tugged at her very soul, and she had to collect her willpower like tiny chinks of iron that she could weave into a protective suit of armor. Every night as she climbed into bed, no matter how weary she was, she repeated the phrase Time heals all to herself over and over until sleep took possession of her brain.

It was early October, and the trees had taken on the riotous colors of autumn before succumbing to the drab desolation of winter. Reds, golds, yellows, oranges—all sang their song in harmony as they moved in the cooling breezes, embellishing the land with their glorious hues. It was like stepping into a world that could still awe, inspire and mystify.

Nicole had finished at the hospital early, and with no commitments ahead of her for the rest of the day, she looked forward to spending the free time on the back of the chestnut mare. She entered Jake's barn with an air of expectation and strode toward the stall with a light-hearted step.

The warm smile melted from her face, and her amber eyes expanded as they beheld the empty stall. Maybe Jake had needed the stall and had put the horse elsewhere for the time being, she thought to herself, then swiftly went to seek out Jake. On her search for him she looked about the barn, becoming more frantic with every glance at the empty building. When she saw Jake herding the cows up from their grazing field, she ran out to meet him.

"Where's Charm? Did you put her somewhere else?" she asked anxiously, matching her stride to his.

Jake shook his head in despair. "I hate to tell you this, knowing how fond you are of the animal . . ."

"Tell me what? Has something happened to her?" she interrupted.

"Mr. McBride came and took her back up to his barn, gear and all," replied Jake.

"Why?" There was an aching plea in Nicole's voice that she didn't attempt to hide.

"He didn't say and I didn't ask. I guess his wife wanted a horse to ride, and a wife can be pretty persuasive at times."

Jake's words hit Nicole between the eyes like a lead pipe. Jason's gift to her of Charm was no more than an empty gesture, words that had no meaning. She had thought he was a man of his word, but now she didn't know what to believe. The only truth she had to deal with was the fact he was no longer alone in any decision-making process. He had a wife—a mate—to persuade, to alter any judgments he might make. It was a bitter pill to swallow but one she must if she was to function at all. Her misgivings became coated with a twinge of anger as she left the Douglas farm.

When she told Dr. Carey what Jason had done, she was surprised by his reaction to the news. Dr. Carey simply shrugged and told her to forget the entire incident. With stoic determination she tried to follow Dr. Carey's advice, but whenever the image of the heavy-handed brunet using a riding crop on the mare darted into her mind, she became incensed. That she could do nothing about it only served to heighten her fury.

It had been a busy week, and Nicole was glad it was drawing to a close. She had had the station wagon all tuned up and checked, for she planned to use the weekend for a trip home to see her family, even though they frequently wrote to one another.

It was almost four in the afternoon before the waiting room finally emptied out. After making a fresh pot of coffee, Nicole and Dr. Carey sat at their desks and discussed likely candidates for a veterinary position with them at the clinic. Dr. Carey passed her several applications, accompanied by detailed resumés with some penciled commentaries.

"This one absolutely refuses to work on large animals. I don't put him high on my list, for there will be times when they'll have to go out to a farm, although I'd try to keep him busy on small animals as much as possible. Now here's a more likely prospect," said Dr. Carey, handing Nicole the application with its attached resumé. "What do you think?" he asked when she had finished reading it.

"Looks good to me. He has all the qualifications and graduated with honors. And he doesn't rule out doing large-animal work," she commented, handing the papers back to him, then sipping her hot coffee.

"All in all, I guess there are about five candidates to interview personally. Would you like to send out the letters or shall I?"

"I will. I've seen your typing," she said with a smile.

"Good. I was hoping you would. My hunt-and-peck system is so painfully—" The telephone interrupted him in mid-sentence. He reached for it and lazily brought it to his ear.

Nicole leaned back in her chair and mentally began to compose the letter she would send to the various applicants while Dr. Carey's voice droned in the background. The click of the receiver being placed in the cradle brought her back from the mental exercise of letter writing.

"I'm afraid you have a call to make before you can end your day," he said, removing his glasses and pinching the bridge of his nose. "I'd take it myself but he specifically asked for you."

"Who was it?"

"Young Tommy Keeler."

Nicole was instantly alert. She had an idea of what was coming, and her blood began to pulse erratically through her veins. "What happened?" she asked in a quiet yet shaken voice.

"It seems Mrs. McBride has taken the mare, and the Keeler boy didn't like the way she was handling the horse. He's worried there will be a repeat of the last time, only he fears it might be worse this time, for she was in a furious mood." Dr. Carey replaced his glasses and peered over the rim at Nicole. "Of course if you'd rather not, I understand and will go myself."

Nicole stood, her fists clenched at her sides. "No. I'll handle it. And if that woman has raised so much as one welt on Charm's hide, I'll have hers."

"Now don't get yourself all worked up. I don't want you to go looking for trouble," he warned.

"Don't worry. I'm not about to do anything illegal. But I will bring charges of abuse if the occasion warrants it, McBride or no McBride." She took off her white coat and slipped her arms into an old corduroy jacket she used on the farms, grabbed her medical bag, then dashed out of the hospital without another word.

Tommy Keeler was waiting outside the barn as she drove up. She bounced out of the car with a verve that was spurred by sheer anger.

"Which way did she go?" asked Nicole heatedly.

"Down toward the pond," replied Tommy.

"Where is Mr. McBride?"

"I'm not sure."

"Is he in the house?" she continued to question.

"Oh, I know he's not in there."

"I'll try the laboratory." Her anger put all fear of coming face to face with Jason out of her mind as she stalked toward the laboratory. The door was locked. She knocked loudly and frantically before deciding he wasn't there. Her only alternative was to ride down to the glade herself. She plodded back to the barn where, once inside, she found that Tommy had Midnight all saddled.

"Do you think you can handle Midnight, Doc?" he asked.

"Midnight is a fraud. He's not as devilish as he would have one think. Of course I can handle him, Tommy, but I will need a boost up. He's much bigger than Charm."

Hands interlocked to receive Nicole's foot, Tommy gave her the lift she needed to swing her leg over the black stallion's back. She leaned forward and stroked Midnight's neck. "It's all right, boy. We have a little business to take care of," she whispered to him, then led him out of the barn with the same ease she used with the mare.

Her blond ponytail bounced in the wind that blew past them as the powerful horse galloped along under her control. She could understand why Jason was so fond of the animal. He responded quickly and obediently to her commands. She felt a strange elation to be governing every movement of the magnificent beast. She would have loved to find out what it would be like to race across the fields with him, but there was a more pressing need to be attended to.

She slowed the animal to a trot as they reached the narrow lane leading to the glade and the pond. She slipped from the black stallion when they came to the glade before he had come to a standing halt, for she had spied Charm nibbling on some grass that had not yet been frosted. Unthinking, she let the reins to the stallion drop to the ground and rushed over to the mare. Her hand trailed over the chestnut's right flank. There wasn't a hint of a welt. The hide was as smooth and glossy as it had been when she had last seen the horse. She moved closer and hugged the animal's neck as the mare turned to stare at her quietly. Relief flooded Nicole, and she wondered if she should unobtrusively ride back to the barn, for no harm seemed to have been done and she didn't want to appear the fool, especially in front of Linda McBride. The thought made her curious as to where the tall brunet might be. She cautiously scanned the glade but saw no trace of the woman. She tenderly patted the mare's nose in a gesture of farewell, then turned to retrieve the reins to the stallion when sheer astonishment illuminated her face.

"Jason!" she gasped. He stood before her dressed in tight black jeans and a black turtleneck sweater, exactly as he had been the first time she had seen him sitting so regally on the fiery black stallion. She swiveled her head and glanced around the glade before returning her gaze to the tall, obviously troubled man who was holding Midnight's reins. Looking at him, she realized something was amiss. The whole setup was wrong. "What's this all about, Jason?"

"I am sorry to have had to play charades like this, but after our last encounter and seeing the way you felt, it was the only way I could think of to talk to you alone and without interference. There are a number of things I want you to know before I leave."

Her heart fell. His words had a finality to them, and she didn't know if she could tolerate never seeing him again even though he was a married man. "Leave?"

"Yes. I'm closing up the place and moving back to California," he said quietly.

"California? I thought you loved this place. What about your dreams of a greenhouse? The horses?" There was a frantic note in her tone.

"That's what I want to talk to you about. I will send Tommy a monthly check for the care and feeding of the horses. I would appreciate it if you would feel free to use them at any time and will trust your judgment as to their medical needs. As to the house . . ." He drew in a sharp breath, then slowly released it. "Well, Mrs. Beaton will see to the necessary tending of it."

"Mrs. Beaton is in California." Her head was ringing. Nothing was making any sense to her. His wife was probably from California and had talked him into moving back there. The thought flooded her with resentment.

"Was. She returned yesterday."

"When are you leaving?" Nicole asked icily.

"The arrangements haven't been completed. Probably not until sometime next week." He gazed at her steadily. His haunting dark eyes searching her face ardently.

"After the warmth of California, it must be difficult for your wife to endure our Vermont winters," she said in a hard, flat voice, forcing a tentative smile to her lips.

"She's not my wife!" cried Jason angrily. He dropped the reins to the black stallion, turned on his heel and walked down to the tumbling waterfall.

Stunned, Nicole stood where she was as if in a trance. Words and visions scrambled around in her brain like a stirred-up ant's nest. That woman was not his wife? What was going on? She moved, hardly aware that her feet were carrying her to Jason's side. She didn't notice the stallion plodding up to the mare and nudging the chestnut fondly with his nose.

"Jason . . . I don't understand. She said she was Mrs. Jason Mc-Bride."

"She would." He ran a hand through his thick black hair. "It's a long and ugly story, Nicole—one I don't think you'd be interested in."

"Try me," she said softly, reaching up to touch the deeply furrowed cheek, the face she knew and loved so well.

Jason took her hand from his cheek, turned it palm up and placed a lingering kiss on it. "You always did have a gentle touch, Nicole." He continued to hold her hand as he led her to the mossy area where they had picnicked so many times in the past. He released her hand and sat down, his knees up and drawn apart as he rested his elbows on them. "Are you sure you want to hear this?"

"I've never been surer of anything in my life," she replied, knowing that her entire future might depend on what Jason had to tell her.

"I was twenty-four and what they called a real comer in the microelectronics field," he began as Nicole sat down beside him. "My work was my life until I met Linda. She was my age, and she captivated me with her knowledge of my work. She had an uncanny grasp of the fundamentals involved in what I was doing. I was duly impressed with her. She painted visions of a new Marie and Pierre Curie, and before I knew it we were married, three months after we met. It didn't take me long to realize that I had made a drastic mistake. I was not in love with her but in love with the idea of being part of an important team in the field of microelectronics. I had the youthful hope of being notable enough to enter the history books. The marriage turned sour, but we remained together. I felt I had made a commitment and it wasn't her fault that I had married her in order to fulfill some childish dreams. Why she stayed with me was another story—one that almost destroyed me." Jason stared off across the pond at some invisible point in the distance and remained quiet for some time before Nicole broke the silence around them.

"You don't have to tell me if you don't want to, Jason." There was an agonized look on his face that made her want to reach out and cradle him in her arms until the sorrow went away.

"No . . ." He sighed. "You may as well know it all now that I've started. We had been married a year when the sky opened and the heavens came crashing down. Unknown to me, we had been under surveillance by the FBI for several months. It came as a dreadful blow when we were arrested for industrial espionage—selling hi-tech information to unfriendly countries, as they put it. Linda had been under suspicion long before she married me. I suddenly found myself in a living hell and had no idea how I got there.

"It was well publicized on the West Coast for a short time; then a lid of secrecy came down on the whole incident. I didn't understand until later. Anyway, the trial was long and arduous. I sat through it, my senses numb, my brain in neutral. My whole life was crumbling around me, and there seemed to be nothing I could do to stop it. Half the time I didn't even know what they were talking about. Finally I was exonerated of all duplicity. Linda was convicted, fined and sentenced. It seems they were using me to reach Linda. They had hoped that if they included me in the indictment, Linda's love for me would force her to name her accomplices to clear my name. When they realized that Linda had no intention of trying to clear me, they brought the lid down on the proceedings, as they didn't want to lose my expertise in the field. I knew I had been used by Linda and by the government. I'm afraid it left me bitter and wary of my fellow man.

"Anyway, I paid her fines, waited for her to serve her sentence, then tried to divorce her. But she contested the divorce, demanding astronomical sums as settlement and blaming me for her clandestine activities. I had had enough. The divorce didn't mean as much to me as peace and quiet. I picked up and left, my only desire to return to this farm and live out the rest of my days in peace. To my relief, the arrangement appeared to suit Linda." He picked up a pebble and tossed it into the water before them.

"Then legally she is still your wife. But why did she wait six years, then come back?" asked Nicole as an eerie hopelessness filled her.

"This spring I decided to pursue the divorce once again, regardless of the cost. It took the lawyers several months to track her down. She moved around quite a bit and on occasion used aliases. When they finally found her and served her with the papers, she flew here to confront me in person with her demands.

"The same morning I received her call informing me she was at the airport, I also received a call from the private investigator the lawyers had used to locate her. He told me he had uncovered some important facts about Linda but he would only reveal them to me in person and when he had five thousand dollars in cash in his hand."

"And that's why you left so suddenly for California?" asked Nicole, her heart bouncing in her rib cage as her feelings alternated between despair and hope.

"Yes," replied Jason. "I didn't even want to talk to Linda until I knew what the investigator had to offer. I also gave Mrs. Beaton airfare to see her daughter in case she couldn't tolerate Linda. I knew how exasperating she could be. I flew up to Montreal, where I could get a commercial jet to California quickly." Jason paused, sadness flickering in his eyes as he steadily gazed at the pond.

"Well . . . what did the investigator say?" Nicole's nerves were stretched taut and about to snap if Jason didn't get on with the story.

"In the course of his attempts to locate Linda, he came up with her full background. She was born in Texas and at the age of seventeen married a local man. She left him after a year, never bothering to get a divorce. I flew to Texas to talk with the man, and it seems he never bothered to get a divorce, either. So you see she was never legally my wife. When I returned, I told Linda of my findings and that my lawyers were proceeding to have our marriage declared a void marriage. Some bitter words were spoken, and she left vowing her undying hatred of me."

Nicole closed her eyes and smiled as a surge of pure happiness coursed through her. The smile vanished, and her eyes flew open at the thought of Jason leaving Vermont now that everything had been resolved. When she found that he was no longer next to her but standing at the water's edge, she scrambled to her feet and went to join him.

"If everything has been cleared up, why are you leaving, Jason?" she asked softly.

He turned and looked down at her, his dark eyes moving over her face like a velvet glove. "I can no longer stay here, Nicole." His finger caressed her cheek.

"Why?" The plea in her voice matched the ache in her heart, and tears trembled behind her eyes.

"I can't bear to see you around and know you are so close but in love with another." He sighed heavily, then quickly continued as he turned to stare at the water again. "When I returned from Texas, I was jubilant until I learned you had resumed your liaison with Stephan Baker. The words you spoke the day I trailed you across the empty cornfield gutted me. A summer romance, you said. I suddenly realized you had been marking time, waiting for Stephan Baker to slough off his latest interest and come back to you."

"Jason—" she interrupted.

He held up a staying hand, not looking at Nicole. "Let me finish. I called your office, hoping to have one last chance to talk to you. When the answering service told me you were at the county fair, I decided to track you down, only to find you sitting with Stephan Baker at the show ring. When you looked at me with love shining in your eyes so brightly, I knew I had lost you and would have to leave Essex Junction. I couldn't stay here knowing you belonged to another. I'm sorry for tricking you into coming here, but I wanted to set the record straight and let you know why I had never wanted to talk about the past. Well . . . I've said my piece, and you may go knowing no abuse will ever come to the horses again." He shoved his hands into his back pockets as his shoulders heaved with an anxious intake of breath. He stared vacantly into the splashing waters.

"Oh, Jason, why didn't you tell me all this long ago? Didn't you think I'd understand? Didn't you trust me?" asked Nicole, a tremble in her voice.

"I wanted to get the matter of the divorce settled first, because even though I hadn't considered myself married for a long time, I was afraid I'd lose you if you thought a legal marriage existed. I can see now I never had you to begin with. Your heart had always belonged to another."

Nicole was more moved than she had thought possible. Jason was so much like the proud black stallion—majestic, confident, bristling with masculine potency . . . yet under it all was a core of gentleness, of caring that demanded respect and engendered love. Her heart was beating so fast she didn't know if she could stand it much longer. She reached out and touched his arm. She could feel him quiver under her fingers.

"Jason . . . you did see love in my eyes that day—a deep, constant love that will endure beyond time."

Jason moved his head obliquely and gazed at her, his eyes heavy with pain. "Don't, Nicole."

"Oh, Jason, don't you know? Can't you see? That love is for you and you alone. There'll never be another man for me . . . only you—you, Jason." One stray tear of happiness could not be held in check as he turned to face her and it burst over her lower eyelid to straggle over her upturned face.

His long, lean finger lifted imperceptibly and wiped the salty drop from her cheek. Their eyes communed, saying all it was necessary to say. His arms enveloped her, and his cheek pressed against the top of her head. An eternity slipped by before he spoke.

"Nicole, I love you beyond reason itself. As soon as all the legalities are disposed of, will you marry me? You're the only Mrs. Jason McBride I shall ever want."

"Nicole McBride," she murmured. "I like the sound of it, and it is the only other name I would ever consider having."

He held her from him and smiled, love glowing in his eyes. His hands left her shoulders, then went to the band that held her ponytail in place and removed it, letting the cloth-covered elastic fall to the ground. His spread fingers combed through her silken tresses with great gentleness as he gazed at her adoringly.

"When you lay in my grandmother's bed, so oblivious to the world, your hair fanned like a golden halo, and I knew then that I loved you and wanted you more than anything else in life. I also knew I would have to settle matters about Linda even though I wasn't sure about the relationship between you and Stephan Baker."

Nicole gazed lovingly into the dark eyes of the man before her and smiled sweetly. "I'll admit I tried to make myself feel something for Steve, but it just wasn't there. I was too hopelessly in love with you, and I guess I always have been. There'll never be anyone else." She coiled her arms around his neck and pressed her head against his strong chest.

"Do you think you could live in that museum of mine?" asked Jason.

"You know I love the house almost as much as I love the owner. I only hope you don't expect me to be standing over the stove baking bread or some such thing," she said, tossing her head back and looking up at him with shining eyes.

"You at a stove? Heaven forbid. No, Nicole. I know you love your work and wouldn't dream of asking you to give it up any more than I could give up my work. Besides, I think we are both partial to Mrs. Beaton's cooking," said Jason with warm humor, caressing her head with tender strokes while one arm held her fast to his body.

"Things won't be quite as hectic. Dr. Carey is going to take on another vet to ease the work load. It will give us more time together."

He clasped her head between his large, fine-boned hands and tilted it upward to meet his, then smiled. "We'll have our whole lives together." He kissed her lightly. "I have your wedding present all picked out."

"Oh?" Her eyes sparkled.

"A matched pair of golden Labrador retrievers—puppies. I saw them the other day and thought of you." His thumbs traced her cheekbones with affection.

"You do know how to win a woman's heart, don't you, Mr. McBride?"

"Yes, Nicole McBride."

They kissed long and deep, as if for the first time. Leaves began to fall in the glade, forming a carpet of wondrous gold at their feet, and birds trilled in the arching trees high above the embracing couple. The rushing waters spattered magical tunes in the crisp air, and horses whinnied in concert with the sounds of nature. But for Nicole and Jason, only their love was real in the tenuous enchantment of the glade.